A FATAL DEBT

BALLANTINE BOOKS

NEW YORK

A FATAL DEBT

A Novel

JOHN GAPPER

A Fatal Debt is a work of fiction. Names, characters, places, and incidents are the products of the author's imagination or are used fictitiously. Any resemblance to actual events, locales, or persons, living or dead, is entirely coincidental.

Published in the United States by Ballantine Books, an imprint of The Random House Publishing Group, a division of Random House, Inc., New York.

BALLANTINE and colophon are registered trademarks of Random House, Inc.

LIBRARY OF CONGRESS CATALOGING-IN-PUBLICATION DATA
Gapper, John.
A fatal debt : a novel / John Gapper.
pages cm
ISBN 978-0-345-52789-9 — ISBN 978-0-345-52791-2 (ebook)
1. Psychiatrists—Fiction. 2. Bankers—Fiction. 3. Physician and patient—Fiction.
4. Rich people—New York (State)—New York—Fiction. 5. Wall Street
(New York, N.Y.)—Fiction. I. Title.
PS3607.A66F38 2012
813'.6—dc23   2011045503

Printed in the United States of America on acid-free paper

www.ballantinebooks.com

2 4 6 8 9 7 5 3 1

FIRST EDITION

Book design by Dana Leigh Blanchette
Title-page photograph: © iStockphoto

To Rosie with love

A FATAL DEBT

1

New York City has a light of its own, a dazzling glare that is utterly unlike the soft, cloud-strewn summers where I grew up. I once found its intensity disturbing, like the city's, but I miss it now. It was glowing on that May morning as I stepped from my apartment building. Sun shone on the budding leaves in Gramercy Park and illuminated the Art Deco gargoyles of the Chrysler Building in the distance along Lexington Avenue.

My gym was nearby, a box with windows on one corner of Irving Place, filled day and night with New Yorkers pounding on long lines of running machines. Some watched monitors and wore earpieces, cords dangling from their ears and swinging in time with the rhythm of their runs. It was a Sunday at the end of a surreal, stressful week—

one filled with fraught events that I hoped had been resolved. I walked slowly, trying to relax, letting those events filter into my subconscious.

Two men were playing chess on the sidewalk as I passed. They were both slim and scraggy with thinning hair, and one had a trimmed white beard. As they played, they kvetched about the state of the city, the rise in subway fares, and gentrification on the Bowery. The one playing black prodded a knight forward at the white king, and as he released the piece, the other swooped his queen across and seized a rook with two fingers. The clack of the white queen's base being slammed on the board echoed across the street.

"Ach," Black tutted to himself.

"You didn't see that?" White cried.

The first ten minutes on the treadmill when I reached the gym were painful—my muscles creaked, my throat burned. At about the fifteen-minute mark, the urge to stop was succeeded by a state of boredom, and my thoughts drifted. I always felt this moment, before I started the countdown to the end, when the experience became soothing. As that small but pleasurable window opened, I glanced over the monitor tuned to Fox News on a nearby machine.

Then I jabbed at the red "Stop" button.

The screen revealed a live feed from a news helicopter—the image of a police chase or maybe a crime in progress. The camera shuddered as it circled, but the scene was clear enough: Harry Shapiro's house in East Hampton. There was the lawn by the dunes, the blue pool, the squares and circles of the cedar-shingled roof, the chairs on which we had sat. The seats were vacant and no one was in sight—only house, lawn, dune, beach, and black-and-white vehicles jamming the drive. His Range Rover was parked by the house, apart from the melee.

"You using this machine, man?" someone asked me from my left. Without noticing, I had climbed off my own and drifted toward the screen.

"No," I said. "Go ahead." Other channels were showing the same image, but I tuned to Fox, with its red banner at the bottom of the screen: DEATH IN THE HAMPTONS. The news anchors, when I put on the headphones hanging on the machine, were talking excitedly but not making much sense, as if in the grip of mania.

"We're going to Bruce Bradley," said a woman's voice, "who is at the scene. Bruce, what can you tell us?"

The shot cut to a man with a blue blazer and a bland face, standing at the entrance to the lane where Harry lived and looking professionally grave. In the distance I could see the low, misty outline of Harry's guesthouse.

"Melissa, I'm in East Hampton, the Long Island beach town known as a retreat of the wealthy," he said sonorously. "Detectives were called to a house down this lane last night, where they found a body, I'm told."

The woman anchor started to ask something, but a man's voice cut over her. "Bruce, this is Jack. Can you tell us the identity of the victim?"

"The police are not saying, but my sources tell me that the deceased is a banker who was well known on Wall Street."

"Jesus," I said—loudly, because of the headphones. A woman on a machine nearby looked over at me reprovingly. "Sorry," I said, holding up one hand. It was shaking from the rush of fear as I put it on the handrail.

For weeks afterward, that anxious feeling of the world breaking up around me was never far away; even now, whenever I'm in New York, a quick glimpse of Fox News can make my heart rattle. It was more than the threat to my livelihood: it was a sense of being wrenched from the frame I had around me, the detachment I had built from other people with all their disordered emotions. Love. Jealousy. Despair.

Hatred.

After pulling off the headphones, I stepped down from the machine and started to walk back to the changing rooms. Near the door to the workout room, I was hit by a wave of dizziness and sat down to place my head between my knees. I didn't need to watch any more: I already knew what had happened. Harry Shapiro had killed himself. I also knew, with absolute certainty, that I was to blame.

When Rebecca was on duty, she would sometimes return home in the early hours and sit silently in the kitchen before coming to bed. I'd know then that a patient had died on the operating table. We shrinks don't lose many patients, so we never get used to it in the way that a surgeon must. Patients of mine had killed themselves before, but, unhappy as it made me, I'd never believed it was my fault. They'd been in a chronic condition, had been battling their death wish for a long time, and I'd done all that I could to help.

Harry was different. I'd known he was in danger, and I'd let him die. I'd allowed myself to be bullied and bribed into failing him.

My head was still between my knees, but saliva had stopped running in my mouth and I could feel the dizziness starting to ease. I raised my head to see a gym trainer looking at me with concern, thinking that I must have overdone it on the machines. I grimaced at him as if he were correct, got up, and grabbed a towel. Then I went to the showers and stood under one for a long time.

2

Harry arrived at Episcopal when I was on Friday night call. I was up on Twelve South, trying to lure a paranoid schizophrenic out of a seclusion room, when Maisie Knox paged me from the psychiatric emergency room.

The schizophrenic had arrived a few hours before on a gurney from Central Park, where he'd been shouting at traffic and worrying the dog walkers. After administering a shot of Haldol and Ativan, the cocktail of antipsychotic and tranquilizer we used to subdue dangerous patients, I'd admitted him on his Medicaid gold card—no need to tussle with an insurance company trying to save money. When he'd revived an hour later, he was quieter but still obstinate.

Maisie was a fourth-year resident with a combination of looks—gentle eyes and an unruly lock of blond hair that she tucked behind one ear—serenity, and, most alluring of all, competence. I was happy to hear her voice, but being paged meant disruption of some kind and I'd selfishly hoped to get through the rest of the shift without that.

"There's a patient here you should probably see," she said when I got to a phone. Her tone was as steady as ever, but I detected something: nervousness? excitement?

"What's wrong with him?"

"He's depressed."

"I'm feeling a bit down myself. Can't he wait?"

"I don't think he can."

I started to get irritated, despite my soft spot for Maisie. There is an order to things in the ER. First a nurse, then a resident, and only then the attending. I was supposed to be in charge, and I couldn't run around after every disturbed person who decided to walk in off the streets. You only had to ride the subway to realize how many of those there were.

"Who is he?" I said, sighing.

"It's a Mr. Harold Shapiro. Harold L. Shapiro. And his wife, Nora Shapiro, brought him in," she said, as if the names settled the matter. And they did.

"I'll be there in a minute," I said.

Don't make exceptions, we were always taught, *it never works out well.* But if there was anyone who had to be treated as a special case, it was Harry Shapiro. I didn't know him, although I'd read something in *The New York Times* about him losing his job as chief executive of a Wall Street bank in the financial crisis. The piece suggested that he'd deserved it, that he'd never realized the risks his bank was running. I knew one thing, however. At that moment, I was standing in the Harold L. and Nora Shapiro Pavilion, a wing of New York–Episcopal Hospital that held various wards, including Twelve North and South.

The Shapiros had donated $35 million to the hospital, allowing it to thrust itself out over the FDR Drive, and a plaque on which their names were etched greeted every driver who drove north through the tunnel beneath. So they were not to be taken lightly, especially if he was ill. I'd experienced what happened when donors came into the hospital they had funded. Furtive calls would soon follow from administrators or even board members. *Don't go out of your way,* they would say, *but do everything you can.* We usually took the hint.

I decided to leave my schizophrenic by himself for a while. He was safe enough, even if he wasn't coherent. When I got down to the ER, I found Maisie in the doctors' room at the end of the corridor.

"Yes . . . yes . . . I'll make sure he knows," she was saying on the phone in the tone of someone already fencing with authority.

Maisie looked at me inquiringly, and I shook my head. I didn't want whoever it was second-guessing the treatment before I'd even seen the patient. She silently held up four fingers: room four. I found Harry sitting on the cot in the room, wearing a Polo Ralph Lauren shirt, pants, and a blazer. His shoulders were hunched, his head bowed, and he was shivering. It could have been a symptom of anxiety, but it was ice cold in there. I swear they kept the rooms refrigerated. We often asked maintenance to fix it, but they never had.

Room four was identical to the others on the corridor: it had a hard cot dummy-proofed to prevent anyone from using it to harm themselves or the staff, a plastic chair, and a glass panel facing the hallway so the nurses could examine the occupant at leisure. Its distinguishing feature was a bad oil painting of a red-roofed Italian seaside town, screwed to the wall in case anybody tried to do some damage with it, on which one literacy-challenged occupant had scratched: "Train to Tijooana." Maintenance hadn't fixed that either.

The fact that Harry was still in his clothes was a cause for concern, and I noted the hovering presence of Pete O'Meara, the ER security guard, who was standing by the door looking unhappy. He had a big, jowly face and was capable of subduing most patients who looked threatening, but he'd met his match in Harry.

"Hello, Mr. Shapiro," I said. "I'm Dr. Cowper, the attending psychiatrist. I'd like to have a chat, but would you mind changing into a gown first? It's hospital procedure."

Harry raised his head and I saw his dark eyes for the first time. I knew then why Pete had backed off. They were like the embers of a fire that had died down but would flame up if prodded. Of all Harry's qualities, his ability to intimidate was the most striking. Even then, in that state, I wouldn't have tangled with him. He was powerfully built and trim, as if nervous energy had burned off all excess fat. His eyes were set deeply into a lean face with a sloping forehead and an aquiline nose. He looked like a Roman centurion who headed a merciless legion that had just fought its way through Gaul, taking no prisoners.

"This is bullshit," he muttered. "I'm not a lunatic."

"Of course not," I said. "But we have rules in place to protect everybody. You've been in the security line at the airport, haven't you? You don't want to be the one guy who makes a fuss."

That was my usual line, and it wasn't a bad analogy—we were also wary of hidden weapons. Harry hadn't been to LaGuardia in a long time, I later found out, but it worked. He gazed at me for a few seconds before nodding.

"Okay, let's get on with it," he growled.

"Good. Mr. O'Meara will take your things and get you a gown, and I'll ask the nurse to take some blood. Then I'll return."

Back in the doctors' room, I found Maisie examining Harry's chart, which had just been spat out by the computer. All the patients got their blood pressure taken and their insurance checked before they reached us.

"I don't think he'll have trouble paying the check," she said.

"See if there's room at the Four Seasons, just in case."

That was our name for York East, a six-bed ward on the thirteenth floor that was a high-rent version of Twelve South for those who paid $700 a day on top of insurance for better amenities. The food was fancier and they got their own rooms, with en suite bathrooms, although the doors were locked just as firmly against their departure. It was more like a hotel, but there was no checking out.

"Who was that on the phone?" I asked.

"Sarah Duncan. Mrs. Shapiro rang her before they came in and she wanted to know what was happening. I said you had things under control."

Sarah Duncan was Episcopal's president, a silver-haired Chicagoan who had elevated her briskness to a managerial art. I recalled that Nora Shapiro sat on the Episcopal board, which muddied things further—it meant that Duncan's career was in her hands. Glancing at Harry's chart, I saw that he was fifty-eight and had been treated at Episcopal before, but only for routine things such as colonoscopies. His blood pressure was a little high and he was on Lipitor, but he was otherwise in good health.

Back in room four, Harry was still on the cot but now in a gown, and a nurse was wheeling away the phlebotomy cart, having drawn his blood.

"So," he said. "Dr. Cooper, is it?"

"Yes. It's spelled Cow-per, but the w is silent," I said, feeling as ridiculous as I always did when I had to explain my name.

"Some fancy British thing?" he said acidly.

"Perhaps you could explain why you're here," I said.

Harry paused to consider and his head dipped. He looked flat and he talked slowly, both symptoms of depression. I was already getting a sense of what was going on in his head. It looked like a male midlife crisis of the kind we dealt with day in, day out. I'd have to check what was under the surface, but I wasn't too concerned. He was probably in more mental pain than he'd ever experienced in his life, but it would pass.

"Not so great," he said glumly. "Things have been tough. I lost my job."

He stared out into the hallway and I waited in case he had more to say, but he remained silent. He wasn't telling me any more than he had to, which made getting an exact fix on his condition more difficult. I ran through the standard list of questions.

"I'm going to ask some things about your state of health, Mr. Shapiro. How's your appetite?"

"Okay. I eat."

"Do you drink?"

"A little. A glass of wine with dinner."

"Take any drugs?"

"Nothing like that."

"How much sleep do you need at night?"

"I can get by on five hours or so. I used to be in the office by six a.m., get ahead of the day."

"Before now, have you been through long periods of feeling sad or hopeless?"

"I've never been that way."

"Ever had prolonged periods of feeling excited, with lots of energy, as if you were on top of the world?"

Harry regarded me levelly, having realized where I was leading. Many patients who arrived with depression had undiagnosed bipolar disorder, and their manic phases had been mild enough to be adaptive—to take them to the top. I'd known a few Wall Street patients like that, and a couple of doctors, too.

"I'm not crazy. I told you."

"I don't mean to suggest that. I have to ask you one more question. With all you've been through, have you had any thoughts of ending your life?"

He paused as if he needed to consider the question carefully, which was telling in and of itself. *That's why his wife brought him here,* I thought.

"I couldn't do that to Nora," he said at last.

"Good," I said, although his answer hadn't been straightforward and he was not telling me everything. I had enough to make a start on helping him to feel better, anyway. "I'm going to prescribe you a tranquilizer that will help you to relax. I'll ask the nurse to bring it. Meanwhile, I'll have a word with your wife, if that's okay."

I walked out of the cubicle and went through a locked door at the end of the hallway to the waiting room beyond. There, perched on a dirty chair under a dismal fluorescent light, was Nora Shapiro. Harry hadn't come as a surprise, but his spouse did. She was younger, perhaps forty-five, but she didn't fit the archetype of a thin, blond second Wall Street wife—she looked more like a teacher or a professor. Her dark brown hair spilled out over a catlike face with wide, high cheekbones, and she wore studious tortoiseshell glasses. She looked up at me gently, her eyes soft and melancholy.

Some wives I'd seen in that chair had been gripped not only by the uncertainty and anxiety of a spouse whose loved one is ill, but by barely controlled anger. *You don't understand,* one of them had told me. *This wasn't the deal.* The woman had tolerated long hours alone, having to bring up their children by herself, run the household, and attend boring dinners and look as if she were enjoying it. In return, she'd had the status of being married to an alpha male who kept her in wealth and status, with New York foundations and boards competing for her favors. She hadn't signed up to find her husband transformed into a weakling who'd lost his self belief.

Nora didn't look like that. She displayed no anger or resentment at her enforced presence in the ER. The only thing that emanated from her was love and concern for Harry, as if nothing he could do would sap her affection for him. There was something about her, patiently awaiting news of her distressed mate, that touched me. That was how a spouse should be, I'd always believed: my mother had been like that. Until she'd been betrayed.

"Mrs. Shapiro? I'm Dr. Cowper. I've just seen your husband and I've come to have a chat, if that's all right."

"Thank you, Doctor."

Nora twisted her hands together nervously as I sat down by her. She wore an antique silver ring on one finger with an intricate pattern etched on it. It looked as though she'd found it herself in an out-of-the-way shop, not just snapped it up automatically at Tiffany's. She gazed at me plaintively, as if we were old friends and she trusted my counsel.

"I thought I should bring Harry in, just in case," she said. "Was I right?"

"I'm sure that was best. Can you tell me what worried you?"

"I don't know how to describe it. He lost his job, you know. It was so unfair what they did to him. That was last fall. After that, he seemed to deteriorate, to drift out of reach. He got much quieter than he'd been before, and he looked as if he was in pain all the time. He kept on waking up in the night. I sometimes found him pacing around our apartment at three in the morning. He couldn't stand what had happened."

"What made you come here?"

"We went to East Hampton for the weekend. We've got a place out there. I went out for a walk on the beach this afternoon, and when I came back into the house, I heard music from his study. I went through and he was sitting there staring out of the window. He was holding a cocktail glass and . . ." She rummaged in her handbag. "This was on the table."

As she said it, she pulled a shiny object out of her bag and passed it to me. I looked down to find a nickel pistol with a walnut grip lying in my hand. It had a stubby barrel with a notched sight at the end of the barrel. I noticed that it said MADE IN ITALY on the side. It felt cold and heavy, and I almost let it fall to the floor in shock.

"Pete?" I called, getting up from the waiting room chair with the gun still in my hand and taking a step backward. I rapped on the locked door. Pete opened it and I held the gun out grip first, not aiming it at him. I didn't know gun etiquette, but I sensed that wouldn't be the right thing to do.

"Is this safe?" I asked.

Pete took the gun and examined it, then slipped a catch and slid the magazine out of the stock. He handed the two parts back to me separately.

"That's fine. The safety's on," he said. "Beretta Cheetah. Nice weapon."

I couldn't think of a reply to that, so I just nodded and he stepped back inside the ward. I sat next to Nora again and tried to carry on with our conversation as if nothing abnormal had just happened. It was common for Pete to find knives on patients as they came in, but I'd never been handed a gun before.

"Whose weapon is this, Mrs. Shapiro?"

"It's supposed to be mine. I mean, I've never used it. I wouldn't know what to do with it. The permit's in Harry's name. There were some break-ins nearby and he said we needed one in case I was alone. He kept it in his study, locked in a drawer—"

Nora gasped, unable to complete her sentence, and her eyes filled with tears as her pent-up distress overwhelmed her. I felt sorry for her, having to carry this responsibility for a man who'd never needed to be protected before.

"I need you to store this somewhere safe," I said. "It's important that your husband can't get at it for now."

She nodded, still gulping. "I can do that. I've got a safe for my jewelry. Harry doesn't know the combination."

"Please put it there right away," I said, handing her the gun and the magazine and watching her put them back in her bag alongside her makeup and her ordinary things. "You were absolutely right to bring him here."

An understatement, of course. A middle-aged white male with several symptoms of major depression including suicidal ideation who'd been drinking and had a gun? Never mind his importance to the hospital and Duncan's involvement: if that was not a slam-dunk admission for danger to self, nothing was. The women who talked about suicide weren't generally the ones to be worried about—it was the lone man who never said anything but walked into the woods one day and ended it all. The only issue was whether it would be voluntary or if I would have to commit Harry against his will.

"You've been very understanding, Doctor. I'm so grateful to you," she said.

She reached forward and placed her hand on the back of mine. Her palm was warm, and as she rested it there briefly, I could see tears in her eyes. I wished that I could cure her husband for her then and there, but I believed we could bring him back to decent health within a month or two. After excusing myself, I went to check with Maisie. Good news: there was a bed in York East. I dreaded to think of Duncan's reaction if I'd had to force Harry to bunk in a shared room on Twelve South with a psychotic.

Some people, however, are hard to please.

"No fucking way," Harry responded to my suggestion that he sign himself in. He was still in room four, now standing in his gown. It trailed halfway down his legs, leaving his calves bare, and his shiver had gotten worse.

"Mr. Shapiro, I do understand your feelings, but I'm in no doubt that it's best for you to be admitted so we can help you immediately."

"What if I refuse?" he said, glaring truculently at me.

It was a tough question, to which the true answer was: *I'll have to lock you up.* I tried to phrase it more gently. "To be honest, I'm very concerned about your state of health, and it's my duty to protect you. We do have powers to admit you involuntarily."

"That sounds like a threat," he said, his nostrils flaring.

"I wouldn't put it that way," I said soothingly. "I really do think it is best, for all sorts of reasons, for you to be with us. Your wife told me that she found you with a gun this afternoon, and that concerns me greatly."

I hoped that my mention of the weapon might extract the truth about what he'd been thinking in that room, but he didn't respond directly. His head dipped until it hung limply between his shoulders. He sighed, the fight leaving him.

"I need to talk to Nora," he said.

Ten minutes later, the deal was done and I was on the phone to the charge nurse in York East. We didn't send ER patients up with a full report, just a summary of the initial diagnosis and a mental status exam. Danger to self, danger to others, unable to care for self— whatever was our reason to admit them to a closed ward, rather than just send them away with some pills and an outpatient appointment. When they were assigned to an attending and a team resident, they would be examined again. My job was almost done.

"I'm admitting a fifty-eight-year-old male with a differential diagnosis of adjustment disorder with anxiety and depressed mood, or major depression," I said, running briefly through Harry's symptoms and affect. "His spouse is supportive and will visit tomorrow."

Stepping outside, I saw Pete pushing Harry in a wheelchair toward the elevators as Nora watched their retreat. Everyone we signed in was wheeled up to the wards with their notes on their laps to make it harder for them to escape on the way. It was the last I thought I'd see of him.

3

There were plenty of others like Harry around that time. Not as well-known or as powerful, with their names carved on the hospital's walls, but all with the same crushed and baffled air of highfliers who'd fallen to earth.

When I'd been a resident, I didn't know how many cases I'd treat of clinical narcissism, but suddenly it was all around me. We were taught about a condition called narcissistic injury, a blow to the egos of the self-centered and manipulative. Their personalities had been formed by a parent they'd been able to please only with achievement, who'd never given them unconditional love. Wall Street must lure such people because the hospital was full of them—all wanting special treatment, claiming to know more than I did about therapy, and generally being insufferable.

To have their status stripped away was a terrible blow. They came through the ER and the clinic in agony after the crash had triggered their plummet into anxiety or depression. They sat silently by themselves, pale-faced and shaking, their brains whirring to make sense of how it had all gone wrong. One thing was clear: They didn't want to be treated by a thirty-three-year-old psych a couple of years out of residency. I looked too young, although I was as old as some of them. I wasn't important enough.

One of them, a man in his thirties who'd run a real estate fund on Madison Avenue, had been there a couple of weeks before Harry. The fund had $2 billion at its height but was down to nothing, being squeezed by the banks that had lent him money. A friend of his brought him in one night after fetching him from a hotel room where he'd holed up, high on Ketel One vodka and cocaine, screaming at the room service waiter. I'd admitted him, but the next day, sobered up, he wouldn't look at me. He'd demanded to see a real doctor.

Which was why, when I returned on Monday for morning rounds on Twelve South, I didn't expect to be paged by Jim Whitehead, the York East unit chief and head of inpatient psychiatry. I couldn't afford to alienate Jim if I wanted to get on in my career, but when I called him back, he sounded irritated.

"I have a patient here who'd like to be seen by you, Doctor," he said formally. "Mr. Shapiro."

Jim was tall and solemn and had stiff black hair with a few gray flecks distributed throughout: even those were carefully delineated. His shirt and suit were always clean and pressed, as if dirt and crumbs slid off them. It beats me how he kept pin-sharp creases in his pants despite being seated for most of the day. When not on York East, he had a lucrative private practice into which he gathered quite a few of his Episcopal patients. *He probably wants to shift Harry over there,* I thought, *and doesn't want me in the way.*

Despite Jim's mood and the difficulties I feared it could cause me, the news that Harry had asked for me gave me a thrill that I tried to keep out of my voice. I'd thought of Harry a few times that weekend and had even let myself fantasize briefly about him becoming my patient—hadn't Nora hinted she wanted that? Despite his temper, Harry had many attractive qualities. He was wealthy and well known, and having the whole wing named after him made him a trophy asset that other doctors would covet. Besides that, he was intriguing. There was another story there, behind the headlines, which I wanted to hear. Best of all, I was confident that I could help him, since middle-aged depression is highly treatable. My fantasy was coming true.

I left the Twelve South residents to get on with running things and made my way out of the ward, unlocking and relocking the secure double doors with the jangling bunch of keys that hung at my belt. We referred to patients slipping out as "elopement" rather than "escape," as if it were a romantic adventure, but I felt like a jailer. York East was one floor up, with a view over the river toward a new condominium block in Long Island City topped by a sign that said FOR RENT. I found Jim in his office by the ward, reading notes on the clipboard he always carried with him. I walked in and sat in front of his desk.

"Mr. Shapiro?" I said.

Jim carefully finished what he was doing before looking up, signaling that he wasn't going to be distracted by the affair. "Mr. Shapiro," he said before waiting silently, as if his job were to listen and mine were to explain.

"I don't know very much about the case, I'm afraid. I admitted him from the ER on Friday. Danger to self. It was the first time I'd seen him, so I'm surprised he's asked for me. Has he been assessed?"

Jim furrowed his brow, which was as close as he got to an open display of annoyance.

"Not for want of trying," he said. "I was told of his admission on Friday night and I came by on Saturday morning so we could start treatment immediately. It sounded as if he was in distress."

So Jim came in on a Saturday, I thought. Not many patients got that treatment. Harry had been unhappy, but so were most of those who got admitted to the ER on Friday night—just as the psychs were leaving for the weekend. With the nurses watching them, there was no need to hurry, so they had to sit it out on the wards until Monday with tranquilizers to soothe them. Yet Jim had taken the time to see Harry the morning after his admission. Either Sarah Duncan had made him give our new inpatient the VIP treatment or he'd spotted the potential in Harry himself.

"He wasn't cooperative?"

"When I arrived, his wife was with him and they wanted privacy. I came back yesterday, but Mrs. Shapiro said he'd wait to see you today. She apologized, but said it was typical. He always puts his trust in a small circle of people, and he's taken a liking to you, it seems."

"Interesting," I said, trying to portray Harry's rejection of Jim as an insight into his personality we could examine together. But Jim still looked irked. Harry was used to others being at his beck and call, I imagined. He probably hadn't noticed the significance of Jim's arrival to see him on the weekend.

"There we are," Jim said, looking at his watch. "I'm due in Westchester early this afternoon. I'll leave him in your hands."

We had a facility in the New York suburbs for the well-off who wanted to recuperate in more bucolic surroundings. I'd wondered on Friday whether to send Harry there, but it had been late.

Jim unlocked the unit and guided me to Harry's room, which was about the best we had at Episcopal—the medical equivalent of a penthouse suite. It had a wider bed than the cots on Twelve South and a couple of soft chairs in institutional brown next to a window that overlooked the East River. Harry was pacing up and down by them, clenching and unclenching a fist. He was wearing a crisp monogrammed shirt and looked livelier, but his expression wasn't any more welcoming.

"Dr. Cowper has arrived, Mr. Shapiro. I'll let you two have a talk," Jim said, and he slipped back out. I heard the door to the ward click shut as he left.

"Hello, Mr. Shapiro. How are you feeling?" I said.

Harry glowered at me, his eyes burning.

"I want to leave," he said quietly.

"I see. Well, let's talk about that," I said, crossing to his side of the room and taking one of the chairs.

He briefly stood there glaring before sitting opposite me. It was a lovely morning and the sun was casting a square of light on the floor. There were many worse places to get stranded—an airport, a police station—but his reaction was typical of people who woke up in a secure ward after being persuaded to sign in. They found themselves locked up, with sharp objects removed for safety, needing to ask permission for anything, and they went crazy if they weren't in that condition already. I glanced at Harry's notes. There was little there but a scrip for Klonopin, a longer-lasting tranquilizer than the Ativan I'd given out in the ER. His mental status had not been fully assessed, and he hadn't been interviewed about his history or started on antidepressants. The only psych he'd talked to at length remained me, on Friday night.

"How have you been sleeping?" I said.

"I want to leave," he repeated slowly, as if I hadn't listened the first time. I found it hard to hold his intense gaze.

I tried to prevaricate. "I know it must be difficult to be here, but I think it's a good idea to talk so I can get a sense of how you are. Then we can start on treatment and you can leave, maybe in a day or two. We don't want to keep you in here·any longer than you're comfortable with, believe me."

Harry flinched with irritation and got up to stare out of the window. "I don't think you heard what I said," he growled over his shoulder.

I didn't like what I was seeing. Harry was just as moody as he'd been in the ER, but more agitated, which was a bad combination. Patients who are very depressed may think of killing themselves, but they lack the energy to do it. The trickiest moment is when they start to feel slightly better and more capable of action. He was also angry, which was worrying. Suicide is an act of hostility, not only to the suicide victim himself, but also to the person he blames for his plight.

All in all, I wasn't inclined to release Harry before he had stabilized and I had a better sense of what was going on in his head. Legally, I was in a far stronger position than he. Having signed himself in, he could petition to be let out at any time. But the hospital was allowed to hold him for seventy-two hours before his lawyers could spring him. It would be a disaster if things got that far, given that Harry had paid for the wing in which he was incarcerated, but I didn't imagine that it would. Three days would be plenty as long as he calmed down.

"What worries you about being here?"

"I can't sleep," he said, turning to me. "The bed's uncomfortable, the blankets are thin, I was cold all night. The traffic noise kept me awake. I'm fine, don't you understand? There's nothing wrong with me."

I listened to the buzz of the cars on the FDR Drive. It sounded pretty routine for New York, and fainter than the noise in my own apartment, but that wasn't the point. Anxiety and wealth had made Harry hypersensitive. The thread count on the grayish sheets was lower than he was used to, and there was no goose-down duvet. He wouldn't have noticed either if he'd been at ease.

"I'm sorry, Mr. Shapiro. Perhaps we can discuss all this with your wife and make a discharge plan. We'll try to agree on a way forward."

Harry gave a cynical grunt, but he at least agreed to wait for Nora. On the way back to Twelve South, I considered my predicament. Jim's escape to Westchester had put me in charge of Harry, and he was becoming a difficult assignment despite my earlier wish to get hold of him. I couldn't in good conscience let him out immediately, but he had a lot more power than most patients—and no compunction about using it.

My best hope, I thought, was Nora.

An hour later I was standing in what we generously called the library, a room with a sprinkling of books and a computer on which patients could send email, listening to Lydia Petrovsky, a birdlike patient who had been with us for a week. Unlike Harry, she showed no sign of wanting to leave—quite the opposite—but her insurer was threatening to withdraw coverage and the finance department wanted her out. As I was trying to persuade her to go back to her apartment and attend the day clinic, my pager vibrated with a summons to see the president.

Sarah Duncan's office was in a corner of the Shapiro Pavilion, with a view toward the Queensboro Bridge that went to waste. Her twin assistants were both pale and pretty, in their mid-twenties, and dressed immaculately in short skirts and chunky jewelry. One gave me a bottle of water from a small refrigerator and a pro forma apology for Duncan keeping me waiting, which seemed to be the normal course of events. Then she returned to clicking through emails. Since no one else was appreciating the view, I looked at the cars rumbling over the bridge from Queens to Manhattan. The Williamsburg Bridge and the far reaches of Brooklyn were visible through its girders as a cable car looped its way to Roosevelt Island.

"Dr. Cowper?" said a low voice from the doorway, making me jump in surprise. "Please come through."

Duncan had translucent eyes, silver hair shorn into a bob, and a face that was too smooth to be natural. She scared me. I followed her into a cool corner office that was laid out neatly with no stray papers. There was a sofa, two armchairs, and a glass-topped desk with two inch-thick files resting on it, a fountain pen set precisely beside them. None of the furniture was the standard-issue stuff of the kind that cluttered the rest of the place. She stood by her desk, moving a sheet of paper in front of her and examining it minutely.

"Dr. Cowper, I've just been reading about your work here." She tapped the file. "Very impressive, I must say. You are clearly a highly valued member of the team," she said, as if pinning a minor medal on me.

"Thank you, Mrs. Duncan. That's kind."

"I didn't interrupt you, by the way? You have a few minutes to spare?"

"It sounded as if it was urgent."

"That's one thing I like about doctors—always ready for an emergency," she said with a curt laugh as she gestured for me to sit opposite her on a sofa. There were clearly other things about us that she didn't like. "This must be one of the trickiest situations I've faced in my time here."

"I take it you mean Mr. Shapiro?"

"I count myself as a friend of Nora Shapiro, whom I recruited to our board, so I'm anxious to do everything we can for them. You did the right thing to admit him, but I'm hearing that he now prefers to be discharged."

"He told me so this morning."

"I take it that we can fulfill his wishes," she said, gazing at me firmly.

There was a pause while I thought about what to say, apart from: *Mind your own business. You're a bureaucrat, not a doctor.* I'd taken the Hippocratic oath to heal patients, while she was in charge of keeping the books balanced. We'd always been assured that when the two clashed, Hippocrates won.

"That might not be best immediately. I'm worried about him leaving while in a fragile condition. I'm sure you understand."

She sighed and tapped her finger on the arm of the sofa. "Dr. Cowper, you're a young man and you've got a long and hopefully distinguished career ahead, so let me explain something to you, between ourselves. The Shapiros are very important to the future of this hospital. I recently discussed with Nora our plans for a new cancer wing, and she's talked of making a generous donation that might help to save thousands of lives."

"I see," I said, shifting in my seat.

I remembered not taking Duncan's call in the ER, gesturing to Maisie that I wasn't available. How smart I'd been then and how stupid now to be in the middle of this political mess. How could I balance my duty to help Harry against the lives of others whom his money might help? The trouble with psychiatry was that patients believed they could diagnose their own state of mind pretty well, and the more disturbed they were, the more likely to believe they were fine. It was Harry's view of himself against mine.

"If we lost her support, that would be a tragedy, not just for us but for many, many patients."

"I see that, but—"

"So, look. The last thing I want is to interfere in your treatment of Mr. Shapiro, but surely he can be cared for outside these walls?"

"Well . . ." I paused, trying to think of a way out. "I've agreed with Mr. Shapiro that we'll talk with his wife later and agree on a plan."

Duncan gave me a frosty smile as she got to her feet. "Good. I'll leave you to make a decision." She walked to her desk and, as I got halfway out the door, added in a low voice: "Do ensure it's the right one."

I found Harry sitting with Nora in the patients' lounge in York East, which looked like a hotel lobby. It had halfway decent furnishings and a flat-panel television—an advance on the old cathode-ray sets fixed to the ceiling in Twelve South. There was no one else in the room, just the two of them side by side on a sofa with hands intertwined.

Nora disentangled hers and got to her feet, leaving Harry sitting by himself. "I'm so glad to see you again, Dr. Cowper," she said.

Seeing her, I had the same feeling as the first time. She wasn't like Harry or Duncan, with their easy recourse to intimidation. She didn't behave like a powerful person or someone on a higher social level— her affect was of surprise at being in that position at all. After my encounter with Duncan, I knew the only way I could avoid either doing something I felt unhappy about or making myself unpopular with my employer was to persuade Nora that her husband should stay for a few days. That would require me to be blunt.

"Perhaps you and I should have a chat in private. Would you mind if we used your room for ten minutes, Mr. Shapiro?"

Harry nodded guardedly, as if he were suspicious of my intentions but couldn't think of a reason to refuse. I closed Harry's bedroom door behind us and turned to find Nora already sitting on the bed with her legs crossed and one heel on the ground. It felt too intimate to sit next to her on the bed; I thought of staying on my feet, but that didn't seem right either. I needed to woo her a little to persuade her to keep Harry with us, so I compromised by sitting at the other end of the bed, by the pillows.

"Your husband told me he wants to discharge himself immediately, Mrs. Shapiro. How do you feel about that?" I started cautiously.

"I don't know what's best for him, Doctor. He's very upset, and I think he blames me for forcing him to come here. I only wanted to help."

She looked fragile, and I saw tiny lines form by her eyes as she frowned. I liked the way that she hadn't succumbed to the Upper East Side surgeons the way Duncan seemed to have done. It took nerve for someone in her circle to resist the peer pressure to have a blandly perfect face.

"You did the right thing, but I'm worried about your husband's mood at the moment. I'm sure he'll recover, but I'd feel happier if you could persuade him to stay a few days, just to get his treatment under way."

"Are you worried he'd . . . ?"

Her voice trailed away and I looked firmly into her soft eyes, not wanting to miss my best opportunity.

"To be frank, I am still concerned about self-harm. I'm sure he'd listen to you if you advised him not to leave."

Nora looked down hesitantly. "I don't know if I can do that. He's very unhappy, and he's not listening to me anymore. Can't he be treated as an outpatient? I'll make sure he's safe. I've locked that gun away, like you told me."

I pursed my lips as I thought. I didn't feel happy about letting Harry leave in that state, but if Nora couldn't help, then I'd have to defy both Harry and Duncan to keep him there. It was the slim chance of Harry killing himself against my certain career suicide if I stood in his way. Nora looked at me pleadingly and I felt myself weaken. She'd shown that she would look after her husband, I reflected. It wasn't as if I would be discharging someone who had no one to guard him.

"Well, if you believe that you can't change his mind . . . But we need to have a plan in place, and he would have to enter treatment immediately for his own sake. Do you know a psychiatrist he'd agree to see regularly?"

"Harry wants you to be his doctor," she said. "He likes you."

That gratified me, I have to admit. Harry did want me to treat him, as I'd hoped. Jim wouldn't be happy, but I didn't care. It was also a relief, which is how I justified it to myself. If I had to discharge Harry, I'd at least be able to watch over him. Anyway, there was no alternative: he had both Nora and Duncan on the run. I put him on Lexapro, an antidepressant that wouldn't make him more agitated, and half a milligram of Klonopin twice a day. I arranged to see him in two days at my office and gave her my number to call if his mood worsened.

Then, signing my name on the release, I let him go.

4

On Tuesday the phone rang just after dawn, jolting me from sleep into the gray bedroom light. I fumbled for the receiver, which still sat on Rebecca's side.

"Ben?" said a high voice that I recognized as my father's second wife. "Were you asleep? Or is it evening?" Jane had a shaky grasp of time zones and often added the five-hour difference between London and New York instead of subtracting.

"No, it's fine. I'm up," I said, lying instinctively and squinting at my alarm clock. "It's six. Six in the morning."

"It's your father," she said, ignoring the implausibility of the denial. "He's had a heart attack, but he's okay, I think. He's in West Middlesex Hospital. . . ."

She trailed off uncertainly, as if unsure of where she was or what to do, and I felt a pang of sympathy for her, which was unusual. My doziness had evaporated, and I struggled to grasp what had occurred while my emotions jostled uncertainly in the background. I wanted him to be okay, but there was something murkier, too—a guilty satisfaction that he was mortal. Even he could be knocked off his triumphalist course.

"He was fine when he woke up. He was in the kitchen making himself coffee, talking to me about a case. Then he said he was getting a pain in his arm. He tried to sit down, but he fainted. I called the ambulance."

"Is he conscious now?"

"Yes, he came round in the hospital. They're doing tests. Is Rebecca there? I thought she would know what to do."

My girlfriend—or former girlfriend, as I was coming to accept—had removed her stuff a couple of weekends before, taking her bewilderment and hurt out on the apartment wall. In the living room, I'd found her desk and shelves gone, leaving a dozen holes in the wall for the resident—in this case me—to stitch up. I'd peered at the wounded plaster in places where she'd clearly lost her composure and ripped out screws, and I'd thought how unusual it was. She was noted for her calm precision as a surgeon.

"She's away. What did they say about his condition?" I said, feeling the sting of being judged not a real enough doctor to contribute.

"Just that he'd had a heart episode."

"Are they planning to operate?" I knew enough about cardiac illness to know it was good news that they had not wheeled him straight to the catheter laboratory to open a blocked artery. They still had to be assessing the damage.

"I don't know. I should have found out more, but I couldn't grasp half of what the doctor said."

"No, it's not your fault," I said insincerely. I knew there was no point in quizzing her further. She'd told me all she could.

I'd always been baffled by what my father saw in Jane, beyond her youth, a fine pair of breasts, and her hero worship of him. They had met when he was forty-two and Jane was a thirty-year-old pupil at his chambers, and soon afterward he'd left my mother, a woman of much greater taste, kindness, and sensitivity than her usurper. Maybe a son is just a terrible witness, but it used to infuriate me that she'd accepted the betrayal so passively.

"Don't be too hard on your father, Ben," she'd admonished me one day.

"*Hard on him?* How can you say that after what he did?" I had shouted back, and rushed out of the room, blinded by anger and guilt for my own role in the affair, which I hadn't confessed to her.

"Where's Guy?" I asked Jane. My brother was a branding consultant who was highly in demand in exotic countries around the world.

"I think he's on business somewhere. Malaysia, or perhaps it was Vietnam. Roger asked me to find him, but I haven't managed yet."

"Does he want *me* there?" I asked, irritated that I was so clearly at the bottom of the list, below even my ex-girlfriend.

"Oh . . . Yes. Of course," she said.

"I'm coming. I'll try to find a flight this evening," I said.

I lay back and slapped the duvet in frustration. Even in hospital, four thousand miles away, my father had an unrivaled ability to rile me. But I wasn't going to let that prevent me from getting involved: it sounded as if he might actually need me. I was already hauling a suitcase across my room when I remembered Harry.

My father was lying on a bed in a surprisingly pleasant private room in the West Middlesex Hospital, wearing a short gown over his pajamas and reading the *Daily Telegraph*. Some of the cash that had flooded into London since I'd left had found its way into the National Health Service, and he was being treated in a clean, light building that squatted amid the other Victorian buildings like a spaceship.

"Hello, mate. Come in," he said as I tapped on the door and put my head round.

He'd picked up this mockney use of "mate" for his friends and colleagues in the past year or two, as if to compensate with demotic familiarity for his wealth and success. In his late career, he was paid outrageous amounts by companies that wanted to curb their tax bills and needed his slippery yet watertight legal advice on how to launder money through small Caribbean islands. He reached across with a pale hand and shook mine as I sat down by him, the plastic tag on his wrist shaking with the movement. I cast a professional eye over him. His face was wan and his thinning gray hair was askew, but he didn't seem to be in pain.

"Hold on, I want to see your chart," I said, reaching to the end of the bed where it sat in a frame. My instinct had been right. He'd had a mild myocardial infarction, and they'd run blood tests before putting a catheter into an artery in his groin and clearing a blockage near his heart with a stent. He was on Plavix, aspirin, and a beta-blocker. They would release him soon.

"You're going to live," I said.

"I reckon so, if I've got any blood left. They kept taking more of it. Bunch of vampires, I reckon."

"They have to do serial blood tests to check for enzymes. It shows whether the heart muscle is damaged." I could feel myself straining to prove my medical expertise, but it didn't impress him.

"They seem to know what they're doing. I like my doctor, I've got to say. She knows her stuff, put the fear of God into me about exercise and what I have to eat. Very capable. Reminds me of your Rebecca."

"Well, you should listen to her," I said, ignoring the mention of Rebecca. Both he and Jane appeared to regard her as some kind of savior, but what business was it of theirs? I'd thought my mother was a good wife, but my father hadn't agreed with that. "It was a close call. I was worried about you, Dad."

He looked at me as if unsure of how to treat my expression of emotion, so used was he to our avoidance of intimacy, and cleared his throat. "All's well that ends well, eh? You got here fast."

"I was lucky with the flight," I said, avoiding his eyes. "Where's Jane?"

"She was here this morning and then she took Lizzie to school. She usually goes by bus these days. Quite the young woman."

Lizzie was my stepsister, a sixteen-year-old who seemed *au fait* when I had taken her to Madame Tussauds on my last visit, with an impressive array of C-list celebrities.

"They grow up fast, don't they?" I said.

"They sure do."

The immediate crisis over, we had relapsed into talking to each other like strangers in a pub. I was starting to feel duped that I'd over-reacted by flying in so quickly when he could clearly do without me. It was an old feeling—that I was naïve to care for him.

It's easy to lie, and it's simple to betray the person you most love. I found that out when I was twelve years old, and the man who taught me was Roger Cowper.

He must have started his affair with Jane when I was eleven, I once calculated. Perhaps it was at my birthday party, to which she came one afternoon to drop off some files from the office. There was a clown performing in our garden, and my mother made Jane tea. Then they came out and stood by the kitchen together, looking along the garden and smiling at the clown's antics and at each other.

A few months later, I came home from school early one afternoon with a cold that had worsened during the day. It was a windy fall, and the horse chestnut trees had strewn half-open spiky green capsules across the pavement, a field of conkers waiting to be found by children coming home. That afternoon there was only me, running between trees and stamping on the harvest to prize loose the glossy brown seeds.

When I came into the house, letting myself in with the key my parents had given me, I banged the door shut and went through to the kitchen to scavenge for some cake. I came out again into the living room and heard a noise on the landing, then my father's footsteps and another set of feet behind his. Jane's face was flushed, I remember, but I wasn't old enough to appreciate what I'd stumbled upon.

It was strange to find my father home at that time: he told me that he'd had a case in west London. I remember her being awkward, not knowing how to talk to a child in the way that most adults I knew—my parents and my friends' parents—did. She had an alien quality about her, which I know only with hindsight was sexual.

We went back into the kitchen. My father was unusually cheerful, I remember, slicing more cake for me and asking me what had gone on at school, while Jane hardly said anything. After a while, she got up and said she ought to get back to the office, and my father showed her out. Then my brother came home and we watched television before my father said he was going to fetch my mother from Paddington station.

"I'll take Ben with me," he said, "and Guy can mind the store."

My father had bought a Rover and he let me sit in the front, which he hadn't done before. The seats were leather, and I smelled them as we drove, the wipers squeaking on the windscreen in the drizzle. I watched the colored segments of the dashboard display until we got to Paddington and waited across the road from the entrance to the station, where my parents had arranged to meet. The radio was on and he leaned over to turn it down.

"Listen, Benny, will you do one thing for me?" he said.

"What, Dad?"

"You know Jane, who you just met? Don't mention her to Mum, will you? I think it's better kept between us."

I looked at him, not quite understanding what he meant, and I saw his awkwardness, the pleading expression on his face that I hadn't known before. It was an adult face, different from a child's, with its folds of flesh, its pockmarks, its stubble and sweat. I thought of him as huge—impossible to knock off course from sheer bulk—but he seemed vulnerable in that moment. I was pleased to be taken into his confidence, for my agreement to be needed. It seemed like a small thing not to reveal the presence of another woman in our home.

"Okay, Dad," I said.

My mother came out of the station just after that, and she ran across the road, in the gap behind a bus. She put her head through the rolled-down passenger-side window when she saw me and laughed with the relief of being reunited. She was only a few years older than

I am now. She'd been born in Virginia, although she'd lived all of her adult life in London after meeting my father as a student in the 1970s. The British are supposed to be genteel and Americans boors, but she disproved it. She'd taken up British habits—gardening, visiting seaside towns—but not the rudeness.

"How are you, boys?" she said gaily.

"We've just about coped without you," my father said.

"You haven't missed having a woman about the house, then?"

"What do you say, Benny?" my father asked me, a warning look in his eyes.

"It's been fine," I mumbled.

He drove us home, with my mother insisting on me sitting in the front while she chatted happily from the backseat. She'd been to visit a friend in Oxford for a couple of days. We stopped to pick up fish and chips on Chiswick High Street as we neared home—a reward for good behavior, my father called it.

For a time I forgot it, basking in the glow of my intimacy with my father—the fact that he relied on me for something that mattered to him. Jane was filed away in my mind until a few months later, when my parents' arguments, which had been occasional and brief, became loud and vituperative. From my bedroom, I heard terrible threats and recriminations being exchanged.

My brother, three years older than I, was contemptuous of my frailty and taunted me for crying in the middle of one volcanic eruption. Half-fascinated and half-scared himself, he passed on gossip from his forays halfway down the stairs to overhear what my parents were shouting about. Some woman called Jane, he reported.

I was tempted to flaunt my knowledge of her, but something told me not to. It would have revealed that I'd kept a secret, not only from him but also from my mother. As my father's affair progressed to its inevitable conclusion—my parents calling us down to give us a stilted explanation, my father leaving with a suitcase and hugging us in the hallway—the ball of my guilt and complicity swelled inside me.

My mother hid her distress from us after he'd gone, except once. One day, when I was sixteen and the postdivorce arrangements for weekends, birthdays, and Christmases had become routine, I found her in our living room. She was looking at a photo of us four together, my father with his arms around us.

"I wish I'd realized, Ben. I could've done something," she said.

My heart twisted again. She wasn't crying: I think her tears had long been shed.

"It wasn't your fault," I said, my teenage self unable to conjure up more.

From that moment on, I had an uneasy sense around my father of being trapped together in our deception, him not knowing whether I had blurted out the truth to her. It was too difficult for either of us to acknowledge, so our secret was buried with her.

Ten years later, my mother had died of cancer while I was at medical school in London. It was the catalyst for me to depart for New York, escaping my father's guilt-ridden bonhomie and Jane's relief that she no longer had to compete. Jane sat a couple of rows back at the service, while my father occupied a front pew with my brother and me, and edged up to stand beside him only at the gravesite. It hadn't made her presence there any less painful.

I bumped into Jane on the way out of the hospital, in the store that sold newspapers, sweets, and shiny helium balloons bearing cheerful messages for the patients. She was squatting with her back to me to pick up a magazine, and the white strap of her bra was pressed up against her cream blouse in a way that provoked in me desire mixed with hostility. That wasn't, I'd come to realize in adulthood, a contradiction. I kissed her airily on the cheek, barely grazing her skin, and told her that my father looked well.

"Have you got time for a cup of coffee, at least?" she said, as if it were typical of me to be rushing off.

Look, I've just flown across the bloody Atlantic to see him, I thought, but I kept it to myself and nodded. We found a seat in the hospital's atrium, holding two cups of foamed milk sprinkled with brown powder. The space was lit from above by a cloudy sky.

"How *are* you?" she said. "We haven't seen you for *ages*. I hope you told Roger he'll have to change his diet. You know what he's like."

"I sure do," I said, matching her smile despite the tug of rivalry I still felt when she talked of my father proprietarily. We remained in temporary harmony while I explained what had happened to his heart in terms she grasped, and she looked appreciative.

Our détente didn't last. "When will we see Rebecca again?" she said, licking the foam with her tongue. "I think she's great, Ben. Don't you let her go."

"I'm afraid we're taking a break," I said stiffly.

"Oh, *Ben*. Why? She's such a lovely girl."

That was Jane. No sensitivity, no sense that there were things she shouldn't push. I hadn't paid for a psych to probe into my guilty secrets—I just wanted to be left alone. I felt a prickle of sweat and longed to be out of there, no longer held to emotional account.

"Yes, she is. You're right, Jane. It's all my fault," I said, standing up.

My heart was starting to race with all my long-held resentment against her. It didn't take much to trigger it, and I knew that I had to finish our conversation before I said something I'd regret. As I did so, I looked up and saw a black Audi that I recognized halting outside the entrance. It shouldn't have been there, but I was glad it had flouted the rules.

"I've got to go. I'm getting a lift," I said to her upturned face. "I'll call later to see how Dad is. Take care."

I hurried across the atrium before Jane could stop me, the doors at the entrance sliding obediently open to let me escape.

5

As I reached the Audi, a slim young man in a dark blue uniform got out and opened the rear passenger door, revealing a man sitting comfortably in the back. He was in his mid-fifties, long-legged and broad-chested, with a pink face. His mottled gray hair was unkempt for a banker's, brushing his collar at the back and flopping over his forehead so that his nose protruded like a mole's. His dark gray suit looked expensive but slightly crumpled. He had a rich voice, the product of an English public school, and the self-assurance that went with it.

"Hello there," he said, shaking my hand. "I'm Felix."

He'd called earlier that morning as I'd arrived at the hospital, saying that he'd be sharing my flight home if I didn't mind. His name was Felix Lustgarten, he'd said, and he was an old colleague and friend of

Harry's. I hadn't felt in a position to refuse, not that there was any reason to, and I was still absorbing the shock of what had happened after I'd called Nora on Tuesday morning.

I'd told her that I wouldn't be able to see Harry on Wednesday after all, and she ought to take Harry to see another psych—Jim Whitehead, I'd suggested. Nora had been sympathetic but implacable. After asking about my father and expressing her regret, she'd promised to sort it out. After half an hour, she'd called back to say that she'd arranged for me to fly to London and be back to see Harry as we'd arranged on Wednesday. I hadn't thought she could be serious, but she'd been as good as her word.

"Nora told me your father's been poorly. I do hope he's recovering," Felix said.

"He's doing better, thanks," I said.

The Audi pulled away from the hospital and turned onto the A4 back toward London as Felix adjusted the rear air-conditioning. The car was as hushed as its driver; sitting in those deep leather seats was like being swaddled. I could feel myself relax as the driver accelerated silently past an obstructive truck. This was the cocoon I'd yearned for as Jane had poked tactlessly at my raw emotions. Even Felix's presence was soothing: he had an air of amused detachment that I liked.

"We can shoot you back in comfort, anyway," he said. "Nora insisted I take good care of you."

"That's thoughtful of you, Mr. Lustgarten."

"Felix, please. No one calls me Mister, not even the doorman at my apartment. Actually, I wish he did. Perhaps I should tip him more for the holidays." He leaned forward to address the driver. "How does the traffic look, Frank?"

"A bit nasty along the Embankment, but we're going against it," the man replied.

"Jolly good. You might tell George we're on our way and we should be wheels up by eleven." He turned back and regarded me quizzically. "Now then, I understand you're not allowed to tell me anything, but I can talk, can't I?"

"I can't stop you," I said.

"Hah! Well, nobody can, apart from my wife, bless her. Anyway, Nora told me about Harry, poor chap. He's in a bit of a state, isn't he?"

"That's what Mrs. Shapiro told you?"

Like Jane, Felix was pushing me about things I didn't want to talk about, but I didn't find it uncomfortable because it wasn't about me. It was a patient whose privacy I wanted to protect, not my own. I was used to that.

"Christ, you don't give much away," Felix muttered.

"Do you work here?" I said.

"Nope. New York, where the action is. Mind you, there's been a bit too much of it lately. Every time I look up, another bank has disappeared. At this rate, there won't be any money left for my bonus."

He lapsed into silence for a few minutes, thumbing at his Black-Berry, and I looked out of the window. We reached the Embankment and passed the London Eye, heading east. The hum of the tarmac under the tires was hypnotic, and I could feel myself slipping into a doze when Felix's BlackBerry rang shrilly, making me start.

"Oh dear," he said, looking at the name on the screen. "Have you read *Wind in the Willows*? As soon as Toad goes to jail, the weasels invade Toad Hall. We've got company." He held his BlackBerry to his ear. "John? . . . Delighted to have you on board. Lots of room. We'll be there soon."

He clicked off and looked balefully at me. "Hell is other people. I'm afraid a couple of investment bankers want to cadge a lift. They've been here holding out the begging bowl to the Arabs for capital because Harry lost it all—our new masters, I'm afraid. So much for our chat. I wouldn't trust John with a secret, although it's supposed to be his job to keep them. In fact, I don't trust him, period."

"I thought *you* were an investment banker," I said, puzzled by his contempt for his colleague.

"A banker? Not me, Doctor. I'm just a humble PR man, paid to make them look good. It's a dirty job, but someone's got to do it. Where were we? Oh, Harry. Yes, poor old Harry, my boss and protector. Without him, I'm not sure how long I've got left at Seligman. I don't imagine the new guard will approve of our little jaunt. I'd hoped to keep this under wraps, but fat chance now."

We'd passed north of Tower Bridge and were coasting along by the Thames with Canary Wharf ahead. Felix pointed at it through the windscreen.

"See there? Second tower from the left, a third of the way up. That's where I worked twenty years ago. We were the only ones in the building, it felt like. Desolate bloody place. The London end was in an awful mess. New York sent Harry over to pull the Brits into shape. God, he nearly screamed the place down. It was a shock for the others, but he took a liking to me."

"Did you like him?"

"Strangely, I did. He's a warm-blooded creature, Harry, not a reptile like some of them. He's got a heart."

Felix thumped his chest with a fist, on the spot where most people imagine the heart to be. Then, as the golden fish on the roof of Billingsgate Market swam by, he reached out and traced a pattern on the window with one finger.

"You know Harry's mistake?" he asked. "He reckoned he'd rebuilt Seligman single-handedly—which he more or less did. He thought he could rescue Wall Street and America, too, could take on anything. He stopped watching out for trouble because he thought he couldn't be beaten. Mind you, he wasn't the only one who was smoking his own dope. Turns out none of us are as smart as we thought."

As he spoke, we swung left past some blue concrete blocks and a security barrier on the edge of City Airport. Just ahead, parked in front of a low building, was a small white jet with two engines perched next to its tail and large oval windows running the length of its fuselage. The driver halted next to a man wearing a yellow overjacket and carrying a clipboard. I was back where I'd arrived that morning, in Harry's Gulfstream IV.

Harry's jet felt only distantly related to the regular kind, like a Thoroughbred horse next to a donkey. As we taxied over to the runway and lined up behind a turboprop, I sat in a leather armchair with a cup of coffee beside me in a cork-lined holder. The cabin was covered with gold fittings, from the air-conditioning nozzles to the edges of the walnut panels. Michelle, the blond attendant who'd been my only companion on the way over, hadn't bothered to give us a safety demonstration. I'd latched my seat belt instinctively, but neither Felix nor the two bankers in the rear, immersed in BlackBerrys, had bothered. Together, we occupied a third of the aircraft's dozen seats.

"Tell him to cut the bullshit and talk to me. I thought we had this deal done," the senior-looking one hissed into a phone as the Gulfstream aligned itself at the start of the long runway. "They said they would offer thirty-one, so why don't they offer thirty-one? . . . No, you're not listening . . . No."

He kept talking as the engines fired, but I was lost in the adrenaline rush of takeoff. Instead of the rumbling, straining effort to pick up speed of a passenger jet laden with fuel for an Atlantic crossing, we galloped along the tarmac so rapidly that my head was pushed into the rest. Then we were up and off. As we twisted over Canary Wharf, the city scrolled up the window, making me light-headed. We rose so fast, with a goldfish bowl view of sky and city, that my brain jammed with data.

The jet punched through clouds into clear light, our rate of climb hardly slackening. Across from me, Felix glanced at the *Financial Times,* looking bored, while the men to my rear resumed thumbing through their emails. We leveled out at forty-seven thousand feet in a layer of sky I'd first been introduced to on the flight over. It was a deep azure, and white tendrils spiraled lazily upward from the clouds below.

"Nice, isn't it?" said Felix, glancing over.

"I could get used to it."

The coffee had awakened me, and my sense of being safely coddled was fading, squeezed out by anxiety at the way I was being absorbed into the Shapiros' world. By the time I'd worked out what Nora had meant by her offer, it had been too late. A car had been dispatched to take me to Teterboro Airport, just across the Hudson, for the flight to London. There had been no schedule to keep. The Gulfstream had soared into the night sky, bearing Michelle and me, as soon as I'd waltzed through security.

That night I'd slept on a bed made up by Michelle, without sound or motion to disturb me. The pilots guided the Gulfstream through the skies as she watched over me. I'd felt like a lotus-eater in a gilded world that I might not have the energy to leave. Even as I luxuriated, it troubled me. Psychiatric treatment has a frame. The patient must turn up on schedule and pay the check on time—he must make a commitment to his cure. We didn't let the wealthy dictate their terms any more than the Medicare brigade, yet here was I, drifting away from the protocol with every step I took to help Harry.

"We're above the turbulence here," Felix said. "Concorde used to fly this high, but now it's the guys with their own jets. Come on, I'll introduce you."

He led me three paces down the aisle to the bankers. The older, more talkative one was tall, and his swept-back blond hair was graying at the temples but luxuriant. His face was long and watchful, and he had chiseled features that should have been handsome but were slightly too perfect. Sitting by him was a man in his early thirties, wearing a suit, dark tie, and spectacles. He was viewing a spreadsheet on a laptop computer, and he nodded at me silently, in the manner of a junior partner.

"Ben, this is John Underwood," Felix said, indicating the older man.

"Good to meet you, Ben," Underwood said. "This is Peter Freeman, he's on my team." He gestured toward the younger man. "Felix, I thought we were going to Teterboro. What's all this about Bangladesh?"

"Not Bangladesh. Bangor. Maine," Felix said patiently. "We're going through customs there to drop Ben on Long Island. It's quicker. No one else around."

It was the first I'd heard of Long Island—I'd assumed I would return to New York—and it added to my unease.

Underwood turned to me. "I didn't catch your second name, Ben," he said.

I hesitated. I didn't want more people to know who I was or my connection to Harry. It was already too open a secret for my liking.

"Ben's a friend," interjected Felix. "Let's grant him his privacy."

"Ben the mystery man, then," Underwood said, a glint in his eye.

"John's a fig banker to the stars and confidant of our new chief executive," added Felix, making both sound suspicious.

"Fig?" I asked.

"Financial Institutions Group," said Felix. "A banker who advises other bankers. Go figure." He shook his head. "So here we all are, a happy band of brothers. It sounded as if you were having some trouble there, John."

"Unfortunately, yes. Deals that used to take weeks go on for months now. Nothing's simple anymore."

Freeman tapped a pile of documents. "I've found something on the recap," he said to Underwood. "We might be able to shed the tax liability."

"Two bankers devise a clever way to avoid tax," Felix whispered to me. "What could go wrong? We should leave these wizards to it."

After an hour, Michelle laid out some plates of meats and cheeses, and Felix sipped a glass of red wine as he read. I took a nap. Soon Maine's greensward appeared below, with its ridged coastline and leopard-skin lakes, as if God had picked up Cornwall and splattered it on the other side of the Atlantic. The aircraft floated over a pine forest and a small town dotted with the blue circles of backyard pools before settling gently on a runway.

We had Bangor Airport to ourselves. Apart from a couple of USAF air tankers sitting by corrugated steel hangars, there were no other aircraft in view. We taxied across to the terminal and halted. Michelle opened the front door, and Felix carried on reading without acknowledging that we were no longer in the air. Then a van drove up and a chubby official with a buzz cut entered the cabin.

"Hello, Officer Jones," Felix said, reading his badge. "What's the weather doing today?"

"Going up to about seventy, I believe," the man said, leafing through Felix's passport. He pronounced "about" as "aboot," and I figured we must be close to the Canadian border. Having glanced at our papers, he went to the back to give the bags a cursory glance.

"How are you enjoying the flight, Ben?" Underwood asked, approaching up the aisle and placing his arms on two seats to examine me better.

"I wish I had one of these myself."

"Friends of mine do, but then they worry about the things sitting on the tarmac, costing them money. If it flies, floats, or fucks, rent it—that's what I say."

"Or just cadge a ride, eh, John?" said Felix. His BlackBerry rang. "I'm in Maine. . . . Yes, Maine. Checking out summer camps," he said. *My wife,* he mouthed at me.

"You gentlemen have a good flight," said Officer Jones, and he departed. I seemed to have passed through U.S. Customs and Border Protection while seated in a chair. Within a few minutes, we were aloft again and following the coast south.

"Felix, where are we going?" I said.

"Oh, didn't I mention it? So sorry," he said, turning his head to check what the others were doing. They were heads down in work again, and he spoke quietly. "Nora thought it would be best to take Harry back to East Hampton. I said I'd drop you there."

"Okay," I said, feeling control slipping from me but unable to stop it. Episcopal didn't expect me back for a couple of days, so I was free to visit the Hamptons, but this was a further step into the unknown. I'd started by suspending my judgment to discharge Harry, and then I'd found myself on board his jet. Now I was being taken to him, when convention said we should meet at Episcopal.

"Is this *really* Mr. Shapiro's jet?" I asked Felix.

"Not exactly. It belongs to the bank. We've got a few, although it's awfully politically incorrect. But one of the Gulfstreams is the chief executive's and Harry got to keep it for a year when he left. Smoothed the deal, you know. Mind you," he said, nodding at the two bankers, "some people treat it as public transport."

It was lunchtime as we headed over the ocean to Long Island, and there were few clouds. I saw the tip of the South Fork reaching into the Atlantic like a beckoning finger and the strip of sand lining the coast all the way to the Rockaways. An airstrip stood out below us, like an encircled gray "A" against the green.

"It's been a pleasure, Ben. I do hope everything goes well. Give my best to Harry. I think Nora's sent a car to pick you up," Felix said.

We made a low pass over the ocean and then sank over woods and fields to the tiny bump of our landing. Michelle opened the door at the front with a sad face, as though she were going to miss me terribly. Freeman was talking on a phone as I got up to depart and gave another silent nod.

"I'm going to get a breath of fresh air," Underwood said, following me along the aisle and down the aircraft's steps. He halted at the bottom with one foot on the tarmac as I pulled up the handle on my suitcase.

"I wish I was getting off, too," he said. "I've got a place in Sag Harbor. Harry's in East Hampton, isn't he?"

I shrugged in mock ignorance.

"There's one thing you ought to know, Ben," he said. "Don't you believe Felix's sob stories. Harry brought this thing on himself. He's the one to blame."

"Good to meet you, Mr. Underwood," I said. I walked off toward the low clapboard terminal building, determined not to stay for long.

6

I'd been to the Hamptons a few times to visit friends with summer rentals or to hang out on the beach for a day, but I'd never penetrated those high hedges and pristine gardens. How could I have? Staked by each house on the roads south of Route 27, where the wind rustled the tall trees, were foot-high signs with security company logos and white heraldic boards with black script: *Private Property. Private Way. No Trespassing.*

So as I sat in the front seat of a stone gray Range Rover, scanning white wooden gates and broad driveways, I enjoyed being welcome for once. I glanced to my left every so often, not only to observe a cottage or mini-mansion, but also to take a glimpse at my driver. I knew only her first name: Anna. It was all she'd given away.

When I'd emerged from the airport building into the parking lot, she'd been standing by the car, one black flip-flop-clad foot propped against the driver's door, chewing a stalk and refixing her straw blond hair in a ponytail. She'd been hard to miss because there was no one else in sight and she'd given me a wave and a broad smile, pulling her lips so far back to show her teeth that it looked like a contortionist's trick. I'd grinned back stupidly, wondering what someone like her was doing there—I'd have expected to find her in the city.

She was in her late twenties, I guessed, but had a girlish affect, from her unbridled smile to her dewy skin and red fingernails. She wore a lime green T-shirt, and as she'd turned away to climb into the car, I'd seen the tiny blond hairs on her swanlike neck. She seemed to straddle the border between innocence and experience.

"Beautiful gardens, aren't they?" I said, looking out to my right.

She laughed. "They're crazy, some of them. Look over there on the right, by that white house."

We swung round a corner and passed a long hedge with a tall gate in the middle. Arrayed along both sides of the hedge were six plane trees, each trunk held vertical by three duckbill cables pegged to the ground.

"None of those trees were there last week. They all went up on Sunday."

"You're joking."

"That's how they do things here. They don't believe in delayed gratification."

"There's a lot of security."

She laughed. "You're telling me. They're all paranoid someone might break into their little paradise. I went with Nora to a cocktail party once, a place over near Water Mill some billionaire owns with his blond Hungarian model third wife—she's about seven feet tall. We were in a room at the back and they had these giant screens showing shots of the beach and the ocean. Nora asked her what they were for."

Anna put on an Eastern European accent. "'Our security is *gut* from the bay side, but we are *wulnerable* from the south,'" she said, then switched back to her normal voice. "Ha! Wulnerable from the south! What was she scared of? A platoon of Marines and a beach landing?"

We were getting close to the ocean. I could smell the sea air, and the light had gone a milky white, as if the sun were being refracted through frosted glass. We turned down a lane with a line of houses on the ocean side, perched along a high dune. Anna slowed at the end by a gray split-rail fence. Two weeping willow trees flanked the entrance to a pink gravel drive, which she followed as it curved back on itself and up the steep rise of the dune. Nature had been tamed on this side of the slope. It was planted with sculpted bushes and lawn, divided up the middle by a stone path. We passed two gardeners giving a hedge a morning shave and halted on a square of gravel by one of the prettiest houses I'd ever seen.

It was more cottage than house, like something out of a fairy tale: an oblong stuccoed in pale green, the same color as the lichen spreading over the stones on the ocean side. The roof was tiled in brown cedar shingles that curved over the eaves and around the top of each doorway like a thatch. To the west, where we stood, was a small tower topped with a wizard's hat of shingle. On the side facing the ocean was a pristine lawn ending at a ridge from which the dune tumbled to the beach. A swimming pool edged with white stone, no more than thirty feet long, was cut into the lawn, and beyond was a view of dunes, pristine beach, and ocean that ran for miles.

Sitting on the lawn, gazing out to sea, was Harry.

The girl walked toward a small sign by the side entrance that read SERVICE. I wasn't sure whether it was a comment on our status or just the easiest way to go, but she led me into a light-filled, slate-surfaced kitchen with big stainless-steel appliances. She went over to a brushed-steel intercom on the wall and prodded a button.

"Nora, your guest is here," she said, hardly louder than her normal speaking voice, and gestured to me to pass by her through another door.

On the far side was a large living room with two white sofas facing each other across a broad wool rug with a geometric pattern in gray and black. There was a low table on which sat an antique brass sculpture of a hand grasping a ball. Above was a light housed in a globelike shade studded with colored tiles that looked like a piece of art. The room led out onto a veranda facing the lawn with a long wooden table, set with white napkins and glass candleholders like a ship's lanterns. The whole thing was perfectly ordered and restful, an aesthetic intelligence behind it.

After I'd stood there by myself for a minute, Nora entered from the far side. She wore a pale linen shift with an embroidered front and linen pants, and she looked far more at ease than she'd been at the hospital. She walked across to me and, before I could shake hands with professional formality, kissed me on the cheek. It left a pleasant impression of soft skin and expensive scent.

"How is your father? I've been worried about him," she said, gesturing to me to take a seat on one of the sofas. It seemed unlikely that she really had, since she'd never met him and she hardly knew me, yet she sounded genuine.

"He's doing okay, thank you. I think he'll recover all right if he follows his doctor's advice."

Nora smiled knowingly. "Getting middle-aged men to do what they're told can be hard, can't it?"

I found her hard to argue with, but I felt the need to restore some of my authority after the manner in which I'd been brought there. I tried to sound stern.

"It was kind of you to arrange the flight, but I'd expected to see Mr. Shapiro back in New York, as we'd agreed."

Nora gave an embarrassed grimace. "I'm sorry. Harry wanted to come here to rest, and I didn't want to agitate him. I hope you understand. Would you like to see him now?"

I walked through the living room to the conservatory and onto the lawn. It was a blissful sensation to step straight out of that ordered house into an infinity of nature and ocean, with the breeze blowing in my face. Harry had his back to me and was reading a book through half-moon glasses. As I reached him, he looked up and studied my face for a while. His own was tense but less agitated than before.

"Sit down," he said.

There were chairs at the table, all of them soft and cushioned. I looked around for a solid seat—something suggesting formality—but there was none in sight, so I sank into one of them. I tried to compensate by perching forward on the edge with my hands clasped.

"Move around so I can see you," Harry instructed.

I dragged my chair over to the spot he'd indicated and found myself squinting at him with the sun in my eyes. It was an old maneuver of his, I suspected. It irritated me, but it was at least encouraging that Harry was getting his game back.

"How have you been feeling, Mr. Shapiro?" I asked.

He had a cup of tea resting on the arm of his chair, and he pulled at the string of the bag a few times while he mulled the question. Then he laughed bitterly. "I've had better weeks. You try being locked up, having your razor taken away every morning, and someone shining a flashlight in your room during the night."

"Patients often find the precautions difficult, but there are reasons for them."

"Maybe for some people. Not for me."

He did some more stage business with the tea bag and gazed away from me out to sea. He was talking faster than in hospital, which was a good sign—the psychomotor retardation was easing as his brain started to function better.

"How are you feeling?"

"I've slept some more."

"You haven't had any thoughts of death?"

He glanced at me with a creased brow, as if he couldn't grasp what I was getting at. Then he frowned, gazing down at the lawn.

"I'm not going to kill myself."

He hadn't looked me in the eye, but it was at least a firm declaration of the kind he hadn't given before. A good thing. Harry levered himself upright and looked across the lawn to where a row of flower beds lined the edge of the dune. "Let's take a walk," he said, striding to a break in the beds, through which lay a wooden platform.

Joining him, I saw that it marked the top of a stairway leading down the dune onto a line of cracked, weathered planks. The planks formed a rolling path up and down the sand and sea grass until they ran out after thirty yards, leaving only a sandy path the rest of the way to the beach. It would have been a wonderful place for children playing hide-and-seek, an amorphous territory between habitation and nature. We walked down the steps in silence: it was so narrow that I had to follow behind him.

He had the beach to himself. In the distance, where the road off which Anna had turned to reach the house ended, a woman in a head scarf was throwing sticks for her dog. Apart from her there were only sand and waves, crashing on the beach and throwing up spray. The sand near the dune was fine and hard to walk across, but down by the ocean's edge it formed a smooth, solid surface. When Harry reached that area, he started to walk westward.

"Tell me more about what happened," I said as I followed him.

It was hard to keep up with his long strides, and his renewed sense of purpose reassured me. He remained silent for about three hundred yards and then grunted a couple of times as if preparing to say something. The disadvantage of walking by him was that I couldn't see his face to observe his reactions, but it provided detachment, like an analyst's couch. The silence extended as we walked, and then he halted, facing the sea, where tiny waves foamed into the sand.

"It could have been a great deal," he said. "A great deal. It wasn't a sure thing, they never are, but if the market hadn't tanked, it would have worked out fine. There was no way I could have known. I couldn't have known."

He gazed at the horizon, and he seemed to be responding bitterly to the voices in his head. I had no idea what he was talking about. Then he bent down to pick up a shell and scraped sand off the underside with his thumb as he spoke.

"It was about a year ago, I guess. Things were going so well for Seligman, it was great. There were rumblings over subprime and some hedge funds had closed, but it felt like our time had come. We'd turned that little place into something. You know what I'd always wanted it to become? I wanted us to be like Rosenthal. They were never going to let it happen. I know that now."

Even I had heard of Rosenthal & Co.—everyone had. It was the one Wall Street bank that had escaped the housing crisis, had come through the crash without collapsing or even being bruised. Everyone seemed to admire it, or be jealous of it, or think it had some unfair advantage. I didn't know the difference between one bank and another, but I could grasp what had driven Harry. There was an outfit like that in every field—the place for which everyone wants to work. Episcopal was the Rosenthal of New York medicine, or so we convinced ourselves and so the patients believed.

"I knew a guy who'd run private equity in Europe for Rosenthal. Marcus Greene," Harry said. "Knows his stuff. Hard-assed on deals, would squeeze you for a dime, but I thought he was a good guy. Nora was friends with Margaret, his wife. We'd see them on weekends out here. They've got a place over in Sagaponack."

"Greene left Rosenthal in the mid-nineties and started his own firm. He called it Grayridge, after a hill in Georgia he knew as a child. So he says, anyway. Felix thinks Greene made it up. He's never met anyone who's heard of the place. It was good timing, when LBOs and hedge funds were getting big. A decade later, he was a billionaire. He had the Rolling Stones at his fiftieth birthday. It was fun," he added wanly. "He calls me one day, supposedly to chat about CDS clearing or something. 'You know, Harry,' he says, 'it's time for us to talk. I think Seligman and Grayridge would make a great fit.' I thought it was a terrific idea, it could put us up there with Rosenthal, so I said, 'Sure, Marcus, we'll take a look.' I'd heard talk that things weren't going well for him. They might be in trouble."

"What did you find?"

"I'll tell you what I thought I saw: a firm that had grown too rapidly and had a few problems, but nothing we couldn't handle. We'd close down a couple of funds, inject maybe a billion in capital, and have a good business. Plus, we wouldn't have to pay a premium, and there wouldn't be any messing about with who was in charge. Marcus would take the number two spot and we'd see how things went from there."

"It didn't work out?"

Harry sighed. We had reached a rivulet that ran down from a pond behind the dunes and couldn't go farther. He scored a curve in the sand with the toe of one shoe, and the bottom of the tiny trench filled with water like the moat of a sand castle.

"We did the deal, but the market went bad and it turned out Gray-ridge had bonds on its books that Greene hadn't told me about. Mortgage paper that everyone thought was safe. We held the triple-A, for fuck's sake, stuff the ratings agencies loved. It all turned to junk and we lost billions. I felt like I was being dragged down, like I was drowning. You don't know what it feels like to see everything you've built falling apart."

He shuddered at the memory, and as I looked over at him, I understood for the first time what had brought him to Episcopal. Loss is hard on the psyche. We aren't built to cope with it immediately: it takes a period of mourning. The worst thing is feeling trapped and helpless, unable to fight or flee. It made sense of everything—even Harry's gun. Harry turned at the rivulet and started walking back. I followed, catching up after about ten yards.

"What did you do when you found out?"

"We had no choice. The share price had gone to shit and we were in trouble rolling over repo funding. Not just us—half the Street was in distress. I've never known anything like it. We ended up one week-end at the Fed begging them to help us out. They agreed to it, but Treasury demanded a sacrifice."

He swept his right hand across his throat in a slitting gesture. As he did it, he closed his eyes and tightened his jaw, as if his hand were cutting his throat like a blade. He looked as if he were experiencing the agony of death.

"That's when you lost your job?"

"I lost everything. They ruined me."

"And all these losses. No one realized?" I said. I'd thought that people who worked on Wall Street were smarter than that. It was the people like me who made stupid mistakes with money, not bankers.

"A couple of hedge funds made money out of it, and Rosenthal did fine, of course. Treasury made sure of that," he said stonily.

I felt sorry for Harry at that moment, realizing what Felix meant by him having a heart. He radiated a baffled sense of loss, as if someone had stolen from him everything he'd had. He walked slowly up the path toward the steps without me. I stayed where I was to take in the view of the house, now arrayed on the dune above me. Nora was in the room where we'd talked earlier, reading a magazine on one of the sofas. Farther along, I saw a room with bookshelves lining one wall and a desk with a twin-screened computer. It had to be Harry's study, where Nora had found him with the gun. By the time I got back up to the lawn, he was in his chair again, looking tired and downhearted.

I sat by him. "There are a lot of things I think it's worth us talking about."

"Analysis, you mean?" he said with an edge of contempt, either at me for being a psych or at himself for being vulnerable.

"I wouldn't suggest therapy at this stage, more of a conversation, but a regular one, two or three times a week at first."

"I guess that's okay. I've got time. All I've got is time," he said.

I walked back to the house. It was the third time I'd talked to him and the first time I'd felt better as a result. My discomfort about having discharged him from the hospital was easing, and I thought I was starting to gain some insight into his condition. There was even a prospect of getting Harry back to Episcopal and into treatment. *This could work out fine,* I thought.

7

I found Nora in the kitchen talking to Anna, who was perched on a countertop in bare feet, crunching a green apple. "You two met before, didn't you?" Nora said, and Anna nodded silently, her teeth embedded in the fruit.

"Anna kindly drove me here," I said.

"I can take you back to the city, if you want," Anna said, having finished her bite and lobbed the core into a trash bin. "I'm going to see a friend."

"Are you sure, Anna?" Nora said. "It would be wonderful if you could. I know he wants to be back soon. You can take my car." She stepped one pace to her right and draped an arm over Anna's shoulders as if they were friends rather than employer and employee. "I can't tell you how much I rely on her."

Anna looked across the room at me with a cool, appraising stare that made me lower my eyes. The prospect of spending several hours in a car with her was unnerving, but she intrigued me more than I cared to show.

"I'll wait for you outside," she said, then slipped off the counter-top and padded softly out of the room.

Nora waited until the door had closed behind her and then looked at me tensely. "How was he?" she said.

"Good, I think," I said. "His mood seems to be improved and he's agreed to see me on Monday. As long as he keeps taking his medication and comes to see me regularly, I think the prognosis is excellent."

I hoped to reassure her after everything she'd suffered, but it was true. Harry didn't seem to be chronically depressed, and there were already signs of life in him. With luck, he might be experiencing the only episode of his life, and the gamble I'd taken in discharging him would have paid off. He'd have to adjust to the loss of his job, but most people did that in time and the Shapiros weren't exactly on the streets. Maybe I'd just launched a career as a therapist for Wall Street billionaires.

"That's great. That's a relief," Nora said, exhaling and letting her shoulders relax. I was glad to have brought her good news—she deserved it for her loyalty.

"You must keep a close eye on him, however," I said. "We don't want anything to go wrong now."

"I will, Doctor. Absolutely," she said, beaming.

When I went outside, Anna was standing by the Range Rover with her back to me, gazing at the sea. I stole another look at the graceful curve of her neck before she heard me and turned around. Her eyes looked pale blue in the ocean light.

"Ready to go?" she asked.

"All done. It's kind of you to give me a ride. If you just drop me at the rail station, that'd be fine."

"You'd be waiting a long time if I did. People commute by helicop-ter around here, you know." She walked across to me and laid her left index finger on my lapel, gently prodding me backward. "Get in the car, Doc."

I obeyed her, remembering the pleasurable sensation of the brief contact between us as she guided the Range Rover down the drive and out along the lane. She knew my profession, I noticed, even if the way she'd demonstrated it had been playful. There clearly couldn't be many secrets between her and Nora. She gestured over to my left as we passed a low cottage set back from the lane.

"That's the guesthouse, in case they summon you out here again. I sneak over for yoga or a nap sometimes. Like Goldilocks."

"Ever been woken by a bear?" I said lightly, excited at having left the Shapiros' estate and feeling as if I'd finally regained control of my life. Of course, I should have realized that it was an illusion. Sitting in Nora's car with Anna driving wasn't much different from sitting in Harry's Gulfstream with Felix as my guide. It was all in the family.

She giggled. "Not even a small one. Anyway, Nora doesn't have to look far. He has the whole estate wired. I'm never out of reach."

"What's that like?"

"Uh, excruciating? It's nice to escape to the city for a night. Look over there. That's the big news around here," she said, gesturing out of my window. We had snaked along a maze of roads with vast lawns and reached the junction to the main thoroughfare. There was a long curved pond surrounded by neat lawn.

"What?" I asked, unable to see anything noteworthy.

"The swan mother is on her nest on Town Pond. She had five cygnets last year and it was all anyone talked about. I felt like I was losing my mind."

As she said it, she pushed down on the accelerator and we sped out of the village as if we were being chased. Like me, she seemed to perk up just to be leaving the place behind. We were both silent for a while as we whizzed up Route 27, and I tried to catch glimpses of her face without her noticing me. Something was going on inside me that I hadn't felt for a long time. It was foolish because I couldn't do anything about it. The last thing that made sense was to start an affair with Harry's housekeeper, even if I stood a chance, which I probably didn't. But I wanted to prolong the thrill I felt when I was with her even if I couldn't act on it.

I thought of the look she'd given me as she stood in the kitchen, one that suggested she knew all about me although we'd only just met. She could see all of the bad things inside me—my cruelty, my coldheartedness—and she didn't care. It was only my fantasy, but that was how she made me feel. It was like the first time that I'd fallen in love as a teenager, the sensation of adoring someone for reasons I couldn't articulate and of craving her physical presence. Laura Kendrick had been her name, and it had lasted a year. As I sat there, I thought of Laura, now married with two kids, and smiled to myself.

"What?" Anna said. I hadn't noticed her looking at me.

"Nothing."

The sad thing was that it didn't remind me of Rebecca. I'd been fond of her, admired her, even loved her, but I had never craved her in that desperate, chemical way. There were things I'd always kept from her, and I'd felt guilty that she cherished me so much. *He isn't me,* I wanted to say to her. *That man you love. He's a better person than I am.* I'd never said those words because she was my best friend and I'd been afraid to hurt her, but she'd realized it and she'd left. She'd saved me the heartache of jettisoning her.

I'd been having a recurrent dream about Rebecca. I was on the steps of the Metropolitan Museum of Art, standing next to my mother and seeing her gray hair and her soft, kind face. We were talking—I didn't know what about, but it made me happy. Then I glanced up the steps and saw Rebecca wearing a summer dress. "Come on," I said to my mother, and we set off after her. We couldn't find her inside, and we started hunting through galleries, my mother now leading the way. Then we came to a gallery where there was a party, with a crowd of people drinking champagne around a painting.

I walked up to the painting and saw that it was a nude of a woman lying on a sofa. She was beautiful, and I reached forward and felt one of her breasts, which was soft and warm to my touch. Then my mother called to me, pointing toward a window through which Rebecca had climbed. I saw that Rebecca had scrambled down a rope into Central Park and was running across the grass to a clump of trees.

"Becca!" I shouted, but she didn't turn round.

That was how the dream ended.

We'd met at Episcopal two years after I'd arrived in New York, so my mother had never known her. I'd always believed they'd have got on well—both of them were sweet and loyal. On our first date, she told me I was different from the other shrinks, which I took as a compliment. We were sitting in a restaurant on the Upper East Side, one of those Italian spots that are institutions, although they don't deserve it anymore. I spent most of the meal enjoying her presence, and as we left, she turned to me to be kissed.

I'd chosen psychiatry despite the questions it raises. They screen for a degree of empathy when they admit you to medical school: they don't want scientists who can't talk to other people. But the competitive spots are for cardiology, radiology, or ear, nose, and throat, the entry point to plastic surgery—anything that involves expensive procedures and minimal chat. Other residents suspected the psychs of being lazy or crazy. Lazy because psychiatry involves little night work apart from emergency shifts. Crazy because many were drawn to it by some affinity with their patients. Either they were odd themselves—working out an inner demon by finding one in others—or they had a family history. Guilty on both counts.

After a while, with no sign of Anna wanting to break the silence, I did. I was puzzled by what she was doing in East Hampton, especially given her skepticism about the place. It didn't appear to be her natural habitat.

"How come you work for the Shapiros?" I asked.

"How long have you got?"

"Until we reach the city, I guess."

"It shouldn't take that long. Let's see. Grew up, went to liberal arts college in Massachusetts. Very pleased with itself, but I thought it was kind of crappy. I came to New York, got a job as an assistant to a magazine editor, and turned out to be good at that, weirdly good."

"That's great." I noticed that she'd taken one open-ended question and given me a brief rundown of her entire adult life.

"Except I was working so hard, really hard, and holding myself to such an insanely high standard that I started to go a bit nuts. I was having panic attacks in my cubicle, sweating and freaking out."

"Did you seek treatment?"

"I took drugs. They calmed me down a bit, but I knew by then that I wasn't happy, so I quit."

"That was brave."

"Brave, reckless, stupid—all the things I've always been. Anyway, I thought I could teach yoga instead, so I took a course. That's how Nora found me. I was covering a class for a friend at the Ninety-second Street Y and she came along. It went from there. Now I'm everything—housekeeper, cook, indentured servant. My job is to make things easy, whatever that takes." Her voice was lightly satirical, but I heard a note of bitterness.

"What are they like to work for?"

She turned her attention from me to check her mirror and merge onto the Long Island Expressway. We passed low pine forests on either side as we headed into the city. She overtook two trucks and then, pulling into the right-hand lane, answered my question as if she'd been considering it since I'd asked.

"Nora's great. I love her and she treats me like family. It's almost too cozy with her sometimes."

"And Mr. Shapiro?"

"Harry's fine," she said tonelessly. "Anyway, you know all about me now. What about you?"

There was a glint in her eyes as she looked at me. She seemed to find me entertaining, which was a start.

"What do you want to know?"

"Okay, you're a psychiatrist, right? Nora says you're treating Harry."

"I can't talk about that, I'm afraid." Even as I said it, it sounded stiff and ponderous, and I wished I didn't have to rebuff her.

"Wife, children?"

"No."

"Girlfriend?"

"Can we change the subject?"

Anna grinned. "Why? That's all my therapist wanted to talk about, my old boyfriend. Him and my childhood and whether I was seeking a father figure. Nathan would have been a terrible choice if I had been."

"So you've seen a therapist?"

"I admit it."

"And you had a boyfriend?"

She laughed, giving me an amused glance that made me feel good, but then stopped talking as we passed under bridges with ragged American flags fixed to them in memory of soldiers who'd died in Iraq. When she spoke again, she was quieter.

"He was borderline, my therapist reckoned. He hooked me, and then made me suffer for loving him. I would have talked about it forever, but I had to stop in the end. You guys charge a lot for a forty-five-minute chat. You know why I really ended it, though? One day I was listening to myself talking and I thought: *I could be making all of this up.*"

"Were you?"

"No, but I might have been, right? He'd listen to me each week and take everything I said seriously and try to find a meaning in it, but how did he know any of it was true? He thought he needed to make me feel good—explain away everything I'd done as a reaction to my past or something. I could have been a terrible person. He wouldn't have known."

"You're *not* a bad person, are you?"

"I don't know. Honesty matters to me. I've always got into trouble for trying to tell the truth. People think I'm just a bitch. Maybe I am. Anyway, I didn't think he could keep me honest, so I stopped."

She laughed sheepishly, as if she had given away more about herself than she had intended. Dusk was falling and taillights were glowing in a red line ahead of us as we passed the big-box stores and projects of Queens. The vehicles around us gradually adopted New York driving habits and started to weave in and out of the lanes, making her curse softly. We popped into the Midtown Tunnel and out onto the city streets. I'd done that swift border crossing a dozen times, but it always surprised me. Despite my halfhearted protests, she drove down Lexington and around Gramercy Park to deposit me on Irving Place by my apartment building.

"Bye," I said, holding out my hand as she idled the Range Rover at the curb.

She grasped it and gave it a satirical tug, as if I were being absurdly formal. Then she pulled out a scrap of paper, wrote a number on it, and gave it to me.

"Call me if you like. I'm in the city sometimes."

I felt the urge to justify to myself asking her out, but I resisted. It was a bad idea, no matter how tempting.

"I don't think I should. Business and pleasure, you know," I said awkwardly.

"So," she said. "You think I'm pleasant."

I laughed despite myself as I climbed onto the sidewalk. Then she eased the Range Rover into the traffic while I stood and watched her disappear.

8

That Saturday, I went to the greenmarket in Union Square, and when I returned, laden with paper bags, I was halted in the lobby by Bob Lorenzo, the head doorman of my apartment building. Bob had a neatly trimmed beard, bloodhound eyes, and an air of fortitude under pressure. We got on fine, though I tried to avoid discussing the Mets or the co-op board, both of which were painful topics.

"Dr. Kaufman came by, Dr. Cowper," he said, holding up an envelope with "Ben" written on it in Rebecca's round script and then underlined. "You just missed her. She asked me to give you this."

"Thanks, Bob," I said. I had once tried to persuade him to call me by my first name, but it had not stuck. The envelope was weighed down at the bottom by something, and I felt the shape inside: her key to my apartment. Bob regarded me with a look of disapproval, as if he knew what the package signified.

"She said she wouldn't be here so much anymore. I'm sorry to hear that."

"I'm sorry, too," I said. I felt a surge of irritation at his silent judgment, compounding my guilt. *What was wrong with these people?* First my father and Jane, and now I couldn't walk into my apartment building without being made to feel ashamed. That probably would have been my mother's reaction, too. *Are you quite sure, Ben?* she'd have said with an undertone of reproach.

Back in my apartment, I lay on the bed, took a breath, and tore open Rebecca's envelope with my thumb. Inside was a sheet of paper folded over upon itself, with her key attached with Scotch tape.

Ben,

I'm sorry I had to go. I miss you already but I think it's for the best. I expect I'll see you at work. I'll be the one who looks like she's been crying.

R.

I wanted to weep, but nothing came—my emotional tank was empty. It would have been easier if she'd been angry with me. Her affection and sad dignity were a kick in the stomach. If I hadn't known her so well, I'd have thought that she'd calculated it to cause me pain, but she wasn't like that.

I got up and paced around the room for a while, but the desolate feeling wouldn't pass. I felt weary, but I didn't want to stay at home, feeling bad about my ill treatment of Rebecca and entanglement with Harry, and worrying about my father's heart. I needed something to distract me. I laid her note on the bed, walked into the living room, and called a friend from the hospital. He was a party animal who'd known in our first week of residency which bar to drink at and where to go afterward. Sure enough, he was heading out to a gathering later on.

"A guy Emma knows invited us to his apartment in TriBeCa. His parties are great, they say. He works on Wall Street," he said.

"I don't know, Steve. I don't think I want to spend my Saturday night with a bunch of bankers."

After my week with Harry and his entourage, it didn't feel like relaxation to be plunged back into his world.

"Right. You've got so many other choices, don't you? That's why you're calling me at six o'clock. Come on, it'll be fun."

When the sun had set and the lights had gone on in Union Square, casting a glow over the rooftops, I went into the bathroom. I opened a medicine cabinet above a jar of seashells that Rebecca had collected on a vacation we'd had in Cape Cod. I poked among the lotions and deodorants, behind the Ambien that she'd sometimes taken to help her sleep. I found a bottle full of orange ovals—30-milligram tablets of Adderall. Doctors shouldn't self-medicate, especially not with amphetamines meant to treat attention deficit disorder, but Steve did and sometimes I did, too. At that moment, I craved anything that would blank out the thoughts in my head.

By the time I'd hailed a taxi downtown, my skin was prickling and a sheen of sweat had broken out on the backs of my hands as the amphetamine salts filtered into my blood, tampering with the norepinephrine and dopamine inside my brain. My mouth was dry and I felt the worry of the past few days drop away, leaving a light-headed fascination with the colors and shapes around me. All of the emotional clamor, the buzz of discomfort, grew muted. The discordant groans of the taxi's air conditioner congealed into a pleasing harmony. I lowered the window as we shot along Broadway and the lights streamed behind us like a vapor trail in blue sky.

I pushed fruitlessly at the buzzer on the metal door to the building for five minutes before a couple rolled down the stairway on their way out and admitted me. It was obvious why I'd been ignored when I reached the tenth floor of the building and heard the roar of voices from inside the apartment. It was a vast multifloored loft with white-painted iron columns and a crush of guests shouting over hypnotic music being mixed on an Apple laptop by a DJ. Urban wealth was on display everywhere, from the canvases of rusting bridges and desolate landscapes on the walls to the black-uniformed waiters pouring Krug champagne into flutes. I walked out through the doors onto a terrace with a glittering view of nearby towers and, in the distance, City Hall. Steve was standing in a knot of people, and I walked up to him.

"So you made it. Ben, this is Lucia," he said.

The young woman by him smiled. She was pretty—dark cropped hair, mascara, and gleaming eyes. She wore a silk dress, and the amphetamines made the straps over her shoulders appear to sparkle in the light.

"Great to meet you," I said, feeling her soft hand in mine.

"Isn't this apartment awesome?"

"Amazing."

"It's Gabriel's. He's over there with Josh."

She pointed to a corner of the balcony where two men were talking. The man she indicated had a ruddy face, a flat jaw, and alert eyes. He seemed amused by the whole event, as if he were a guest rather than the host.

"I'm going to find a drink. Can I get you one?" I said.

Later on, back at her apartment in the East Village, after she'd gone to sleep, I stood at her bedroom window overlooking a dark alley and stared at the brick wall opposite. It was two a.m. and the Adderall was wearing off, making me shaky and paranoid. I remembered my walk on the beach, Harry telling me how he'd lost everything in the crash, and shivered, my faith in him evaporating along with the drugs. He'd told me he wouldn't harm himself. *Why should I trust him?* I thought.

Hot water cascaded over my head and down my body on that Sunday morning as I stood in the shower at the gym, trying to absorb the news. I'd just watched it on television, the thing I'd feared. I'd left Harry in what I'd believed was a stable condition, and he had taken his own life. If I'd stuck with my instincts—the treatment in which I'd believed—instead of giving way to Duncan, I could have saved him. I thought of Nora and the distress she must now be in. After all she'd been through to save him, Harry had abandoned her. How could I face her again?

After a few minutes, I turned off the faucet and stepped out of the shower to dress. The treadmill runners were still panting on their machines as I'd been half an hour before, oblivious to the outside world. Walking out of the gym, I saw the same spring scene—the chess players on the sidewalk, a couple walking a dog, an old lady talking to a doorman—but my pleasure in it had gone.

Back home, I lay on my bed for a minute, thinking about Harry's death and what it meant for me. I couldn't talk to Rebecca; I didn't want to worry my father in his convalescence; I couldn't face calling Episcopal. Reminding myself that I advised patients not to wallow in their misery, I got up and paced my living room for a while. Then I decided that I had to find out exactly what had happened. *Felix*, I thought. *He'd know.* I looked through my jacket for my phone and scrolled through the Calls Received list to the previous week. There was the cellphone number from which he'd called me to fix the return trip on Harry's jet. Pushing the key to redial, I waited.

"Lustgarten," a voice said smoothly and evenly after two rings.

Had it been anyone else, and I hadn't heard the sound of raised voices in the background, I would have thought it was the tone of someone having a relaxed Sunday afternoon. By his standards, however, he sounded edgy.

"Felix, this is Ben Cowper."

"Ah, Dr. Cowper. How are you?"

"Fine, thanks. I'm sorry to disturb you. It sounds as if you're busy."

"Just a little, yes. Could you hold on a minute? I'll be right with you."

"Sure," I said.

He put his hand over the phone, but I could hear his muffled voice call across a room.

"Andrew! . . . Andrew! Tell him he'll have to wait. We'll have a statement in ten minutes. . . . No, I don't care. I don't care if it's God Almighty."

There was a rustle as Felix removed his hand and spoke to me.

"Sorry about that. The roof's fallen in, as you might expect."

"Are the papers calling?" I asked densely.

"A few. That happens when the chief executive of a Wall Street bank dies violently. The vultures circle."

If I'd been thinking in that moment, if my brain hadn't been frozen with shock, I would have caught it. *Chief executive,* he'd said, not *former chief executive.* But I pressed on with my questions blindly, and it took another few seconds for Felix to deliver the news unambiguously.

"How's Mrs. Shapiro coping?"

"Nora's in quite a state, very traumatized. She's with the police now. She thinks she can get Harry out on bail. Best of luck, I say."

"Get him out? From where?"

"Out of jail, I mean. Where else?"

"But he's dead, isn't he? I saw it on the news."

Felix made a strained gurgling sound, half mirth and half horror, at my words. Then he told me. The peculiar thing is that when I first heard the words, my first, instinctive reaction was relief. It turned out I hadn't let my patient commit suicide after all. *I'm not going to kill myself,* he'd promised me on the beach in East Hampton, and he'd told the truth—just not the whole truth.

"Harry?" said Felix. "No, Harry's absolutely fine, apart from being under arrest for murder. It's Marcus Greene who's dead. Harry shot him last night."

9

The Riverhead Correctional Facility loomed from the mist in the cold morning. I saw a couple of trailers set back in the woods off the Long Island Expressway and the eyes of a startled deer, then I was pulling up to the security gate. It was a gloomy place, six or so floors high with a few narrow slits in the walls to let in light. The walls were covered with rolls of shining razor wire, one piled on another, and patterns were molded on its façade in a halfhearted effort to make it less drab. *Don't get yourself locked in here,* the building said. The blue-uniformed guard glanced at my license and waved me on.

Inside, a thin, dull-eyed correction officer told me to take off my belt and jacket and put them in one of the lockers. I sat on one of the bucket chairs fixed to the floor in the waiting area with a knot of visitors—mostly women and children who looked as if they knew this ritual well. On the hour, a shift of visitors drifted out, a couple joking idly with the officers.

The entrance to the visiting room was a cage with red barred doors on two sides. Visitors had to walk into it and have the door locked behind them before the guards released the other. They weren't taking chances. Before I entered the cage, an officer stamped the back of my hand with a small green circle.

"What's this?" I asked.

"Ultraviolet," he said, shining a flashlight on it to light it up. "We don't want the wrong guy leaving."

The visiting room was large and dimly lit, with long trestle tables running its length. Each table had a Perspex screen in the middle, perforated with holes to let through the sound of voices. Prisoners in yellow jumpsuits with VISITING written in black on the back sat on the stools on one side, awaiting their visitors. As wives and girlfriends approached, they stood up to hug or kiss them briefly before sitting again. I didn't see Harry at first, but then I spotted him in the far corner, away from the others, sitting on a stool by himself and looking toward me with a placid expression on his face. A bulky officer stood by him, like his personal bodyguard, as I walked over to greet him. He stayed seated, as he'd done on his lawn two weeks previously, but thrust up one hand over the Perspex to shake mine.

"Hello, Doctor. Sorry about this," he said, pointing across at the other inmates. "Not much privacy here."

"It's all right, Mr. Shapiro. How are you?"

"You know. Keeping busy."

I looked at him through the screen. It was only the fourth time I'd seen him, but it felt as if our relationship had lasted months. I'd have said that we'd become intimate except that he'd so obviously deceived me. We were also back together in an institution, this time with him in a yellow uniform instead of blue. Since his arrest ten days before, he seemed to have changed in a way I hadn't expected. I'd imagined that he would be feeling desperate and unhappy, but the tightness in his jaw had gone, his eyes were alert, and his skin was ruddy. Despite having been detained for murder, he looked better.

I'd put in my request to see him as soon as he'd been arraigned. An all-star legal team and an offer of $20 million bail had not been enough to win him release. The correctional facility was to the rear of the Suffolk County Court, where serious crimes on Long Island were tried. It was an enormous holding pen for those in criminal purgatory, awaiting trial or a jury's verdict. To my surprise, the request had been promptly approved and I had been given a time the following week. Harry wanted to see me.

Perhaps he craves a familiar face, I'd thought on the drive. A media frenzy had erupted since the killing, and every paper and cable show was full of speculation and opinions about Harry's fate. The fact that a Wall Street baron had been arrested for murder rather than a white-collar crime had provided the public spectacle that people craved as revenge on all bankers. I'd informed the jail that Harry was my patient and he seemed to have played along with that, but I didn't believe it was true any longer. I knew that he'd see a jail psych to get his meds—he had no need for me.

Yet I felt we were now kindred spirits: he was locked up and I was in limbo. The explosion of Greene's death had been succeeded by an eerie calm. When I'd arrived on Monday at Episcopal, having watched people around me on the 6 train reading about Harry on the front page of the *Post,* it felt like a forbidden topic. The others were surely talking about it behind my back, but no one dared mention it to my face. The most honest was Maisie, who hailed me with a sympathetic look and a "How are you doing?" that sounded genuine.

Jim Whitehead had finally made clear what everyone else was thinking when, unable to take it any longer, I walked into his office after lunch.

"Ben. How are you?" he said.

When Dr. Formality used my first name, it had to be bad.

"I've been better," I said.

"Has Mrs. Duncan spoken to you yet?"

It was evident from the way he said it that they'd discussed the case. She'd be the one to let me know the hospital's verdict.

"No one's said anything."

"Well," he said, standing to head off the possibility of a long conversation, "I believe she'll be in touch."

With that, the Episcopal omertà had resumed and I'd reached Friday without anyone uttering a word. Even Steve, when I'd called him, had no parties to offer for the weekend. I was left to myself, thinking over the previous week and seeking the clues that I'd missed. If Harry had planned to kill Greene all along, he'd done a good job of hiding it, or I was incompetent. I preferred a third possibility, although it didn't reflect well on me either—that he hadn't known what was on his mind until he'd confronted his victim. That wasn't much better, but at least it wouldn't make me feel such a fool.

"You look well. How are the conditions?" I said.

Harry chuckled at the question as if he were holed up in summer camp rather than a jail. "It's not like being in my own bed, but I've made the best of it. The other guys on the tier treat me okay. I'm spending time in the gym."

This was a change from the Harry of York East. That bed hadn't been good enough for him although it was the best we offered, yet a jail mattress was fine.

"I wanted to see how you were, after all that's happened."

"I'm good. No need to worry about me."

I was finding the conversation unreal. Not only were we glossing over the fact that Harry had just killed someone, but his mood had changed entirely. An enormous weight seemed to have been lifted from him. He'd been shattered by losing his job, but the likelihood of spending the rest of his life in jail didn't appear to bother him. I glanced at the officer, but he was looking at the gray sky through the room's high window and didn't seem to be listening. All the same, I leaned forward and spoke quietly, my breath misting a patch around the Perspex holes.

"Mr. Shapiro, I must ask . . . Did you kill Mr. Greene?"

Harry didn't hesitate or bother to keep his voice down. "I did," he said, nodding calmly. "I was angry. I lost control. He called me that morning, said we needed to talk about something. I was in the city, but he made me anxious, I couldn't stop thinking about it. I told him I'd drive out there."

"What did Mrs. Shapiro say about that?"

"I didn't tell Nora. I knew she'd try to stop me. You'd got her so worried, she didn't trust me."

With good reason, I thought. Nora had promised me that she'd keep an eye on Harry, yet she'd let him escape and kill someone. I remembered her telling me in the psych ER that she'd keep the gun out of Harry's way, the shock and unhappiness etched on her face. She'd said the same thing when I'd asked again in East Hampton. *Absolutely,* she'd assured me. I'd trusted her, but she'd let me down.

"You met at your house?"

"He said they were taking the Gulfstream away and they weren't going through with the settlement we'd agreed upon. He was getting heat from Washington, he said. It didn't look good. He was a coward—he wouldn't stand up for me. I was mad at him."

"So you shot him? Just like that?"

Harry rubbed the palm of his right hand up and down a couple of times on the surface of the table, his knuckles flexing. He gazed at me and there was no longer any fire in his eyes, not even an ember. The life that had once been there had died along with Greene.

"I wasn't acting normally, you know that. Those pills you gave me affected me. I didn't know what I was doing. I was crazy."

I was shocked by how blatantly he'd just blamed it all on me. He didn't look ashamed at having fooled me or for having forced me to release him. *It was all my fault, was it—nothing to do with him?* I felt like reaching across the Perspex screen and shaking him, but his corrections officer loomed nearby.

"But you feel better now," I said, not bothering to hide my skepticism.

"Much better."

He leaned back, and I knew that was it. I wasn't going to get any more out of him. The truth was that I'd never known what was going on in his head, not from the first moment I'd seen him. I'd been blind right from the start. A knot of officers by the cage called time and started to beckon the inmates out row by row.

Harry thrust out his hand. "I don't know if I'll see you again, Doctor."

"I don't know either." I took it, feeling his hard, decisive grip.

"Thanks for your help."

"I don't think I helped, Mr. Shapiro."

"Oh, you did," he said, smiling slightly as he turned away.

When I reached the parking lot, a man and a woman in their forties were waiting by a black sedan. He was ruddy-faced, with plush cheeks, thick shoulders, and a belly that bulged over his belt—a high school football player gone soft. His partner was in better shape: her neck muscles were taut, as if she worked out. Her hair was curly and her face olive-skinned—Greek or Italian, I guessed.

"Dr. Cowper?" she said, halting me as I got to my car and pulled out the key. They had parked next to me—they'd known which one it was.

"Cooper, yes."

"Okay," she said in an unruffled tone. "I'm Detective Pagonis and this is Detective Hodge. We're with Suffolk County homicide. We heard you were here, thought we'd take a drive over. We'd like to ask you a couple of things. You're Shapiro's shrink, aren't you?"

"Why do you say that?"

Hodge grimaced but didn't say anything. Pagonis seemed to be in charge.

"Hey, come on, Doctor. You've just been to visit him, haven't you? That's what he told us, anyways. It's all in his statement."

She reached through her passenger-side window and pulled a sheaf of papers from under the windshield. It was a photocopy of a long document written neatly by hand and signed by Harry on the last page. Pagonis pointed to a passage halfway through.

I received psychiatric treatment at Episcopal hospital from Dr. Ben Cowper. Dr. Cowper was responsible for admitting me to a psychiatric ward and then discharging me on Monday, April 27.

Pagonis pulled the papers away.

"I see," I said, trying to look unimpressed. "How can I help?"

"Just a few questions at Yaphank. It's not far—on the way back to the city. Won't take long. You're not under arrest."

I hadn't considered that possibility until she mentioned it, but the sight of my name inscribed on Harry's confession made me realize it wasn't out of the question. Things were starting to crumble around me, and I couldn't think of any excuse to disobey her.

"You understand I can't answer any questions about my treatment of Mr. Shapiro. I have a duty of confidentiality."

"For now," she said dismissively. "We'll take the expressway. You can follow us." She climbed into the passenger seat while Hodge took the wheel.

We turned off the expressway twenty minutes later on a flat road with low buildings on either side. I was concentrating on keeping a safe distance from the back of their car, but I looked up at the surroundings as they turned right into a lot with a two-story building marked SUFFOLK COUNTY POLICE DEPARTMENT. The Stars and Stripes hung by the entrance, and I saw cops walking through a reception area lit in sodium yellow. I prepared to halt, but Hodge kept going round the side of the building, passing ranks of cars, and parked close to the rear.

"We can go in this way. It's easier for our offices," Pagonis said, leading me to a metal freight door at the back of the building.

It was isolated, with no one in sight, and I felt even more like a suspect. Hodge pressed a red button by the door and I could hear the elevator creak into life somewhere inside. He pulled the door open with a screech and we stepped into the metal box, which deposited us at the second floor on a hallway with a biblical commandment written on the wall in large letters: THOU SHALT NOT KILL. I wondered which bright spark had adopted it as the squad's motto: if everyone obeyed, they'd be out of business.

Why did I agree to this? I thought to myself as Pagonis led me down a hallway and into a narrow room, maybe nine by thirteen, with just one desk, a couple of chairs, and a floor-to-ceiling mirrored wall on one side. An interview room, I knew from a hundred cop shows, and I looked for the voice recorder but there wasn't one.

"Have a seat," Pagonis said, unbuckling her gun belt from around her waist and passing it to Hodge. "Coffee? Milk, sugar?"

I sat in the seat she'd indicated and, looking down, saw a three-foot chain bolted to the floor under my feet. There was a pair of handcuffs attached to one end, and I realized they were shackles. *Christ,* I thought. *Did they chain Harry when they brought him to this place?* Hodge reentered with two paper cups of coffee and sat down silently by Pagonis's side, giving me a glare of suspicion. Her face was lined with exhaustion, but adrenaline was keeping her going—it had to be the biggest case of her career.

"We're investigating the death of Marcus Greene," she said, stirring sugar into her brew. "We aren't called out to East Hampton much. The village police deal with most things there—tennis permits, break-ins, that stuff. We don't get a lot of business, so this is a change all right. Shapiro probably told you what happened."

"As I said, I can't discuss that."

"Sure, sure. Listen, Mike, why don't you get the photos? Dr. Cowper's a professional, right? He'll want to know what his patient did."

No, I won't, I thought, but there was nothing to do but wait as Hodge heaved himself to his feet again and wandered out of the room in search of the evidence. Pagonis gazed at me with superficial friendliness, as if all of us were in this together. A couple of minutes later, he walked back into the room, spilling half a dozen photos on the desk.

"Messy, eh?" Pagonis said, looking at me.

Reluctantly, I picked up one of the images and looked at it. I recognized the Shapiros' living room right away. The shot was taken from roughly where I'd sat talking to Nora. Had it been only two weeks ago? It felt as if it had been forever. The sofa on which she'd sat was in the background, with their conservatory behind. In front was the gray-and-black wool rug, on which a man's body rested, with his left arm splayed out to one side. The right one was clasped over his chest, as if in a useless effort to stop up the wound that had killed him. I could see a small entry mark in his chest on the left-hand side, a few inches above the heart. Behind his back, blood had flooded out, encrusting a wide pool of dark red soaking into the rug. It looked as if the bullet had taken out an artery on the way through. If his death hadn't been immediate, it must have come within minutes.

"This is him," Pagonis said, handing me another photo.

I'd seen Greene's face in newspaper photos since the killing, and I recognized it inert on the rug, photographed from above. His face was white and his eyes stared out unseeingly. His upper lip was twisted in a rictus, as if frozen as he forced out his last words—he looked both scornful and desperate. His head rested in the pool of blood, to which a few strands of his graying hair were glued. I was used to seeing the faces of the dead in Episcopal, but this was different, more personal, as if it were a relative of mine whose last agony had been preserved there. I felt saliva drip inside my mouth and tried to control my nausea.

"What do you think of your patient's handiwork?" she asked. *Your patient. Your fault.* Pagonis wasn't subtle. "Shapiro had a nine-millimeter. Not a bad shot. He must have been a few yards away. There's no powder on the clothes. He fired twice, but we haven't found the other bullet. Must have missed once and got him the second time. Here, look."

She pushed the photo toward me and tapped it, as if I hadn't seen enough the first time. I reluctantly examined Greene's face again. Those cold, staring eyes told me the error I'd made—I'd caused this man to die in agony.

"We'll show you the weapon," Pagonis said relentlessly. "Mike?"

Hodge lumbered to his feet again and she gave me the same thin, hard smile as we awaited his return. I stared at her blankly, but inside my mind was in turmoil. I thought of the gun I'd held in the ER when Nora had handed it to me—a Beretta Cheetah, I remembered Pete O'Meara telling me. *My fingerprints must be on it,* I thought. *That's why Pagonis has got me here. I knew there must be more to it than just Harry's statement. They know everything that happened—the signs that I ignored.*

Minutes passed as we waited for Hodge. Pagonis looked as if she could sense my discomfort and was gratified by it. I heard his footsteps in the corridor and saw a familiar shape grasped in his right hand as he walked over to us, a gun held securely in a plastic evidence bag to prevent contamination.

"There we are," she said as Hodge placed it on the table. "A Glock. Shapiro's fingerprints were all over it and powder on his hands."

I didn't say anything, just reached forward and pulled it toward me. It wasn't the same gun. It was a similar shape, but it looked a little bigger and it was dull gray with a square barrel, like those the New York police carry. *Thank God,* I thought. I'd misjudged Nora after all. She'd kept the gun safe, as I'd told her to do. Then I thought of Harry. I wondered how he'd got hold of this gun. Nora hadn't mentioned another weapon, so where had it come from?

"You're a shrink at Episcopal?" Pagonis said.

"An attending psychiatrist, yes."

"Shapiro says you admitted him to the hospital, right?"

"I can't tell you, I'm afraid."

"Did you think he was dangerous?"

"Again, it's privileged."

"But you let him out again," Hodge said, his eyes flat.

I wondered if he distrusted all psychs or if he felt a particular enmity for me. Probably the first: most cops thought our job was to concoct bullshit excuses for criminals.

"I've told you that I'm unable to discuss this," I said with an edge. "There are strict laws on patient confidentiality in New York State."

"What you did was very convenient," Pagonis said, ignoring me. "You take him into the hospital, establish he's not right in the head, then let him out. A couple of days later, he goes on the run and pulls this gun on Greene. Then he calls up his wife back in New York and tells her. Next up, he calls the East Hampton police to hand himself in. We've got a record of both those calls. It looks nicely planned to me, not at all crazy, but you gave the guy the perfect defense."

Her voice was laden with cynicism, and I couldn't say I blamed her. Harry had tried his excuse about my treatment absolving him of responsibility on me in Riverhead. I'd reacted the same way as Pagonis.

"Detective," I said, "I can't help you."

Pagonis treated me to a long, cool look before getting up from her chair. "All right, we'll talk again. Here's my card," she said, handing me one. "Call me if you change your mind. Mike will show you out."

Back at ground level, Hodge pulled aside the metal elevator door and watched me as I walked back to my car. My fingers were shaking as I tried to put the key in the ignition, and I managed it only at the third attempt.

10

Duncan's assistants were buried in their work when I obeyed her summons to her office two days later, as if they'd been stuck in that position since I'd last seen them. The clicking of keyboards was interrupted briefly by one of them opening a can of Coke Zero with a hiss while the other waved me to a chair to wait.

My feelings about her, never warm, had worsened since Greene's death. If she hadn't interfered, if she'd left me to treat Harry, I could have averted this disaster. I'd have kept him in York East until the drugs had started to work and he was less dangerous. He'd fooled me about the person he'd intended to kill—I'd believed it was himself and not Greene—but I'd known he was dangerous and we ought not to risk freeing him in that condition. Although I was angry at the way he'd blamed the whole thing on the drugs and his condition, it would carry weight with a judge. He'd been my patient and I hadn't done my duty.

After my ten-minute quarantine was up, Duncan once again peered around the door and ushered me into her room.

"Well," she said, offering me a tight grimace as she stood and looked at me, "this is a mess, isn't it?"

Her expression was a cocktail—one measure of sympathy to three measures of iron determination that if anyone at Episcopal ended up suffering as a result of Greene's death, it wouldn't be her.

"It's very unfortunate. I—"

"I've had a call from the insurers," she said, cutting me off and walking to a window. "They're expecting a lawsuit, of course. There's always one of those."

I tensed for the worst. "Who's going to sue?"

"The victim's family. Maybe the Shapiros. Wrongful death, malpractice. There's a range of possibilities." She paused briefly. "This has been very upsetting. Nora is my friend and I can only imagine what she's suffering, but I must put my own feelings aside."

I didn't imagine she'd find that too difficult—they would fit comfortably into a small box. *Anyway, what about my feelings?* I thought. She didn't seem bothered about them. She strode back and sat opposite me on the sofa.

"You'll get your own lawyer—our insurer will pay for it. They're not expecting a civil suit until the criminal case is settled, but you'll need to be prepared. Have you been through this kind of thing before?"

"Nothing like this."

A couple of patients had launched halfhearted malpractice suits against me—those were impossible to avoid in New York—but they had not bothered me too much. The cases were weak and the hospital's lawyer had hardly broken a sweat as he'd swatted them away. They'd mainly been legal therapy for troubled souls.

"There is one question I must ask," she said. "Did Mr. Shapiro give any indication of homicidal intent? I've looked over the notes, but there's not much there."

That could have been a neutral observation, but she managed to make it sound like an allegation of professional misconduct.

"I admitted him because I believed he was a danger to self," I said carefully. "That was why Mrs. Shapiro brought him to the hospital, as you know. There were no indications that he was a danger to others."

"That's good. I'm sorry to ask, but I must be clear. There are some aspects of the case that I don't feel fully informed about." She reached forward to brush a piece of fluff from her skirt. "Nonetheless, I want you to know we're right behind you. You've got our full support."

I didn't like the turn the conversation was taking. What was this about me needing to be prepared and Episcopal being behind me? Surely it should be right beside me, or out in front, given her involvement. I decided I couldn't simply sit there passively and allow her to evade responsibility.

"I hope this case won't affect the hospital too much. You mentioned that Mrs. Shapiro was considering making a large donation to the hospital. To build the new cancer wing, you said."

My reminder of how she had pushed me into obeying Harry made her blink a couple of times, like a computer pausing to absorb data. She regarded me impassively, as if from a long distance.

"I don't recall that," she said.

The brazenness of the lie shocked me—she didn't appear at all embarrassed by it. It was as if she'd managed to rewrite the past so quickly and so neatly in her mind that there was no memory left. Professionally, I would have called it adaptive, the ability to suppress threatening reality.

"But we talked about—"

"What I remember," she cut in, "is that Nora spoke to me as a friend about her husband's distress, and we discussed it. At no time did I instruct you, or place you under pressure, to discharge Mr. Shapiro. In fact, I specifically emphasized that it was a matter of medical judgment, for you alone to decide."

We gazed at each other for a few seconds and I saw nothing but cold determination in those gray eyes. *Fuck you,* I thought. *That's why you got me up here so fast. Not to reassure me or stand behind me, but to force this false version of the past on me and to wriggle out of responsibility.*

"That's not how I remember it," I said.

She stared at me and the room temperature seemed to drop several degrees. She spoke slowly, as if she'd rehearsed what she had to say. "I've gone back over the events since then, and I'm confident I acted correctly. I'm sure that once you've had a chance to reflect, you'll realize that's true. You wouldn't want to place any wild accusations on record, I'm sure, Dr. Cowper. That wouldn't help your career."

Her threat was as blatant as her original lie, and I had to struggle not to lose my temper. "I wouldn't say anything untrue about Mr. Shapiro's case. I'd tell the truth."

Duncan opened her mouth as if about to say something more but seemed to have second thoughts. Instead, she leaned back and breathed out, deciding not to take the confrontation any further. She'd let me know how tough she was prepared to get. Instead, she rose and walked back to her desk, resting the fingers of both hands stiffly on the surface.

"Don't be upset about this, Dr. Cowper," she said, as if it were my intemperate nature rather than her lie that had caused the trouble. "The insurers will be in touch and hopefully it won't get to court. We have a strong defense."

"Yes, Mrs. Duncan," I said, getting up. I wondered whether we were supposed to shake hands, but she didn't make a move in my direction. After a couple of seconds, I retreated to the door in confusion.

"Thank you for coming," she said, gazing at a file on her desk rather than at me and reaching for her phone. On the way out I passed her two assistants still rooted to their spots, unwilling to look up.

There was a plop as Felix drew the cork on a bottle of red wine. He poured out two glasses, then took one and rolled the wine around before taking a gulp.

"It's a 2005 Pomerol. Not a great year, but good enough for pizza. A purist would insist on beer, but I'm not one of those. I brought two bottles because I reckon we deserve it. Cheers," he said.

We were in my kitchen and I was putting out plates, knives, and forks on the table for the food Felix had brought. He'd called earlier in the day to suggest that we meet, and I'd told myself it was important to find out more about Greene's death. But as the day had worn on, and I'd straphanged my way back home from the hospital on the 6 train, I'd realized I also wanted his company. Most people at Episcopal had stopped talking to me except for a few pleasantries, out of embarrassment or suspicion, and Rebecca had left me at precisely the moment that I turned out to need her. The people who had talked to me at length—Harry, Pagonis, and Duncan—had all made me feel worse than before.

"Oh, good, cutlery. I knew this was a civilized joint," he said, squeezing along the banquette. "I *am* glad I came. Not that it wouldn't be a pleasure to see you anyway, Ben, but my wife's tired of all the furor and taken the kids off to visit their grandparents, so I'm on my lonesome."

"I'm glad. Thanks for all this," I said as I lifted slices of pizza onto his plate. "How are you doing?"

It wasn't an idle question. Felix was looking wearier than when I'd last encountered him on the Gulfstream. His face was pasty and his hair needed a trim. He sighed and picked up a fork, with which he speared a slice of pizza. He got it most of the way to his mouth before lowering it to speak.

"You know what? I'd say I was keeping my head above water. The place is in chaos, the last two chief executives having been taken out in one go, and I spend my working days going to meetings with lawyers. What is wrong with this country that you need an entire legal team even if you're only a witness? When I drag myself home at the end of the day, I get bombarded with calls from journalists."

"So what *did* you witness, Felix?" I asked.

He looked at me, munching the pizza, as if I were being tactlessly direct, but I didn't care anymore—I didn't have the energy for small talk. He had a smear of tomato sauce on his upper lip, and for an uncomfortable moment the red reminded me of the blood spilling out from Greene's body in the crime scene photo.

"Not a nice memory, I've got to say. Nora called me that afternoon. She was pretty distressed, said Harry had given her the slip somehow and she needed help to find him. He'd vanished from their apartment a couple of hours before. She had visions that he'd topped himself. We almost called you, in fact."

"I wish you had."

"It was about five o'clock. We tried Harry's mobile and the house. Nothing. Finally, at eight, he called from East Hampton. Nora answered. It was dreadful." Felix closed his eyes and shuddered as he recalled the moment. "Utter fucking mess. I drove her out myself. I didn't want her to face it alone. When we arrived, there were cops swarming the place. They'd taken Harry away from there already. Nora was hysterical, kept saying it was all her fault—you'd warned her."

"That sounds terrible." It did, but there was one consolation. Nora obviously knew that she should have listened to me and was prepared to acknowledge it openly. I hoped she might protect me a little—I needed it.

Felix put some pizza in his mouth and chewed it thoughtfully for a minute or two. "It was. So how's it going at the hospital? I imagine they're shit scared about the whole thing, aren't they? I hope they're supportive."

"Not exactly."

"That bad?" He winced, then pushed his plate aside and poured more wine into our glasses.

"I discharged him. My signature's on the release and no one else wants to share the blame. I only hope it doesn't get to court."

He shrugged and raised his eyebrows, indicating that I was out of luck. "I don't think you should count on that. Put it this way: I think Marcus married Margaret because she was the only person on earth who scared him."

"I'm screwed, then," I said gloomily, taking a glug of my wine.

"There's always Nora. Maybe she could prevail on Margaret. The Wall Street wives' club. Even if her membership's expired."

He glanced at me, not sure whether he'd gone too far, but then we both snorted with laughter, like children sharing a joke out of adult earshot. I stood up and we walked to the living room, where he lounged in an armchair with his shoes off. There was a hole in one of his socks, through which a toe poked.

"Why do you think Harry did it?" I asked. "He didn't tell me much in Riverhead, just that the bank was going to take the Gulfstream away. I suppose that felt like punishment, but all the same, shooting the messenger was extreme."

Felix looked into his wineglass as if he might be able to read the sediment like a fortune-teller. "One thing I'll say about Harry, Ben. You've only known him since he's been ill, but he's a delicate soul. He's always felt like an outsider to Wall Street, not part of the club. When he was pushed out, he imagined that everyone was laughing at him."

He seemed to have a talent as a psych. That might have been what had made Harry flip, I thought—the feeling of being dispossessed by the man who had taken over his bank. It made as much sense as anything in this affair.

"Marcus could be pretty tough when he wanted to be," he went on. "Maybe he said something that got under Harry's skin—the guy wasn't stable."

I knew as he said it that he didn't mean any harm, but it made me throw my hands in the air with despair. "God, if anyone else says that to me, I think I'll scream out loud. I *know* he wasn't stable. I shouldn't have discharged him."

Felix winced. "I'm sorry—ought to have been more sensitive."

I gave myself a moment to breathe. "Forget it, I'm on edge."

"I shouldn't say this, but I don't miss him. You can watch him in action if you want. They made Harry and Marcus give evidence together to the Senate last year. There's a video up on C-SPAN still. That'll give you the idea."

Felix left after midnight, when we'd drained both of the Pomerols and half a bottle of whiskey I'd found in a cupboard. I didn't sleep well, turning back and forth under the duvet as I passed in and out of consciousness. I got up to take an Ambien, hoping it would knock me out, but it only pushed me into a disturbed sleep.

I dreamed of driving down the lane to the Shapiros' house and turning up the drive at night. The front door was open and I walked into the house from a side I'd never been. The carpet was soft under my bare feet after the pebbled drive. The living room was dark, only a dim light coming from the ocean. Harry was sitting on the living room sofa in a blue gown, with head bowed. As I entered, he looked up. Blood poured down his face from an open wound and he stared at me fiercely, his eyes burning as they had in the ER. He opened his mouth, but no sound emerged. *He's trying to tell me something. I need to get closer,* I thought, but my feet wouldn't grip the wooden floor.

I woke up sweating from the dream and the alcohol. It was three a.m. and I sat up in bed, my arms around my knees. *I have to protect myself—I can't let them sacrifice me,* I thought. I reached for the phone and dialed.

"Dad, it's me," I said when he answered.

"You're up late. Is everything okay?" replied his smooth baritone. I heard Jane's voice in the background. "It's Ben," he told her. "Hold on, I'll take it in the other room."

After thirty seconds, he picked up the phone in his study. "Hey, Benny, we're just having breakfast. You rushed off the other day. What's up?"

"I'm in trouble, Dad," I said, my voice starting to shake. "A patient killed someone and it's being blamed on me. I couldn't have stopped it. It wasn't my fault."

I felt myself babbling with exhaustion and stress, triggered by the sound of his voice and my nighttime loneliness.

"Whoa, slow down. I'm sure it wasn't, but take it from the top."

I told him the whole story. It took twenty minutes, and he interrupted occasionally to ask me a question, but he listened. Just talking to him made me feel overwhelmingly grateful to have someone on my side.

"Hmm," he said at the end. "Listen, I've got a friend over there who'll be able to help you, but you must promise me something. It's important."

"Yes, Dad," I said, a child again.

"Don't talk to the hospital or the insurers or the police until you've spoken to him. And don't go visiting any more prisons. You need a lawyer."

11

In New York City, the Shapiros lived in a tower on Central Park West near Columbus Circle that had been built in retro-classic Manhattan style, all limestone and marble. It had become famous for the bankers and hedge fund managers who'd bought apartments there just before the crash. The address was a symbol of the city's new wealth, and magazines recorded each $30 million apartment sale in awed detail.

I'd called to arrange a time to see her, and she'd sounded grateful to hear from me. Despite my father's warning about not talking to anyone, she was—or had been—the wife of my patient and I owed it to her. Besides, I wanted to find out what had gone wrong. She'd kept one gun away from Harry, as I'd insisted to her, but he had slipped away from her and found another one to kill Greene. I still sympathized with her, but what she'd told Felix was true. She should have listened to me and not her husband.

Dusk was falling when I arrived, making the Mercedes sedans and BMWs in the courtyard glow. Everything was polished and shiny, down to the buttons on the coats of the doormen inside who scanned all visitors. After one of them had called upstairs to announce my arrival, another pointed toward the elevator to the thirty-seventh floor. The elevator gave onto a private lobby with a large oak door, which was opened by Anna. She was barefoot and wearing a blue flowered dress, and she gave me a small, pained smile.

"Dr. Cowper?" said a voice from somewhere inside the apartment. Then Nora emerged from a room and walked up to us. Anna stepped a few paces back, ceding her position, and paused briefly before turning away.

"Call me," she mouthed silently.

I'd hardly had time to register that before Nora kissed me on the cheek again—her flesh cooler than it had felt in East Hampton—and stood back in acknowledgment. She wore gray pants and a cream blouse, and she looked pale and fragile, like a widow in mourning.

"It's good to see you, Doctor," she said, her voice wavering.

"And you, Mrs. Shapiro. I'm sorry about everything that's happened. It must have been very difficult."

"It has been," she said simply. I wondered if she was going to cry, but she recovered and gestured for me to follow her inside.

The apartment was grand and high-ceilinged and seemed to recede through endless rooms like a manor house. It was flanked by floor-to-ceiling windows through which I saw the sun casting a glow along Central Park South, its line of hotels and apartment blocks bordering the green block of Central Park. Nora led me to a walnut-paneled study with walls that displayed a mosaic of modern paintings. I saw a Jasper Johns and a Warhol-like lithograph that I couldn't place. A large photograph hanging over the black marble fireplace dominated the room: a Marlboro cowboy galloping against a vast and cloudy sky.

"It's a Richard Prince. I bought it for Harry," Nora said, seeing me look at it.

"It's great," I said politely.

"I don't know what Harry thinks. He was shocked at what I paid."

"You're the collector?"

"My mother was a sculptor and I picked up the habit from her, although I couldn't afford to buy much before I met Harry," she said. She was sitting on a sofa with the Prince behind her, a shadow cast on her face, and she smiled for the first time. She seemed to want to talk.

"How long have you two been married?"

"Ten years in June. June ninth. Not how I expected to spend our anniversary."

"How did you meet?"

Nora smiled. "Harry's first marriage had broken up. He'd waited a long time to end it. They'd been college sweethearts and he'd never been happy. That's what he told me." She laughed faintly.

"Perhaps it was true."

"Maybe. I was kind of a mess then—nothing was working out. I was in my early thirties, no kids, no relationship, a job I hated. A friend invited me to a party in the Hamptons, and I ended up chatting to this twelve-year-old boy in a back room. It was Harry's son, Charlie. He's at Harvard now. Harry was a guilty father, grateful that I'd entertained his son. He latched on to me. He'd been married for so long, he had no idea how to talk to women."

"You liked him, though?"

"I did. I was seeing this guy in his twenties and Harry was such an *adult* compared to him. On our second date, Harry said he wanted to marry me. I was living in this tiny apartment on the Upper West Side. He came over once and refused to come back. He booked a suite at the Pierre and moved me there instead." She laughed at the extravagance. "My boyfriend was young and he was like, 'I want to be an artist, but I'm not sure. I love you, but I'm not sure.' Harry never had second thoughts. He liked seeing you the other day, by the way," she said.

I'll bet he did, I thought, but I tried not to let my resentment show. "He seemed to be bearing up well."

The fragile look came back to her face and she turned away from me to examine a steel sculpture on a side table. She brushed a tear away with one finger.

"He's happier with something to work on—his defense, I mean. That's what I wanted to talk about. We've talked to the lawyers and they think he has a strong defense. He wasn't thinking clearly, that's obvious to anyone. He was in a bad way, and seeing Marcus was too much. Poor Marcus."

Poor Nora, poor Harry, poor Marcus. What about poor Ben? I thought. I liked Nora and felt for her, but I suspected that she wouldn't be any more use to me than Harry or Duncan when it came to it. Her first loyalty was to her husband, and I was Harry's alibi for killing Greene, his best hope of evading life in jail. I'd let him out of the hospital, and as Pagonis had observed, it had been very convenient. If it came to a choice between Harry and me, I knew she wouldn't hesitate. Love would triumph over sympathy.

"I spoke to the detectives. They told me Mr. Shapiro left without you knowing. How did he manage that?"

It was a blunt question, and I meant it that way. I wanted to shock her into acknowledging her failure to heed my warnings. It had the intended effect, for she paled.

"I'm sorry, Dr. Cowper. You told me to keep an eye on him. I know you did. I was in the kitchen and Harry was taking a nap. I heard the phone and him answering, then nothing. When I went to check on him twenty minutes later, he'd gone."

"So Ms. . . . ." I hesitated, not wanting to sound intimate but realizing as I started on the sentence that I didn't know her second name. "Anna. She didn't see him leave?"

"She was with a friend in East Hampton. I wish she'd been here— things would have been different. Anna wouldn't have let it happen, I know she wouldn't." She looked at me sadly, but I wasn't ready to let her off that easily.

"You called Mr. Lustgarten?"

"He came over, but we couldn't find Harry. The men downstairs said the car was gone from the garage. They've got a way of knowing.

It was evening before he called. It was terrible. I still don't understand where Harry got that gun from. You told me to lock up the Beretta and I did that. It's still in my safe in East Hampton. He got hold of another somehow, I don't know who from."

Who from, I noticed she'd said. Not *where from.* I wondered if she was telling the whole truth or if she had more of an idea than she'd admitted. Sometimes in therapy, a single word is a clue to what the patient is hiding.

Nora looked at me penitently. "Dr. Cowper. Ben. I want you to know how sorry I am that I didn't take your advice in the hospital. I've thought about that a lot since then, and I'll always regret it. If I can do anything to make it up to you, I will."

They were only words, but after the aggression and blame that I'd faced over the previous few days, they meant something to me. She sounded genuinely mortified by her blunder.

"There is one thing," I said, not wanting to miss the opportunity. "You know Sarah Duncan, don't you? She told me you're friends."

She looked anxious. "She scares me, to tell you the truth. I tried to leave the board once, but she wouldn't let me. I guess she saw Harry's money leaving, too. She took me out to lunch and forced me to stay."

I smiled at that—I could imagine the scene in some Upper East Side restaurant and how implacable Duncan must have been.

"It's very important for me that the hospital supports me. If there's anything you can do to persuade her, I'd be grateful," I said.

Nora's face lightened as I said it, as if she welcomed the chance to expiate her guilt. "Of course. She has to do that. It's only right."

She walked me out of the apartment to the elevator, and on the way, I glanced into their kitchen in the hope of spotting Anna again. The room was empty. She was somewhere else, deep inside.

Harry sat at a green baize–covered table, his face rigid, his right hand clamped stiffly over his left. In front of him, a scrum of photographers—some standing, others crouching, and two leaning forward so that the tips of their lenses were a couple of feet from his nose—was clicking away, sounding like a swarm of cicadas. Harry looked as if he were only just restraining himself from punching one of them.

He was in banker's garb, which I hadn't seen him wearing before— black suit, white shirt with a button-down collar, and a red tie with a pattern it was hard to make out on my computer screen. I'd located the recording of the Senate hearing, as Felix had said, in the C-SPAN archive. It had taken place the previous fall, just after Seligman had been rescued and Harry had resigned. I sat alone that night, searching the past for what had driven Harry to murder.

The man to Harry's right on the screen was at ease. He was tall—or looked as if he would be standing up—and trim. His brown hair was so neat that it looked molded, like that on a Ken doll. He had pale, clear skin and a strong jaw with a cleft in his chin. The snappers were mauling him, too, but he didn't look stressed. His bearing suggested that he was sure everything would work out fine for him. He leaned forward and minutely adjusted the card in front of him: MARCUS GREENE. I hardly recognized him alive.

The snappers hurried back to crouch in front of a curved table on a dais at which the twenty senators sat. The room was vast and cer-emonial, richly paneled in mahogany and marble, and above the dais was a spatchcocked eagle and the American flag. Pasty-faced staffers in boxy suits who looked light- and sleep-deprived were passing through a brass-engraved door beneath the eagle. The chairman looked unhealthy—plump and rumpled, with thick white hair, jowls, and a pug nose—but he exuded satisfaction at being the center of at-tention, as if this moment were enough to repay his slog to seniority. He rapped his gavel.

"I will remind everyone that this is a hearing, so we will not have any disruptions, no matter what they feel," he said croakily. "Believe me, I feel as strongly as anyone here about curbing the excesses we've witnessed on Wall Street. We will ask the Treasury secretary about that later, but our first panel has many questions to answer. I urge them to talk openly, not to attempt to hoodwink the American peo-ple."

The camera cut to Harry and Greene and showed the lawyers and officials arrayed to their rear in mute support. Just left of Harry's head, about two rows back, was Nora. In the front row, precisely between Harry and Greene, as if to emphasize his neutrality between his old and new bosses, was Felix. Sitting in my apartment, months after this show trial had been enacted, I found myself urging Harry to stay calm. It was useless to try to influence the past, but I couldn't stop myself. As if hearing me, Harry nodded as Greene took the microphone.

"Senator, I pledge the full cooperation of Seligman Brothers in uncovering the mistakes that were made, because there were significant errors that we all regret, and in ensuring that the taxpayers' investment is repaid," Greene said sternly.

Not having bothered to follow a congressional committee hearing before, I didn't know what to expect, but it turned out that the first order of business was to let all the senators make a speech while the witnesses sat silently. Greene composed his face in a supportive expression, while Harry glowered. I skipped through this interlude until I saw the camera focus on Harry, who was reading from a piece of paper clutched in both hands, wearing his spectacles. Once I'd slowed down the video to listen, his speech sounded good. I assumed that Felix had drafted something contrite.

"I would like to assure the committee that, while I regret bitterly what happened, I always did what I believed was best for Seligman Brothers and for this country." His voice was calm, but his shoulders slumped in relief as he came to the end of the sentence. He'd obviously been tensing himself to get through it.

The first senator to ask questions had a crew cut, a beaky nose, and a rough gaze. He stared at Harry and Greene as if they were beneath him, not just physically but morally, and thrust a hand up to scratch his temple as he spoke.

"Mr. Shapiro, that all sounds dandy, but I'm puzzled by one thing. If everything you did was fine, then why did you step down?"

"Senator, I believed Seligman needed a fresh start after—"

"Come on, you didn't resign, did you? You were fired. You were forced out because you'd made a mess of it, hadn't you?"

Harry flinched, but then the accusation seemed to fire him up. He tilted his head toward the senator like a bull getting ready to charge toward the matador's red cloak and spoke in a fierce, controlled tone.

"Given the failure of the firm and our need to accept capital from the taxpayer, I resigned as a matter of honor."

Good line, I thought. As the camera lingered, I peered past Harry at Felix, but his face was inscrutable. The questioning passed to the Republican side of the table, led by a roly-poly senator with a bulging shirt who lolled back in his chair. He smiled at Greene apologetically, as if he'd been shocked by the preceding rudeness.

"Mr. Greene, you told us in your opening statement that you came from a middle-class family?"

"That's right, Senator Highfield. My father was not a Wall Street guy. He worked as a mechanic. I managed to win a college scholarship and I supported myself by working during vacations."

"I expect you worked hard," the senator said encouragingly.

"I did, Senator. My father always wanted me to get a good job, to achieve more than he'd been able to. He was a GI, fought in Normandy. He was a hero to me."

"So you got to Wall Street. How'd that happen?"

"I was lucky. Rosenthal recruited me out of Rutgers. They had an open mind, took people from all kinds of places as long as they were bright and scrappy."

A few of the senators released a rumble of laughter, but others stayed stony-faced, not wanting to be seen sympathizing on television with Wall Street, I imagined.

"Then you were enterprising enough to start your own bank. It says here that you got to be a billionaire, is that right?"

"On paper, that might still be true. I don't feel as rich as I used to," he said. A few more senators joined in that time.

"So why did you sell your bank to Mr. Shapiro last year? I'd have thought you liked being independent."

"I didn't see it that way, Senator. Harry and I joined forces to make a bigger firm, one we believed could compete in the big leagues. I believed I could learn from Harry. He'd teach me a few tricks."

Harry shot Greene an ambiguous glance, half appreciation for the remark and half unease. I thought of what had happened just six months later—the mess that Harry had made of Greene's body. Perhaps I wouldn't have noticed the tension if I hadn't known the outcome, but there was something unnerving in the stiff way they sat next to each other, as if divided by an invisible barrier.

The next senator was a Democrat, a woman in her sixties who was technocratic and stern. She spat out her questions crisply, hardly looking at the witness who was answering, but Greene didn't appear bothered.

"Mr. Greene, can you explain to some of us who are still baffled exactly how your bank came to need the taxpayers' assistance?"

"Senator, it's complicated and I don't think that anyone here, myself included, fully understood the risks we were taking. As I said before, mistakes were made and I bear full responsibility for those errors."

"I'm glad to hear you say that—" she interjected sharply, but Greene carried on talking, and she gave way.

"Let me try to explain this as best I can," he continued. "Our trading desk held mortgage paper that it considered entirely safe. It was triple-A paper that no one believed was in danger of default. Those positions were not reported to the risk committee."

"You mean you didn't even know they were there?"

Greene sighed heavily and closed his eyes for an instant, as if the blunder still pained him. "Unfortunately not. There were flaws in the risk management procedures at Seligman. It examined what it believed were risky assets, and it didn't include any of these CDOs. That stands for collateralized debt obligations, by the way. There are many abbreviations on Wall Street, I'm afraid."

Greene had something, I thought. Imperceptibly, he'd managed to seize control of the hearing and was overriding the questions to present the story he'd prepared. He had a natural authority that subdued others without them realizing it. It sounded as if he were giving a lesson to an appreciative audience, rather than defending himself.

"What happened to these CDOs?" the senator asked obediently.

"This spring, mortgage-backed securities started to fall along with house prices in a way that no one had anticipated. In May, the senior management was informed that heavy losses were occurring on the CDO tranches. I believe the projection was a $5 billion loss. Our estimate now . . ." Greene glanced at a sheet of paper on the desk and read out a figure dispassionately: "is $21.6 billion."

The senator looked at Greene openmouthed. "And you had no idea about this before you lost those billions? You were in the dark?"

Greene held his right hand half-clenched and thrust out to emphasize his words. "Let me address this, because it is absolutely the right question. When I took over as chief executive, I made a complete examination of our balance sheet. I found we had been using too much leverage and didn't have a thorough grasp of some of the instruments we had been trading. I put a halt to it immediately."

The senator still looked astonished, but Greene had managed subtly to deflect attention from himself. He'd become an expert witness explaining the financial complexities, not the one who should be answering for the mess.

"Who ran Seligman while it was doing this and crying to the government for $10 billion to stay in business? Who was in charge?"

Greene paused and looked hesitant. He glanced fractionally sideways at Harry, as if not wanting to say it himself. The camera cut to Harry, who looked crushed. He sat upright and his tongue flicked out of his mouth to moisten his lips, like a reptile. Then, with Greene still silent, he leaned forward to the microphone.

"I was, Senator," Harry croaked.

She shook her head disgustedly. "It sounds as if there was a very good reason why you resigned, Mr. Shapiro. You'd run your bank into the ground."

I could see Felix's eyes focus over Harry's shoulder as he waited to hear the reply. Harry looked on the verge of losing control, but he mastered himself with a visible effort. As he did, and before he could speak, Greene grimaced and reached across the invisible barrier between them. He put a hand on Harry's shoulder, apparently in sympathy.

"Harry did what he believed was right at the time," Greene said. "He wasn't the only executive on Wall Street who made a mistake."

Harry stayed stiffly in position, and I heard the rustle of photographers in the background grabbing their shots for the next day's papers. The camera pulled back to show Harry and Greene stand and huddle in separate knots of advisers. Underwood appeared at Greene's shoulder. Nora moved up to Harry and held his hand as if he were a child who had to be protected from harm, while he gazed desolately into the middle distance.

I reached for my mouse to click off the hearing, but I stopped as the last frames played. A few yards behind Harry, I spotted Anna. She must have gone to the hearing with Nora and Harry, but she hadn't walked forward. Instead, she was standing and talking to a middle-aged woman I didn't recognize, with a sharp nose and gaunt face. They were standing close to each other, as if they were well acquainted, and the last thing I saw before the tape halted and the C-SPAN logo filled the screen was her raising one hand to stroke Anna's arm. It looked like a gesture of comfort.

12

My father's lawyer friend kept his office in Rockefeller Center, high above the honking taxis and lost tourists of midtown. A swaying elevator carried me with a whoosh forty-five floors above the gloomy lobby to the light-filled world aloft. I sat in the reception area for a couple of minutes, then heard footsteps and a shout of greeting. A man emerged quickly around a corner and, as I rose, grabbed me in a hug and slapped my back, although we had never met and he was six inches shorter than me.

"Ben, it's great to meet you," he cried. "I'm Joe Solomon. You're the spitting image of your dad. A privilege to meet you. He's always talked a lot about you. He's proud of you, you know. Let's see what I can do for you."

Up to the neck, he was neatly groomed in a suit and silk tie, but his hair spilled out in gray curls and his blue eyes bulged from a round, ruddy face, suggesting that the clothes were only just holding him in. His accent sounded southern. I'd never heard of him before now. My father had called him a friend, but I didn't know if that was really true or if it was just his term for someone who might be useful. Yet I still found my father's reported words touching. I'd never heard them from the man himself.

We walked to Joe's office, which was on a corner with a view looking south toward the harbor. Whatever he did for a living, it was treating him well. He leaned back in a chair and put his feet on his desk, one leg crossed over the other.

"How much did your father tell you about me?" he asked.

"Just that you were a friend and he trusted you."

He beamed. "Well, that's awful kind of him. He's a gentleman, your dad. We met at a legal conference in Las Vegas a few years back. It was pretty dry stuff during the day, but we had some fun at night, I'll tell you."

I smiled politely. That could mean anything in Las Vegas, and I didn't know Joe well enough to guess—and perhaps not my father, either. I was relieved to be there and by the thought of having someone to protect me, but I was unsure of how much to tell him. I'd been to see my patient in Riverhead, as I was duty-bound to do, and I'd talked to Harry's wife. Neither of those had been improper. But I'd also done something he'd probably warn me against if he knew. I'd called Anna, responding to her silent invitation by the door of the apartment. Discussing the case with someone who might be a witness and was close to my former patient wasn't by the legal or medical book, but I'd been unable to restrain myself. I wanted to know more about Harry. Truth be told, I also craved her presence.

"It's kind of you to see me, Mr. Solomon."

"Hell, forget it. Never mind helping out Roger's son, I'd work pro bono to get on the Shapiro case. Well, on insurance, anyway. It works out much the same. Let me tell you about me. I'm kind of an unusual animal. This firm mostly does civil work, corporate and tax and things like that. Lots of money in it, but no fun. Then they have me.

When any of our clients gets imaginative, I do criminal defense. I'm like those guys who advertise on the subways, except a bit more up-scale."

"I'm glad to hear that," I said, and he giggled and slapped the desk beside his legs as if he and I were already pals.

"It's quite a story, isn't it?" he said, looking serious for the first time. "We'll be seeing quite a bit of each other. Roger told me about what happened. Sounds to me like you've got caught up in something serious, but I know it wasn't your fault. You were doing your best to treat this guy, weren't you?"

"I was," I said. He'd put it better than I'd managed myself. It was comforting to have a professional on my side.

"Roger said you got ambushed by the Suffolk County cops. Next time it happens, tell them you need your lawyer present and nothing else. It's no surprise they've got a ninety-seven percent conviction rate. A lot of people confess to all kinds of things in that place before they get to call a lawyer. And you know what? They don't use any tapes. They write out the confessions and get the poor guys to sign. They don't stand a chance."

I thought of the neat confession Pagonis had showed me outside the Riverhead jail, with its reference to me discharging Harry. It hadn't looked like his handwriting.

"I didn't tell them anything," I said.

"Good, that's always best. So I've talked to the DA's office, who were as helpful as usual—in other words not at all—and to Henry Barber, who's his attorney. He's an old friend and he dropped me a couple of hints. I reckon they'll admit to the killing and plead extreme emotional disturbance. Are you familiar with that?"

"I've heard of it." We were taught mental health law in residency, although I'd just started going out with Rebecca and I wasn't concentrating very hard. "Maybe you could explain it again."

"It's like a weaker version of the insanity defense," Joe said. "If he was mad, say hallucinating or schizophrenic, he'd be locked up in a state psychiatric hospital instead of a jail. The defendant doesn't have to be crazy for emotional disturbance. It's being overcome in the moment and not knowing what you're doing. Like a man who comes home and finds his wife in bed with another guy and kills him. I'd go for that in their shoes, given that he's confessed."

"How does that help?"

"Knocks murder two down to manslaughter if a jury goes for it. I don't imagine the DA would accept a plea. Shapiro could get ten years instead of life, less maybe. Juries don't like it. It suggests the defendant wasn't responsible, and he's not a sympathetic guy, but it could work. The best thing for them is the discharge from Episcopal. They can say the guy was unstable, was on drugs. He'd been admitted to the hospital to protect him from himself. That's good for them."

"Right," I said grimly.

"So that's the criminal case, then after that there'll be a civil suit. Greene's family can sue the hospital and you for wrongful death. They'll wait until Shapiro's been convicted so the cops dig up all the evidence first. They'll say you were responsible for discharging him negligently. There's a doctor-patient relationship and harm's been done, so they just have to show a breach of duty of care and a causal link to the killing. The good news is that it'll take a long time, so who knows what's going to happen? The suit could get settled out of court. Insurers are risk-averse. They don't like to fight."

I felt pummeled by bad news. I'd expected to be told something like this, but hearing him set it out so matter-of-factly, as if there were very little I could do to change my fate, was shocking. Joe had saved the worst until last, though.

"Finally, there's professional misconduct," he said. "Mrs. Greene could complain to the Office of Professional Medical Conduct in New York State that you were negligent, and try to get your license taken away. I don't think that'll happen, Ben," he added, seeing me frown worriedly. "You're young and perhaps you might have made a small mistake. With the hospital on your side, you'll survive."

"I have a question," I said. "What difference does it make that Episcopal's president told me I should release Mr. Shapiro?"

I had the small satisfaction of knocking Joe off his guard with that. He removed his feet from where they had been resting on his desk during his peroration and sat upright in his chair.

"Did he?" he said.

"She. Yes, she did. He wanted to be discharged and she emphasized that the Shapiros were big donors to the hospital. She said to use my judgment, but to make sure that I made the right decision."

"Make sure you made the right decision," he repeated skeptically, and I realized how hollow it sounded out of context.

"She said 'but,'" I said, feeling stupid. "'*But* make the right decision.' It was clear what she meant. She'd called me to her office to make sure I obeyed."

"Uh-huh," Joe said slowly, rubbing his chin. "I don't know. That's difficult. It might help as mitigation in a misconduct case, but you'd have to prove it, and how likely is it that she'll admit that under oath?"

"She says she can't remember it."

He laughed wryly. "I'll bet she can't. Amnesia is a common legal condition. The question is, how much do we want to upset her? We need the hospital to back you up."

"Isn't all this privileged anyway? Can't I just keep quiet?"

"Afraid not. As soon as they present a mental state defense, confidentiality gets waived. Everyone gets to see the hospital records and the notes on the case. If you're called to give evidence, you've got to talk. I'll have to try to make sure that doesn't happen. That's why it's important you don't tell them anything. If they don't know what you're going to say on the stand, they won't call you. Anything else you ought to tell me?"

He looked at me as if he knew there probably was. I thought of Anna again, but I didn't feel brave enough to confess. There was something too personal, too juvenile, about it—falling for a girl in the middle of this debacle. It was embarrassing.

"That's it so far," I said.

As Joe walked me out to the elevator, he cleared up the mystery of just what he and my father had done with their nights in Vegas. It was nothing more incriminating than one evening at the craps tables and two nights in a VIP suite drinking bourbon, or at least that's what he said. The memory seemed to lift his mood.

"Don't worry. We'll think of something," he said, shaking my hand and slapping me on the shoulder before the doors closed. On the ride down, I reflected that people kept on telling me not to worry. That was what worried me.

As I lingered across the street from the Shapiros' building, I saw Anna emerging along the glass-walled corridor and pausing at the front desk to exchange a couple of words with the uniformed guys—they seemed to stand straighter in her presence, to become more animated. Then she headed into the courtyard, wearing a dark green coat with velvet-trimmed lapels, and I stepped forward to greet her.

"What's up, Doc?" she said, reaching me. There was a pause as we both considered an embrace and mutually decided against it. Shaking hands was out of the question after the way she'd treated that as a joke when she'd dropped me off by my apartment, so we settled for nothing instead.

"Too much for my liking," I said.

"At least the paparazzi have gone. There were TV trucks here until last week. Luckily, they never worked out who I was. The neighbors are pissed—it's been frosty in the elevator."

"But you're all right?"

"I'm okay."

She raised both eyebrows and thrust out her chin defiantly, but she looked sadder than before, her bohemian spirit dampened.

"We could try Indian at Whole Foods," she said. "I'm a very cheap date."

We walked down Sixty-first Street and across the knot of traffic by Columbus Circle. I enjoyed the bobbing sensation of her blond head next to my shoulder as she walked, sometimes skipping around obstacles and hopping over the rivulets when we crossed the road. It had rained earlier, the usual brisk drenching, and the drains had overflowed. Passing under the Time Warner Center's jagged towers, we took the escalator that headed down into the crowded Whole Foods, where midtown office workers turned into Upper West Side apartment dwellers, with a last bout of sharp-elbowed aggression at the border.

Anna had found a seat in the café area under the escalator by the time I had fought my way through the lines. As she'd promised, she had chosen inexpensively: a small bowl of vegetables and rice, with dal and pickles. She picked up her fork and pushed rice and vegetables on it to eat, which gave me a chance to look at her. Her hair was gathered at the back, held there by a tortoiseshell clip, and her eyes were downcast. The second she stopped expressing her feelings, she became impossible to fathom.

"Thanks for this," I said.

"My pleasure," she said, and took a sip of water. "I don't get asked out much these days, what with working for a notorious killer."

Had I asked her out? I didn't really know. It had given me the same pleasure when she'd accepted my invitation as if I had, but beneath it was a feeling of anxiety. I wanted to know from her how the disaster had occurred. Nora and Felix had left several questions unanswered, such as where Anna had been while Harry had been killing Greene and what Nora had been thinking about when she'd talked of "who" had supplied the gun. I wished it could simply have been a date, but I had another agenda.

"You never told me your second name."

"Amundsen, like the explorer. My father's family was from Finland; they made it to Minnesota in the twenties. My great-grandfather was a railway engineer."

"Anna *AmUndSen*," I said, trying it out. "Quite a tongue twister."

"My name's like me. One big muddle."

"I wouldn't say that."

"Sweet of you, but it's true."

"This affair must be a terrible shock."

"Duh, yeah. I'll say so."

"When did you find out?"

I felt awkward as I turned the conversation from pleasantries to what I hoped to discover from her. Having experienced her sensitivity, I expected her to look up and call me a hypocrite or worse, but instead she treated my question seriously. She frowned painfully as she thought back, which only made me feel worse.

"They left for the city on the Friday after you'd been there. Nora drove them. I didn't want to be alone all weekend, so I went over to Montauk to see a friend."

"I see," I said, unable to stop myself from wondering who her friend was and then unable to hold back a blush. I've mastered the poker face for therapy, but I've never managed it in life.

Anna smiled. "A *girl*friend, Doctor. Quite innocent. I was there all Saturday. She's a waitress so she was out for the evening and I was watching television—not a very exciting weekend—when Nora called. It was about ten thirty. She was calm, but I could hear police radios crackling in the background. Nora told me what he'd done. By the time I got there, it was chaos. The place was lit up. I had to force the cops at the end of the lane to let me through."

"Mr. Shapiro had been taken away?"

"Leaving a mess behind him. They wouldn't let me in the house. It was full of people in white suits, like there'd been an alien invasion. They'd taken Nora down to the guesthouse."

"How has she been?"

Anna looked at me warily, as if weighing me.

"You're a big one for boundaries, aren't you?" She put on a stiff British accent. " 'We mustn't mix business and pleasure, my dear.' So which one is this? I probably shouldn't be talking to you at all."

"Why do you think that?" I said neutrally.

"Don't give me your therapy bullshit. Answer the question," she said, her cheeks reddening.

I gazed at her as blankly as I could, wanting to avoid the accurate answer, which was a mixture of the two, the very thing I'd warned her against. She was the only one who could tell me the Shapiros' secrets, perhaps help to salvage my career. Yet in that moment, all I wanted was to reach across and touch her.

"Pleasure," I lied.

"Then let's get out of here," she said.

We were walking together in Central Park, the trees around silhouetted against the dusk, when Anna answered my question.

"Nora's all right. She's a lot calmer than I would be, if my husband had just blown my life apart. Sometimes she seems very still and controlled, like she's holding her feelings in check. I hear her crying in her room sometimes."

"You don't sympathize with Mr. Shapiro?"

"He can rot in jail for all I care."

Her voice had a hard edge, and when I looked across at her, her hand nearest me was clenched in a fist.

"That's pretty harsh."

"Is it? Men are assholes. Everything had to revolve around him, the great financier. He's never cared about anyone except himself."

We walked for a while, past boulders massed into artificial mounds and a tourist horse and buggy jingling around the park. I agreed with her about Harry—he was a narcissist—but I bridled at how she'd phrased it, bundling all men into the same category. I was devising a retort when she spoke again.

"He'd already betrayed her," she said.

As she said the words, I went rigid with anxiety. It was the thing I'd been searching for, the truth that had been hidden from me, but I knew immediately in that moment that I didn't want to hear it from her after all—I didn't want Harry's secret to get in the way of our relationship. *Someone else should tell me,* I thought, but it was too late.

"What do you mean?"

"What do you think? He'd had an affair. I saw them together. She was a banker, had a place in Sag Harbor. He got me to drive her to the house when Nora was away on weekends. He didn't even have enough respect for his wife to keep it a secret. You could tell by the way he looked at her."

"You could *tell*? Is that it?" The words came out more fiercely than I'd intended—I was still irked by her condemnation of my sex.

"No, that isn't *it*, Ben," she said sharply. It was the first time she'd called me by my name. "There was something else. She knew the house. When we went in, she knew exactly where to go. And I could have sworn she had a key. When we got to the door, she reached into her bag for something, then stopped as if she'd just realized I was there."

I heard her gulp in the darkness and realized she was upset. I sensed there was something more to her emotions than just the murder. She appeared to have taken Harry's betrayal of Nora personally, as if he'd hurt her too.

"I'm sorry, Anna," I said. "I didn't mean that."

"It's okay," she said, waving away my attention and composing herself. "The thing is, I did something I shouldn't. Can I trust you?"

"Of course," I lied again.

"There was something strange about the way they were together. He said she was there for work, but it didn't look like that. I went for a walk and came along the beach at the back of the house. I climbed the dune stairs to take a look."

Her words brought back the memory of ascending the steps myself after Harry and seeing the rear elevation of the house, with Nora sitting on a sofa reading a magazine. From that spot, you could see anything that was going on inside the house.

"They were in his study. Harry was in a chair, bending forward, his head in his hands. He looked as if he was crying. I'd never seen him like that. She was kneeling in front of him and she had her hands around his head as if she was trying to comfort him. I think she was crying, too. I watched them for a minute and they hardly moved. I went back down the stairs before they saw me."

"When was this?"

"A month ago."

A month. One week before Nora had found Harry in that same room with a gun and had brought him to the psych ER. Whatever had gone on between him and that woman must have still been on his mind. What was more, he'd never told me about it, and I couldn't have known. Harry had lied to me, I realized, but instead of being disappointed I felt a glimmer of relief.

"Does Mrs. Shapiro know?"

"I don't think she does. She keeps saying how sorry she is for him, what an awful time he's had. If she only knew. It makes me so angry. You're the only person I've told, Ben. You have to keep it secret."

Anna stopped walking and put out an arm to halt me, too. We stood in the park under a pale moon, looking at each other. It was an extraordinary intimacy—we were the only ones who knew of Harry's affair, although lawyers, reporters, photographers, and cops were out seeking any tidbit about him and what he'd done. I felt as if we'd been bound together emotionally, although we'd only flirted with a relationship.

She wasn't the only one who was upset. Her description of Nora's faith in Harry had evoked a memory in me of my mother's refusal to condemn my father. The compulsion she'd had to think the best of him had infuriated me. It was something Anna and I had in common apart from the elusive spark between us. We shared a kind of blind faith in marriage and outrage at it being betrayed by a self-indulgent man.

"Who was this woman?" I asked.

"Do you promise me?" she insisted.

"I promise." I didn't want to bind myself, and Anna wasn't my patient so I owed her nothing, but I couldn't refuse. She had a hold on me, and I felt guilty about using her.

"All I know is her name, Lauren Faulkner, and that she'd worked with him once. He told me that. She didn't say much in the car, just hello, thank you. Oh, and she loved being by the sea, I remember her saying. She was there an hour and then I drove her home. At least I didn't catch them fucking."

We looped across the park and returned to Columbus Circle, where we stopped on the side of Sixty-first. She looked up at me, and the lights shining off the towers lit her face like a clown's makeup.

"I'd better go," she said. "I like talking to you."

She faced me, placed one hand on my shoulder, and placed her lips briefly on mine. Then she turned and bolted through a gap in the traffic before I had a chance to respond, leaving that sweet memory behind.

13

I can't recall everything that happened next, but I know I stood there thinking to myself for a couple of minutes, trying to process both the kiss and what she'd told me. Then I turned back the way we'd walked. *I'll cross the park and get the subway at Fifty-ninth and Lex,* I thought. My mind was crammed with emotions—happiness at being with her, excitement at her revelation, and guilt at having deceived her.

I wandered back up to Sixty-third and went through a gap in the boundary wall and down the slope toward the joggers running on the perimeter road. I remember stopping under one of the streetlamps that poked into the branches of a tree and looking at the Art Nouveau ironwork around the lantern, with vaselike shapes cut into each corner. I heard a shuffling sound from behind me, but when I turned there was no one there. It must have been the noise of a jogger approaching down the road, his footfalls refracted off the bushes around me. As I walked farther into the park, those sounds receded and it got darker. The path beneath my feet became gritty as I passed between two softball infields surfaced in sand.

It was quiet there, although the lights of the towers on Central Park South rose over the trees and made a vast stone mound to my right shine in the dark. There weren't many people in the park, and I wasn't noticing much. My mind was caught up in what Anna had told me about Harry. I'd learned something about my patient—my former patient—that he hadn't told me, something that lent a different meaning to all that had happened. It made me feel even sorrier for Nora, who'd been through this torment in ignorance.

I was worried about Anna, too. I could still feel the sensation of her lips on mine, and I touched them with one finger, as if to recapture that moment. Yet our own relationship, if we now had one, had started in the most compromising way. I'd kept her existence secret from my lawyer, and I'd lied to her about my motives for seeking her out. Now she'd told me something Joe would need to know and had sealed my lips with not just a kiss but a promise. She'd given me a choice—whether to betray her or to remain silent.

Cars were passing along a road near the east side of the park, and I walked through a tunnel under it. On the other side, the Wollman Rink had been replaced by an amusement park for children for the summer. It was closed for the evening but a few lights winked in green and red on one miniature aircraft ride and the plastic faces of a pig and a donkey grinned cheerfully from another. I passed to the north and came across a New York scene—a group of dog walkers with their city pooches sniffing one another while their owners stood and talked, in view of the Plaza Hotel. It made me smile, I remember, seeing that gaggle by the rink, then I passed by and walked down into a nook where the reflected light from the buildings around the park was shadowed by trees.

I didn't hear anything until a split second before he struck me. One moment I was strolling peacefully along the path in a hollow by a small lake, and the next moment I felt his shoulder slam into my mid-riff, winding me and knocking me off my feet at the same time. He'd charged at me like a man possessed, running down the slope from above. As he hit me, he wrapped his arms around mine and I could do nothing to break my fall. The side of my head struck the ground at the same time as my shoulders.

My temple smacked on one of the pebbles strewn on the ground and my cheek ground in the dirt as we rolled down the hill toward the lake, out of sight of anyone looking down from the rink or the path. A volcanic eruption of pain surged through my brain, and I was half-blinded by dirt scuffed up into my eyes—all I could see through it were jagged lights. As we slithered to a halt, blood spurted down my forehead.

He'd lost his grip on me as we'd tumbled and I tried to shuffle away and run, but I didn't get far in my dazed and blinded state. I'd managed only a few paces before I stumbled on a stone and he caught me, throwing himself forward and hooking one hand around my an-kles. I pitched headfirst into the darkness and he landed on top of me, knocking the breath out of me again. He rolled my body over to face him.

I was on my back, with my legs above me on the slope and my head half resting on a boulder by the edge of the lake. His left knee pressed down on my chest and he pinned me by the neck with one hand as he raised the other arm above my head. I couldn't hear any-thing, and his face was a black shape, silhouetted against the white glow coming off the rink. Then he thrust his arm down and struck me on the side of my forehead with brutal force. Later, I would realize that he must have picked up the stone on which I'd tripped and used it as a weapon.

In the moment, all I knew was excruciating pain and fear that a crazy person was ending my life, alone in this park, far from home.

Then darkness.

Then nothing.

———

When I regained consciousness a minute or two later, another man was bending over me, holding a wad of tissues to the wound on my head.

"Can you hear me? Are you okay?" he asked.

He had short gray hair and was wearing an orange jacket with SECURITY written on it. His face looked reassuringly worn and experienced. I tried to nod, but it hurt the muscles in my neck.

"I'm all right," I mumbled.

"I've called an ambulance. You're lucky I heard you. That guy wasn't messing around."

My head was throbbing with pain, but the tissue had stanched the bleeding. I reached up and checked my face with my hand, feeling for wounds. My features seemed to be intact, but I felt bruising and swelling around my right eye, where I'd been struck. I tried to remember what had happened, checking myself for concussion. All wasn't clear, but my brain was functioning well enough for me to know that the damage wasn't severe.

After a while, I heard the insistent squawk of the ambulance and its red lights reflected on the man's face as he examined me. They reminded me of the glow on Anna's face only half an hour before, and the memory made me wince. Then the paramedics came and, after checking my pupils for signs of brain injury, carried me up the slope and into the ambulance. I felt it hurtle north through the park and tried to sit up to check with the paramedic next to me where we were going, but I found I couldn't move—they'd strapped me to the gurney to keep me from falling off. I'd seen a lot of schizophrenics brought into the psych ER like that and been happy they were restrained, but I didn't like it myself.

"Don't move," the paramedic said sharply, inflating the pad he'd placed on my arm to check my blood pressure.

The ambulance swung to the right—eastward—and exited the park on the Upper East Side. I knew where we were going then. It was somehow inevitable, and there was nothing to do but lie back and accept the ride, ironic as it was. The paramedic leaned across me casually and took my wallet from the pocket of my jacket, which was strewn across my feet. He seemed to want to check for himself who I was.

"Wow. Hello, Doc," he said, looking at my Episcopal ID card. "Relax, we'll take care of you."

"Who attacked me?" I said.

"Security guy didn't know. Said he'd shouted at him, but he'd run away. You get all kinds in the park. You were lucky."

I saw the tall shadow of Episcopal from the window, and then we drove into the ambulance entrance and they wheeled me into the medical ER. We were greeted by a resident and directed to one of the cubicles. They left me there alone and I rested for a few minutes, wondering what could be keeping them. Eventually, the curtain parted and a female doctor walked in, wearing green scrubs and a blue surgical cap, and picked up my notes.

It was my ex-girlfriend.

"Oh God," I said, craning my head up to see her.

"Great to see you, too," Rebecca replied briskly. "I'm on call and I got paged. For some reason, they thought I'd be worried."

"Why would they think that?"

She paused as if collecting herself and exhaled through her nose, gazing down at me on the gurney. I could see her eyes soften into the old Rebecca. Then she pulled off her cap and I saw that she'd had her auburn hair cropped, making her eyes look larger and more vulnerable. She'd lost weight, too: misery at not having me around, I flattered myself.

"I leave you on your own for five minutes and this happens. Can't you take care of yourself?" She sounded affectionately exasperated.

"I like your hair," I said from my horizontal position.

"Thanks," she said, containing a smile and glancing down at the foot of the gurney. "Can you move your toes?"

"My spine's fine. Everything's working."

"Then sit up and I'll take care of that cut. You lost consciousness, they said. Do you remember anything?"

"Quite a lot. I don't think I'm badly concussed."

"You'd better have a CT all the same."

She let down the side of the gurney and I sat up with my legs over the side to let her remove the makeshift dressing and clean the wound on my forehead. Then she held the two sides of the cut in place and sealed it with Steri-Strips. I could feel her fingers working on me expertly and dispassionately, trying to make the scar as small as possible, and I thanked God for her medical training and professionalism. No matter what she felt about me, I was sure she'd do the job well.

"There," she said, standing back to take a look at her handiwork and stripping off her surgical gloves. "You're not pretty at the moment, but you'll be as good as new in a couple of weeks. Who did this to you?"

"I thought you'd sent him."

"Funny guy. You always told me not to go in Central Park at night, that it was full of your patients. What were you doing there? Night out?"

My head was starting to throb heavily and I didn't have any idea of how to answer that. *A woman asked me to come for a walk in the park and then she kissed me—just before I got attacked.* I didn't think so. I met her skeptical gaze—the look of an old lover with a lingering interest.

"I felt like a walk."

Rebecca looked unconvinced but unwilling to push it much further in case she found out something hurtful. Instead, she looked down and scribbled on my chart, as if to bring our session to a close. As she did, I felt anxious. It wasn't just that I couldn't tell her what I'd been doing in the park. I didn't know why my attacker had picked on me. He'd left my wallet in my pocket, so he was either a bad thief or not a thief at all. Maybe he'd been a paranoid schizophrenic, but it had felt as if he'd known what he was doing.

"Listen, Ben. Are you okay? I heard about that Wall Street guy. I meant to call you, but . . ." Her voice trailed off and she shrugged regretfully.

"It'll be sorted out. Don't worry." It felt better to be handing out that advice rather than receiving it, although no more convincing.

"I hope so," she said, hanging the chart back on the gurney. "They will take you for the scan and then I'm admitting you for the night. We ought to watch you for concussion. You've been acting strangely."

The sheets were welcomingly clean and crisp. Harry hadn't thought much of them, but they worked for me. After the scan, which revealed nothing of concern going on inside my brain, they wheeled me up to a private room on the eighth floor that no one was using that night, rejecting my offer to walk. With Vicodin inside me and the familiar hum of the equipment by the bed, I soon fell asleep.

I didn't take to the breakfast—a floppy pancake with fake maple syrup and apple juice in a sealed plastic container, washed down with tasteless coffee. The stuff had usually been cleared long before I got to see the patients, and it made me understand why some of them were so grumpy about the place by the time I arrived. The sun shone through the corner window, and I lay on my bed with *The New York Times,* waiting for the bureaucracy to grind its way toward signing me out again. My head hurt and I hadn't enjoyed the first sight of my battered face in the bathroom mirror, but I'd survived.

There was a knock at nine thirty a.m. and I put down the paper, half expecting Rebecca to reappear, but Jim Whitehead stuck his head around the door instead. He'd given no warning of his arrival and it didn't fill me with enthusiasm, but I didn't have much choice. I couldn't refuse my department head the right to check on me.

When he wasn't at York East, Jim hung his shingle off Park at Sixty-fifth. I suspected it was his way of making a professional statement, of moving away from Episcopal, which prided itself on being open-minded about treatment—drugs, cognitive behavioral therapy, whatever worked—for the high church of Sigmund Freud. The clue was his couch, a black-leather-and-chrome affair I'd noticed when I'd dropped by his office in an apartment building stuffed with physicians. It made sense: Manhattan was the only place on earth with enough rich neurotics willing and able to spend five hours a week talking to the human equivalent of a brick wall.

Now that he'd got me lying on my back, I wondered if he'd take the opportunity for a spot of analysis, but he stood there with his clipboard for a minute, regarding me with an expression that suggested doubts about my mental stability. Then he took a seat by the bed and rested the board facedown on his lap.

"You had a lucky escape," he said.

I rapped the untouched side of my skull with the knuckles of my left hand. "I'm okay. Last time I go walking in Central Park."

"That sounds wise. You're not having an easy time. If there's anything I can do to help, let me know." He paused briefly before coming to the point. "I came to say that I've met with Mrs. Duncan about the Shapiro case. She's considered all the points on which you might be vulnerable."

I might be vulnerable? That didn't sound like an expression of solidarity. What was it Duncan had said about Episcopal being behind me, just before she'd threatened my career? If they were behind me, they were a long way back.

"She's very professional," I said carefully.

"There is one thing that concerns me. I've reviewed the case with everyone else who was involved—as well as myself, of course. I talked with Dr. Knox and the nurses in the ER, and Mr. O'Meara too. He told me that Mr. Shapiro arrived with a gun. Is that right?"

That jolted me, and I made a show of folding up *The New York Times* and putting it to one side of the bed before I answered.

"Mrs. Shapiro brought one in for safety. She'd found her husband with it."

"Was it the murder weapon?"

I looked out of the window, examining the pattern of steel and glass on the building opposite and conscious of not wanting to face Jim. I thought of Pagonis showing me Harry's gun in the interview room at Yaphank. It hadn't been the Beretta that Nora had brought to the ER, but it no longer felt as though that made a difference. I'd let him walk out of there without knowing what he might do, despite being handed a gigantic clue.

"It wasn't, no. He had another one," I said.

Jim glanced at his clipboard as if longing to pick it up and make a note of what I'd said. Then he gazed directly at me, his eyes boring into mine with the expression of a teacher whose promising pupil has let him down.

"You didn't tell me about that and neither did Mr. Shapiro, since he wanted you to treat him. That worries me. I think it would have changed how I approached the case if I'd known. I wouldn't have been happy handing over responsibility to you like that."

My head started to throb as I grasped the purpose of Jim's visit. He hadn't been worried about my health. He'd come to make sure that I wouldn't drag him into the affair by deflecting the blame to him. It angered me that he had rushed to my side so blatantly to shield himself, just as he'd nipped into the hospital on that Saturday to recruit Harry. He acted deliberately, but he could move fast enough when it suited him.

"Mr. Shapiro is my responsibility, not yours. You don't have to worry about that," I said curtly.

"I want to be clear, that's all. I'll do everything I can to support you through this, Ben," he said.

Jim was the one who glanced away in embarrassment this time: unlike Duncan, he had the decency to look ashamed. As gestures of support went, his ranked pretty low on the scale, however. Even Harry's wife had offered more than that.

It was four p.m. by the time they let me out, and I treated myself to a cab ride home down York Avenue, under the Queensboro Bridge, clutching a paper bag of drugs. I'd taken a shower to wash off most of the blood and mess from having been rolled around in the Central Park gravel, but dirt was still clinging to my hair near the gash on my forehead and the driver had given me a suspicious look when I'd climbed in the back.

I walked into my building warily, prepared to be accosted by one of the neighbors or by Bob, but the lobby was empty. I made it to the elevator and along the hallway without having to explain my appearance to anyone. My luck didn't last. As I neared my apartment, I reached into my pocket for my keys and realized they weren't there. I couldn't believe it at first—nothing else was missing—and I poked my pockets in case I'd stowed them somewhere. But they were gone. There was nothing for it: I had to retrace my steps wearily along the hallway, into the elevator, and down to the lobby. Bob had returned from wherever he'd been, and I walked up to him resignedly.

He looked up and his eyes widened. "My God."

"I got attacked in the park, but it's not as bad as it looks," I said. "Can I have the key to my apartment? Mine's missing."

I went back the way I'd come and got to my front door again, not expecting anything else to be awry. I lived in an apartment building, so the security was good, and I didn't believe the man had taken my keys. It didn't seem likely given that he hadn't been interested in my wallet. They'd probably fallen out as we'd rolled down the slope or had scuffled in the dirt by the pond. Maybe I'd find them if I went back tomorrow, and it wouldn't matter much if I didn't. So I opened my apartment door and switched on the lights without concern.

My mistake was obvious from where I stood. Someone had been through the place like a whirlwind, pulling books from shelves and papers from the desk. Cushions had been tossed to the floor, and a mess of stuff was strewn chaotically on the rug. I stood there in shock for a minute, trying to take it in. It looked like a room in Twelve South after a schizophrenic or a manic patient had lost control, with objects flung around. The walls and the furniture seemed to be intact; only light things had been cast aside. I shivered, knowing for certain that my assault hadn't been a random act. Someone had been after me.

What if he's still in there? I thought. We were taught to retreat from danger if we were in doubt—to find a security guard and use superior force. Many psychs and nurses got attacked, and it was drilled into us not to take chances. But I wanted to find out what was going on without the need to involve Bob—or even worse, Pagonis—immediately. So I halted, breathing silently and listening for human activity. After two minutes, having heard nothing, I walked slowly down the hallway toward my bedroom, leaving the front door ajar behind me. I needed to be able to get out of there fast if I was wrong about the place being empty. My bedroom door was half-open. I pushed it all the way, my heart thudding, and peered inside.

It was in the same state as the living room. The duvet, sheets, and pillows had been ripped from the bed and thrown around, together with clothes from my cupboard. He'd swept all the objects off the counter in the bathroom—even Rebecca's vacation seashells. A couple of them had smashed, and I crouched to pick them up. I was upset by it, as if the family jewels had been trashed. They were the only material things I had left of our relationship.

Kneeling there, I looked to one side and saw one of Rebecca's dresses, which she'd left behind by mistake in my closet. It was bundled in a heap in the corner of the room. I held it up and saw it was slashed from top to bottom with a knife or a pair of scissors. There were deep rips running through the material, from the neck down to the waist. It disturbed me more than the rest of the mess, and I went back out into the bedroom to examine my own clothes, which he'd also pulled from their hangers. They were rumpled but intact. He'd singled out Rebecca's dress to be cut in half, as if he'd had a reason to resent it. It gave me the nasty sensation of seeing into the mind of someone with a sadistic grudge.

Back in the living room, I piled a few cushions on the sofa and sat down to collect my thoughts. I supposed I should call the cops who'd been called to the scene in the park, to whom I'd described the assault before I'd checked out of Episcopal. Perhaps I ought to call Pagonis and fill her in, too. Yet I knew that I wasn't going to do either. That would be the end of whatever privacy I had left, and I'd be dragged straight into an investigation that would make things worse. I didn't even want to call Bob to inquire how the guy had got past him, although he had a lot to explain. What was the point of a uniformed presence in the lobby if a maniac could just walk past? But if I told him, he'd be up here in a minute trying to explain, and everyone in the building would know within a day.

I walked round putting my things back and finished by checking on the bottles of pills my intruder had pulled from the bathroom cabinet. In the back of my mind, I still hoped it might have been an addict's burglary—the last reassuring possibility—but they were all accounted for. My head screamed and I felt overwhelmed. I undressed, swallowed a Vicodin, and fell into the bed he'd torn apart.

14

Sometimes I think I chose to be a psych to avoid having to answer questions. It's one of the craft's comforts that you can bounce back inquiries from patients about what you think or feel and hide behind a wall of detachment. The trouble is, I'm not sure I could answer the questions even if it were allowed. Whenever I was in therapy myself— which we were encouraged to be, but which I'd lately let slip— I would note all my patients' feelings for me and mine for them, every bit of transference and countertransference. Yet I'd mislaid my feelings about myself somewhere.

There was a rap on the window of my car, making me jump. It was Joe, peering through the glass from a few inches away and gesturing for me to let him in. I had parked in the lot near the Suffolk County

DA's Office, on the side of the Riverhead court complex by the jail where Harry now resided.

"What the hell happened to you?" he said, climbing into the front passenger seat and staring at my battered face.

It had been three days since my walk in Central Park, and the worst of the swelling on my forehead had subsided; but purple bruises had formed around it, making my face look even more alarming. I hadn't told anyone about the apartment break-in, and I still didn't feel like doing so: there were too many unanswered questions. If he had been after me, if I hadn't been picked at random from the park's passersby and dog walkers, why had he been so frenzied and what had he wanted?

"They told me Central Park was safe after dark these days. Looks like it isn't true. I went out walking," I said as lightly as I could.

"Shit. You were mugged?"

It was time for the truth. But if I confessed, his first question would be what I'd been doing there in the first place; then why I'd been with Harry's housekeeper; then what she'd told me. I couldn't admit to any of that because I'd pledged not to—she'd made me give my word as we'd stood together. I knew it was foolish to put my loyalty to her, or perhaps just my weakness for her, ahead of my own defense, that I'd been hunted down and attacked and my apartment ransacked, but I kept my promise.

"I was lucky. Someone chased him off."

"As long as you're okay," he said, not appearing to notice my hesitation. "So, what are you going to say in there?"

"Only what you told me."

"Great. In we go," he said, swinging his legs out of the vehicle. I followed him up the steps of the Suffolk County Court, a piece of 1970s brutalism that looked as if it had been built from square white blocks by a giant toddler. At the top of the steps, by the double doors to the DA's offices, was a vista of the back of Harry's prison that was even more unpleasant than the view from the front. The razor wire was extravagantly piled around bleak exercise yards.

I spotted a familiar figure in the long corridor on the second floor. She was talking to a balding man in a three-piece suit who was carrying a stack of files under his left arm.

"Detective Pagonis," I said.

Pagonis looked at me as if she were sorry she'd let me out of the interrogation room and would like to rectify her mistake as soon as possible. It was a stony glare that had no sympathy in it—the sort of expression detectives must practice to intimidate suspects. She narrowed her eyes as she saw my face, making me raise a hand to my head self-consciously.

Joe saw the silent interplay and stepped forward to interrupt. "I'm Joe Solomon, Ben's attorney. He met the wrong guy in Central Park," he said cheerfully.

Pagonis shook Joe's hand warily, a cat greeting a dog. "This is Steven Baer, the assistant district attorney," she said.

"I think I've seen you on television," I told him. I'd watched him once, standing silently on the court steps as Harry's gray-haired, ponderous lawyer had talked to reporters after one bail hearing. The attorney was impervious to the sound-bite demands of the evening news, but Baer had stood patiently as he'd rumbled away.

"Thanks for coming," Baer said, leaning toward me as he spoke and gazing mildly at us. His face was pale and oval, and he was bald on top, with two panels of hair above each ear. "I don't think we've met," he said to Joe. "You must be from New York."

He led us down the corridor at a stately pace, like someone who did not like to be rushed. I could sense Joe struggling to hold himself back from his natural urge to push ahead. When we arrived, Baer's office had a musty smell from his wooden desk, which was piled high with files, and his stuffed bookshelves. He sat behind the desk, and Joe and I arranged ourselves on the creaky chairs around it. Pagonis stood in the corner, behind my field of vision as I looked at Baer, with a notebook poised.

"This isn't an interview, more like a getting-to-know-you session, but the detective will take notes if that's okay," Baer said.

I looked inquiringly at Joe, who was studying the nails on his right hand. "Absolutely fine," he said, still looking down.

"All right, we're in the preliminary stages of the case, as Mr. Solomon will have told you, Doctor. It will be several months before we get to court. Mr. Shapiro's attorney has indicated that he will plead guilty to the killing but offer a defense of mitigation, that Shapiro was emotionally disturbed."

"I'm familiar with it," I said.

"Very good. So you'll know this involves evidence as to the defendant's state of mind at the time of the killing. We take a look at the medical records, and we appoint a forensic psychiatrist to examine Mr. Shapiro. We'd usually expect you to be called by the defense since you treated him."

"Often doesn't happen," Joe interjected.

"Well, there are exceptions. Anyway, it's not happening in this case. In fact, seems the defense are hiring a forensic psychiatrist to examine Shapiro rather than you. That makes me wonder what it is they don't want you to say on the stand. I guess the most likely is that you think Mr. Shapiro knew what he was doing, isn't it?"

Baer's expression was mild and inquisitive, and the way he phrased it made it sound as if he were interested in untangling a mystery, but he had homed in on the awkward truth without pause—he moved faster verbally than in the flesh.

"I believe I can save some time here by making clear Dr. Cowper's position," Joe interjected. "He feels bound by doctor-patient privilege and does not want to disclose details of his treatment of Mr. Shapiro."

"But privilege no longer applies here, given this defense. It's been waived," Baer said mildly.

"Well, two points," Joe said, sitting up. "First, we haven't been notified by the defense that it is waiving privilege, and we'd need that in writing. But second, even if we were, Dr. Cowper wouldn't want to discuss it on ethical grounds."

"That's right," I confirmed obediently, although ethics didn't have much to do with it. I wanted to keep as far away from the limelight as possible.

"That's his privilege, so to speak. As I said, we're only having a conversation. But when I call him to give evidence, he'll be under oath and he'll have to talk to the jury no matter what he thinks. I plan to do that," Baer said.

"That's *your* privilege. But until then, we can't help you," Joe said.

"This is a shame," Baer said. "A great shame. It's a long way for you gentlemen to come to tell me that. I'd hoped we could find a way for Dr. Cowper to avoid getting into any more trouble than he's already in."

"Very kind, but Ben's not in any trouble since he didn't do anything wrong. I'm sorry to disappoint you," Joe said, standing up to bring the interview to a close.

Baer watched us for a few seconds before he rose himself. He looked thoughtful but less friendly, as if moving me from one category—"potential ally"—to that of "hostile witness." Then he emerged from behind his desk to guide us to the door, where Pagonis gave me a disgusted glare.

"What did you make of that?" I asked Joe as we escaped Baer's inquisition and left the building only half an hour after we'd arrived.

"Smarter than he looks."

"He said he's going to call me as a witness."

He shook his head. "It's a bluff. He's not going to do that unless he knows what you'd say. Too risky. The defense will find a forensic psych to testify that Shapiro was unbalanced and he should have stayed in the hospital. Baer's going to get a psych of his own to say the opposite. The guy's as sane as you and I and he cooked the whole thing up."

It sounded pretty cynical, but I had colleagues who worked as forensic psychs and they usually found a way to give the diagnosis that whoever had hired them wanted. Nothing is cut-and-dried about the human psyche, which leaves room to improvise.

"What do *you* think?" Joe said, halting with one foot on the bottom step and another on the parking lot and swinging around to face me. He wore his usual amiable expression, but he scanned my face attentively.

"I really don't know," I said.

In the psych ER, I'd been sure that Harry was, at worst, suicidal—he'd seemed like a classic case of midlife depression. But our meeting in jail had left me wondering whether he'd deceived me all of that time. We walked past a woman dragging two children toward the court, no doubt going to see their father getting jailed. *Not much of a start in life*, I thought.

"Is that it, then?" I asked.

"I hope so," Joe said, and he clambered back into his Lexus.

He waved cheerfully as he cruised out of the lot and turned left back toward the highway. I waited until he'd driven out of sight before walking to my car, keys in hand, but just before I reached it I heard a shout and saw Pagonis approaching. She'd timed her arrival so that my lawyer wasn't by my side.

"Who attacked you?" she said as she got to me.

"I've no idea."

"You know a lot about Shapiro you're not telling us, don't you?" she said, hardly pausing after getting me off my guard before moving to the next question. "We're going to find out what you're hiding."

I felt my face redden with embarrassment, and I turned toward my car door to hide it from her, pulling out my keys. *I can't tell my lawyer and I'm sure as hell not telling you*, I thought.

"You're wasting your time, Detective," I said.

"I don't think so, *Doctor*."

She spat out the last word as if she didn't believe in the notion of medical expertise and walked away. I climbed into my car and sat for a couple of minutes to calm down, then drove steadily out of the parking lot and turned south.

Mist was blowing off the sea when I reached the Shapiros' house, half covering the houses lined up on the dune. In the far distance, the fields and ponds beyond the house looked flat and bleak. It was my first visit alone—the last time I'd been chauffeured along the lane by Anna. As I came to the willow trees and the entrance to the gravel path, I tried to imitate the way she'd smoothly driven up, but I didn't get the speed right and the wheels spun in the gravel near the top.

Nora was in the garden behind the house, crouching by the flower beds in a gardening smock and clipping some blooms, and as I climbed out of my car, she looked over her shoulder. She walked toward me but halted a few feet away rather than embracing me again.

"Your face," she said worriedly, as if she couldn't take any more bad news.

"Just an accident. Nothing serious."

We were standing by the conservatory at the rear of the house, and I could see white sheets covering the sofas in the living room. The floor was bare, with the geometric rug that had covered it—on which Greene's bloody corpse had lain—removed. Lines were still marked on the wooden boards, along with some dark stains, the last traces of murder.

Nora had called me the day after my attack, as I was resting at home—I had a feeling that the hospital liked having me out of the way. She'd just talked to Duncan, she'd said, and had something to discuss.

"I'm trying to get the garden under control," she said. "It grows so fast and the men haven't been for a while. The police shut the house for a long time. Anna's coming down here to redecorate soon. I don't know if we'll stay."

"Take your time. Don't make any big decisions."

That was what we always advised people who were depressed— don't do anything while they were unstable that they might regret later. I wasn't sure how much sense that made, though. Not doing something is an act in itself.

The ocean breeze was blowing her hair over her eyes, and she brushed the strands away to look at me. "You're a good man, Dr. Cowper. I'm so sorry about this. Let's go and talk, shall we?"

She guided me away from the conservatory along the rear of the house and we went into the building through a door by the bedrooms, then along a hallway into what seemed to be her study. There was an ornate French desk by one window, with a vase of flowers resting on it. She sat in an antique chair near four miniature oil portraits.

"I talked to Sarah, as you asked me last time," she said. "It made me realize how hard this has been for you."

Thank God someone does, I thought. I gave her the professional answer, hoping that she wouldn't take it too literally.

"You must do whatever's right for your husband. That's all you should be concerned about."

"I want to say something about Harry, Doctor. He's a good man and he went through an awful experience. He lost his bearings and did something terrible, but I can't let him spend the rest of his life in prison. He doesn't deserve that."

Nora took off her gardening gloves and rested them on her knee, smoothing them out with one hand. Then she lowered her head and a tear dripped from the end of her nose, leaving a dark spot where it landed on her glove. Her face had turned pale and her mascara was running. I got up and walked over to her desk to retrieve some tissues from a box for her. She blew her nose, then walked to a window that overlooked the drive, through the trees to the guesthouse.

"Sarah's worried about Margaret suing the hospital, but I'm sure I can stop her from doing it," she said. "We'll settle with her over the damages. We've got the money. Our lawyer says we'll be first in line to be sued anyway."

"That's very generous of you, Mrs. Shapiro, but I don't know how much it will help. I could still be accused of misconduct."

"Sarah thinks she can protect you," Nora said, her eyes shining with the residue of tears. "I've told her she must, for the hospital's sake. I don't want your life ruined the way Harry's has been."

It was surreal to hear of this negotiation over my fate, and I wondered briefly about Nora treating my problems as equivalent to

Harry's. But her demeanor distracted me. She was smiling brightly and her hands shook slightly. I worried that she might be on the verge of hysteria, so rapid had been her mood swing.

"Have you eaten anything today?" I asked.

"I haven't, no. The kitchen's that way."

She pointed at the wall and I realized she'd been afraid to go there because she would have to pass the crime scene.

"You should sit down. Is there any food in the house?" I said.

"Anna said there would be," Nora said, obeying.

I walked along the corridor and glanced around as I got to the living room. It felt eerily quiet, with furniture pushed in corners, covered in sheets, and a sharp smell of chemicals in the air. In the kitchen, the cupboards and fridge were full of food and there was milk in the fridge. Anna had kept the place stocked.

I scrambled eggs on toast for both of us and brought them back on a tray. It felt good to be able to help her. Without Anna there and with Harry in jail, she had no one else. She'd regained some color in her face by the time she finished the food.

"I do appreciate your kindness," I said eventually. "I'll have to talk to Mrs. Duncan and see what she has in mind."

"Of course. I just don't want any more suffering, that's all. There's been too much of that already."

She walked me out to my car, skirting the house across the lawn, and stood there as I got in. She was on the exact spot where I'd stood behind Anna three weeks earlier, watching her as she gazed out to sea.

15

On Wednesday afternoons, when my ward rounds were done, I had a three-hour block of therapy in my office. My final session was Arthur Logue, a patient who'd come to see me after a spell of panic attacks. I knew his life well—his scratchy relationship with his wife, his various neuroses. It was difficult to interrupt his steady narrative of trivia, and I'd almost stopped trying. He was light relief from patients in acute distress.

Mr. Logue left my door half-open when he left, and while I was up writing a few notes on our session, Sarah Duncan arrived.

"Can I come in?" she said, looking around. "This is nice."

That was a stretch, but it was better than some other offices along therapy row. I had two windows, which was two more than a couple of the other psychs, and I'd refused to move when building services had hatched a conspiracy to shift me. Duncan walked over to the wall on which I'd hung an old poster for Fellini's *8½*, with Marcello Mastroianni in a hat and thick spectacles, surrounded by Claudia Cardinale, Anouk Aimée, and Sandra Milo. It was at the outer limit of office acceptability, but I claimed it was a reference to Jung.

"My husband loves Fellini," she said unexpectedly. "We rented *Juliet of the Spirits* the other night."

"I haven't seen that one."

"Oh, you should. It's wonderful," she said, looking over at the books on my shelves as if she had a right to examine my possessions. Then she sat in my patients' chair, crossing her legs at the ankle and adjusting her skirt. She looked happier than before.

"I've spoken to Nora Shapiro and she told me she's talked with you. I think she could save us from a nasty predicament. I've told her how grateful I am to her."

"I wasn't sure what it would involve," I said cautiously.

"Don't worry about the details. The point is that we wouldn't face any liability over Mr. Shapiro's discharge." Duncan held out her arms and widened her eyes with astonishment, like a preacher describing a miracle. "Wouldn't that be a relief?"

"Mrs. Shapiro's being very generous by the sound of it," I said, trying to mimic her enthusiasm. "But what about me?"

Duncan sighed and looked at me as if I were a child who had sorely tried her patience but whom she was prepared to forgive.

"We may have got off on the wrong foot, but that shouldn't get in our way. We must stick together if we're going to get through this. I've reviewed the files and there are things that worry me about how you handled Mr. Shapiro's case. I've discussed them with Dr. Whitehead. You made no mention of Mr. Shapiro bringing a gun, and I'd have taken a different view if I'd known that."

You too? I thought. It was plain enough what Jim and Duncan had talked about when they'd met. They'd assembled their excuse—that I'd been negligent in not telling either of them about the weapon, even though it hadn't been used for murder. My anger was laced with contempt for them both. Here was I, faithfully hiding the news about

Harry's lover from my lawyer and Pagonis, while they scurried to cover themselves.

"Anyway, the point is that I'm sure you can learn lessons from this case. I wouldn't want it to bring your promising career to a premature end. Nora will take care of the civil suit and I shall try to prevent any misconduct complaint. Meanwhile, I think it would be best if you said nothing, don't you?"

She didn't wait for my answer but rose and walked to the door, where she turned and nodded to me as if I'd already agreed.

After she'd gone, I stood at a window looking at the hospital's exterior walls, which the architect had tiled in white, shaping the windows in Gothic arches like a cathedral. He had a point, I thought: plenty of East Side matrons treated it as a place of worship. The list of people wanting me to keep quiet was growing—Anna, Jim, and now Duncan. Harry didn't deserve my silence, though. He was a narcissist who didn't care about others, not Nora and probably not his mistress. If I'd got him into therapy and delved beneath his hard-nosed ascent on Wall Street, his two marriages, and his affair, I might have found a shy boy with an unfeeling father who hadn't been able to cope with humiliation. *So what?* I thought. *He's a murderer.*

I thought of Anna's words about her own shrink: *I could have been a terrible person. He wouldn't have known.* Harry was a terrible person, and I didn't want to be his vassal. If I refused to talk, I'd have Pagonis and Baer on my trail, pushing me to tell them everything. The only way I could get them off my back was by letting Joe cut me a deal.

I hadn't told him anything that might help me, though, and why not? Because I'd made a pledge to a girl on whom I had a crush. That wasn't loyalty, it was stupidity. Until she released me, I'd be trapped.

Anna agreed to meet me on the Upper East Side at a Le Pain Quotidien near the hospital where I sometimes took a break. It was a long way from the Shapiros' apartment, but she'd prefer that, she said. She was there when I arrived, sitting at the rear by one of the trestle tables, a paperback in hand. She'd draped her coat over the bench next to her and was dressed in a scoop-necked T-shirt, a silver necklace, and gray pants. It was an ordinary getup and she didn't seem to be wearing makeup, but I still found it glamorous. She was nursing a cup of coffee in one hand and I'd almost reached her before she glanced up.

"Oh, my God. What happened?" she said, putting a hand to her mouth in shock. The sight of my face seemed to hurt her, as if she'd been attacked herself—I found it moving how personally she took it. As I sat next to her, she reached out briefly to touch the side of my head with her fingertips and then withdrew them quickly, as if regretting the intimacy.

"I ran across a man in the park after I left you. He didn't seem to like me very much," I said.

"Jesus, Ben," she said, looking dazed. She seemed to be musing to herself, struggling to understand what had happened. "I took you there. How could I have been so stupid? You've got to be careful. Promise me you will."

Not another promise, I thought—she was one for extracting pledges from people. It still pleased me that she cared.

"I promise I'll look both ways crossing the road."

She didn't smile. "Fuck," she said quietly to herself, as if the news were still sinking in. Her face was stricken and a tear trickled from one of her eyes onto her face, where she wiped it with the back of her hand. I wanted to reach across to hold it, but nervousness defeated me as surely as the Perspex dividing the tables in the Riverhead jail. To fill in while she recovered, I called over the waitress and ordered a cup of tea. We sat in silence for a while until she spoke again, flicking a crumb from the table as she did.

"I'm glad you called. There's something I have to say."

"Oh dear. That sounds bad."

"You said the reason you wanted to see me was pleasure." She looked up at me and her eyes shone unhappily, renewing my guilt at the way I'd misled her. "I don't think I can. Enjoy it, I mean. Not with all this."

"I understand," I said.

That wasn't true. Harry was locked up in Riverhead, but he'd been there the night she'd kissed me and it hadn't stopped her. I didn't want to lose her when I'd only just started to feel for her—I needed her on my side. I'd come there to persuade her to release me from my pledge, but that felt unimportant suddenly. She had that effect on me. When I was with her, nothing else seemed to matter. She was my drug.

"I wish I could," she said.

"I wish you could, too."

She looked miserable and her hand trembled slightly as she picked up her coffee to sip it. Then she put it down and started to gather her things, stuffing her book into the bag by her side and threading one arm through her coat.

"I'm no good at this, I have to go," she said.

"Wait," I said, half rising and putting out a hand to touch her arm. "I need your help. The thing you told me about that woman. It's important. I have to tell my lawyer."

It was as if I'd sent an electric shock through her. She straightened up and jerked her arm back, pulling it free of my hand. She stared with her mouth open and her eyes glossy and hard. Then the corners of her mouth tightened and she spat out her words.

"I *trusted* you. That was a secret."

"But I'm in trouble. The police think I've been hiding things from them. You need to help me."

As I said that, I knew it was a mistake. A strand of her blond hair detached itself from where it was fixed and she looped it back over her ear as she stared at me.

"Right, so your job's important and mine doesn't matter? That's what this was about, Ben? You just strung me along to find out what you wanted. Was that it? You think I'm stupid, do you?"

"Of course not," I protested.

"You listen to me. You promised me and I expect you to keep your promise. You don't want your hospital to know how you behaved."

My guilt and shame, and my wish somehow to placate her so that we could go back to the night she'd kissed me, evaporated instantly. She was no better than the rest of them. As soon as she was under the least threat, she resorted to blackmail. Why had she played with me like that, teasing me with her secret about Harry and then forbidding me to use it? I spoke before I'd thought.

"You don't want Nora to know how *you* behaved," I said.

Anna stared at me hatefully and reached into her pockets for cash, twisting the cloth in her rush. She cursed under her breath as she struggled to extract her hand again.

"Forget it. I'll pay," I said.

"Stay away from me," she replied.

She almost ran out of the café and off down First Avenue, disappearing back into the city's millions. We'd degenerated from awkward fondness to blazing bitterness inside a minute and I didn't know why it had happened. I guessed it was my awkwardness at feeling vulnerable around her, which had expressed itself as rage. She hadn't cared for me, after all: at the first sign of difficulty, she'd fled.

As I got up, I saw a glove beneath the bench. It must have fallen from her pocket when she'd left. I held it to my face to catch her scent and placed it in my own.   *

That night as I got ready for bed, I brushed my teeth, looking in the bathroom mirror as toothpaste dribbled down my chin. My bruises had flowered purple, black, and yellow, there were dark circles under my eyes, and my cheeks were puffy in the halogen light. The only comfort was that Rebecca had done a nice job on the cut, sealing it so neatly that it was fading from sight. I looked and felt like an aging boxer: my days were filled with body blows.

None, however, had felt as bad as fighting with Anna. Something had made her abandon me, something she hadn't told me. I hadn't cared that she'd kept her secret from Nora, but I cared that she was keeping one from me. I remembered how she'd touched my face, the shock in hers, as if she were responsible.

I rooted through my pills, seeking something to put me out for as long as possible. Then I realized I wouldn't need it—I was so tired that I'd only have to lie down to fall asleep. The last thing before turning in, I called voice mail to check my messages. Two were from patients who had to change appointments and one was from a man giving an excuse for not turning up that day. I was about to hang up when I heard a voice that I didn't recognize.

It was Lauren Faulkner.

16

Her footsteps announced her identity from a long way away. Most people in the place, even the doctors, tended to shuffle, but Lauren's heels clicked along the corridor. She rapped loudly on the door with none of the tentativeness of my neurotic patients.

It had been easy to look Lauren up after she'd called, to find her photograph, her age—the same as mine—her magna cum laude education, and her list of jobs. High school in Beverly Hills, then Yale, then a job with a consulting company, then Harvard for an MBA, then to Seligman Brothers and a rapid rise from analyst to co-head of the Financial Institutions Group. I thought of Felix's summary of Underwood's job as we sat in the Gulfstream: *A banker who advises other bankers. Go figure.*

A photograph on her new bank's website showed a woman with

dark hair that curled around her ears before straightening, as if coming to its senses, and an unflinching gaze. There were two other photos, one at a fund-raiser in the city and another at a party in Southampton with a group of blue-blazered men. *She's got nice legs under that dress,* I had thought, but the image hadn't done her justice. She wore a silk blouse and an expensive-looking pantsuit that demurely covered the legs I'd noted. In person, her sleekness lit up the room.

"Dr. Cowper? I'm Lauren," she said.

"Come in, Ms. Faulkner."

Since she'd called, I'd been wondering why she'd tracked me down. Psychs are wired not to believe in coincidence. We quiz patients who claim they missed a train they wanted to catch or happened to meet a friend in the street. Deep down, we think, it was deliberate. The idea that Harry's lover had selected me by sheer chance was ridiculous. I'd been attacked on the evening I'd been told about Lauren, and the man whose house she'd been observed visiting was in jail, accused of murder. This wasn't a coincidence.

"Where should I sit?" Lauren said, glancing around the room. "I haven't done this before, believe it or not. I'm the only one of my girlfriends who hasn't. Man trouble, money, the usual things."

Her voice was low and melodic and her tone unworried, suggesting our meeting was perfectly ordinary.

I indicated my patients' chair. "Let's see if I can help you."

"I'm sure you can," she said, as if it would be a waste of effort to try to dissuade her. She crossed her long legs and placed her black leather bag on the floor. She was more finely groomed than women I knew—so polished that she looked as though she wore a mask. Her red lipstick matched the soles of her Christian Louboutin shoes, and her eyebrows were exactly shaped.

"How did you find me?" I asked.

She paused for a few seconds, and I saw her assessing me. Both of us knew the answer to the question, but she avoided it.

"You're on a list, aren't you? Top doctors in New York," she said.

I knew that *New York* magazine list, and I knew I wasn't on it. She smiled, displaying pearl white teeth against red lips. She gave the impression of being in complete control—she wouldn't reveal anything that she didn't care to.

She didn't look even vaguely ill, certainly much less than Harry when I'd first met him. She was talking brightly and at a normal speed, her face was full of life, and she smiled easily, so there was no depression there. It was conceivable she was bipolar or had another condition, but there were few signs of it. She wasn't manic, and she was lucid and rational. If anything, she seemed less stressed than I.

"Can I ask why you're interested in therapy?" I said. "Is there something happening in your life at the moment?"

She gazed at me as she absorbed the question, but she showed no sign of wanting to answer it. Instead, she leaned back in the chair and expelled a slow breath of air through her nostrils, gathering her thoughts.

"May I ask *you* a question?" she replied. "Can I be sure that nothing I tell you will go outside this room?"

"Of course. It will be in confidence."

"I've heard of cases where personal matters came out in court," she said, gazing at me. "Things a patient had told his psychiatrist."

I looked back at her, both of us knowing what she meant and both knowing that the other one knew. It was absurd. I should have stopped her there, told her that I couldn't treat her. Anything she told me in this room, including her affair, would immediately become sealed. Even if Anna released me from my promise, which she showed no sign of doing, it would have to remain secret and I'd have nothing to tell Pagonis or Baer. I'd be bound as tightly as ever by professional obligation.

I felt as if I were becoming more enmeshed even as I tried to fight my way free, yet I couldn't resist it. The lure was as powerful as when my father had turned pleadingly to me in the car when I was twelve years old and asked me to keep secret Jane's illicit presence in our house. I'd been drawn into Harry's world, and I had to know the truth. Anna had only spied upon it from afar, and she wouldn't tell

me more. Even if I could never find my way out of this maze, I wanted
to proceed.

"It only happens when a patient who's been accused of a crime
waives privilege. It's his choice, not the doctor's," I said.

She smiled. "You've got a duty of care. Like a banker."

"I imagine so. I'm not an expert."

"So you'll take me as a patient?"

"Perhaps you should tell me about yourself first," I said.

"Thirty-three, separated, investment banker. What else?" she said,
as if she'd already exhausted the subject of her personality.

"You're separated?"

She sighed, and her confidence seemed to falter. She looked away
from me, speaking to the bookshelf on one wall.

"Wall Street's a relentless place. You make partner in your early
thirties and you need to work hard just to prove yourself, harder than
the men. Seven or eight meetings a day, work every weekend. My
husband couldn't accept that. He wanted children."

"You didn't?"

"I did. I do. But I had no choice. That's the job."

She gave a brittle smile, and a few minutes later, our meeting was
over. She didn't bother to ask me how much therapy would cost, and
it didn't seem likely to bother her any more than it had Harry. We
arranged for her to return at the same time the following week, and I
opened the door for her. She walked toward the elevators as precisely
as she'd come, bag at her side, head aloft, the legs of her expensive
pants swishing together. I couldn't remember a patient who'd come
for treatment in such good health.

I was at home that evening, eating a sandwich and watching television aimlessly to distract myself, when Bob called up from the front
desk to tell me that two detectives had come to see me.

"Fine, send them up," I said as casually as I could manage, although they hadn't given me any warning.

"Sure thing, Doctor."

His voice had the doorman's guarded neutrality. I couldn't tell whether he believed that it was as routine as I'd tried to make it sound or he expected me to be led out in handcuffs in a few minutes. When I peered out of my apartment, I saw Hodge slouching down the corridor as if he hadn't thought much of me the first time we'd met and had since had his view fully vindicated. Pagonis carried a document that she tapped lightly on one wall as she walked.

"We're here to give you this," she called with a tone of malicious pleasure. As she got to me and proffered it, I saw it was a document in a legal-looking manila envelope, fastened with red string to a buttonlike clip.

"Come in for a minute," I said. The way they'd arrived without warning and looked so self-satisfied wasn't reassuring, and I didn't want them to depart before I knew what they'd brought with them.

Pagonis led the way, Hodge squeezing me against the wall with his stomach as he passed. She was wearing a pantsuit that was less flattering than Lauren's. It was a pale shade of gray, and it creased around her knees and waist. Yaphank detectives had less of a clothes budget than bankers, I imagined. As Hodge examined my bookshelves, Pagonis walked to the end of the room by a window that looked south over another block to a high school and a rooftop jumble of water tanks and air-conditioning units.

"Nice place," she said. "I like these drapes. My husband and I are looking for something like that, but we can't agree, you know?"

"Why don't you take a seat?" I said, gesturing at my sofa. I felt the need to corral them. They were behaving as if they already owned the place.

I sat down and opened the envelope. Inside were three sheets of paper, the first one headed "Subpoena Ad Testificandum for a Witness to Appear Before the Grand Jury of Suffolk County." My heart sank as I saw that the People of the State of New York "commanded" me to be in Riverhead in two weeks' time to testify. It was just what I'd gone to Anna to try to avoid. I didn't really know what a grand jury was, although I'd heard of them, but the document looked genuine—Baer had signed it.

"Mr. Baer wasn't happy with our last meeting with you. The one with that New York lawyer," Pagonis said. "Now you have to testify."

She extended her legs on my rug, bending her toes back to stretch her calf muscles. It had been a long journey just to deliver me a subpoena. Didn't they have better things to do with their time, like catching criminals?

"My lawyer will get back to you," I said.

Pagonis shook her head. "Your lawyer can't come to a grand jury hearing. It's just going to be Mr. Baer and you. We've got new evidence that suggests you haven't been honest with us. You spent time at Shapiro's house in East Hampton, it turns out, just after you'd discharged him from the hospital."

How does she know? I thought. There'd been only three witnesses in East Hampton—Nora, Anna, and Harry. One of them must have told Pagonis about what happened that day, and she'd already started closing in on me. Things felt as if they were moving a lot faster than Joe had predicted.

Pagonis smirked. "I'll bet he poured out his heart to you."

"You shouldn't have come all this way," I said, standing to usher them out of the room and the building.

"It was worth the trip," she replied.

After they'd left, I made some tea and sat at the kitchen table, thinking about what Pagonis had said. Maybe I'd been foolish to provoke her—it had made her go and dig up something to use against me—but she'd probably have discovered it anyway. *What else does she have up her sleeve?* I wondered. She'd seemed very confident it was worth putting me in front of a grand jury, despite Joe's belief that Baer wouldn't risk it.

I thought back to that day on the beach. Perhaps Pagonis was right: Harry had given me a clue about his intentions and I hadn't realized it. All I remembered was feeling happy that he was less depressed and volatile. Maybe there was another way to interpret his mood: he'd made up his mind to kill Greene by then, so he was less oppressed by anxiety.

I closed my eyes and tried to think back. The waves had rolled along the beach, and Harry had walked back toward the house as if defeated. *Why had he been sure that his life was ruined?* I thought. Depressed people often think that, but they have their own logic. They feel trapped by something or someone, unable to break free. Who had Harry believed was trapping him? It had to be Greene, surely. His dead body was proof of that. I pictured Harry standing despairingly at the foot of the dune stairs as he'd told me of Seligman's collapse.

I lost everything. They ruined me, he'd said.

Not *him,* not Greene alone. *They.* Who were *they?* I wondered. Were *they* simply the fates that everyone blames when things go wrong, or had it been someone in particular? Who had he been thinking of when he'd said the words? I remembered him sweeping his hand across his throat—that violent gesture and his tortured face.

Treasury demanded a sacrifice, he'd said.

There was something else—something I'd heard recently—that those words reminded me of. It had been in this room, not long ago. Then I remembered. I went into the living room to retrieve my laptop from my desk and brought it to the kitchen. After firing it up, I found my way to the C-SPAN archive and the Senate committee hearing I'd been halfway through. When I'd spotted Anna at the end of the tape, they'd been about to grill the Treasury secretary.

I clicked on the second video of the morning's proceedings and saw the earlier witnesses walking jerkily offscreen—Greene with Underwood at his side, raising his head in what looked like a laugh. There was a pause while the senators went out of the room to vote. Finally, another group of officials and advisers started gathering in the front row of seats behind the witness table, and one official replaced Harry's and Greene's nameplates with a sign that read SECRETARY OF THE TREASURY.

As I slowed the video, a man in his sixties walked into the shot. He was handsome and tanned, his face comfortably lined and shrewd. His movements were spare and he clasped his hands as the photographers took shots, looking born to the limelight. When he was introduced, he bowed his head, acknowledging the panel's seniority and status. His opening statement was brief, and he leaned back to take questions as if eager to chat.

It was a tricky audience—the Democrats were unhappy because Wall Street had been bailed out, and the Republicans were just angry—but he was unfazed.

"Secretary Henderson, I appreciate your public service, but I must ask why on earth you think Wall Street deserves $700 billion for getting us in this mess?" asked the twitchy senator I'd seen before.

Tom Henderson rearranged the papers before him with his long fingers, his gestures delicate and precise, and gave an exasperated laugh.

"Senator, that's a fine question," he said. "The truth is that the banks did not deserve our money. We would have preferred for them to learn a lesson they wouldn't easily forget. You may remember I used to work on Wall Street myself, and I can tell you, people who made such errors suffered a far deal more."

I used to work on Wall Street myself. Curious, I pulled up another tab on the browser and searched for his biography on the Treasury website. "Before his nomination, Secretary Henderson served as chairman and chief executive officer of Rosenthal & Co., where his career began in 1968," it read. Rosenthal was the bank that had recruited Greene, the place Harry had tried to emulate, and the one that had come through the financial crisis unscathed. *Treasury made sure of that,* Harry had said.

I clicked back to Henderson's watchful face, and then I knew. That was what Harry had meant. "They" was Greene and Henderson's alma mater, the pinnacle of Wall Street's inner establishment that Harry had both admired and despised. *He's always felt like an outsider to Wall Street, not part of the club. When he was pushed out, he imagined that everyone was laughing at him.* Those had been Felix's words. Why hadn't I thought of it before? Harry had told me himself: *I wanted us to be like Rosenthal. They were never going to let it happen. I know that now.*

Perhaps he'd been imagining it. Harry was depressed and angry, and he believed his bank had been stolen from him. Many people came through Episcopal's psychiatry wards with similar delusions, believing that someone was out to get them. Their villain was often the government. Just because Harry had thought the Rosenthal alumni, including the Treasury secretary, had ruined him, that didn't prove it was true. It didn't make much difference, though. Harry had believed that and he'd killed Greene as a result.

The twitchy senator was still talking as I restarted the tape.

"Why did you bail them out with our money, then?"

Henderson smiled imperturbably. "Our responsibility was to stop the financial system from collapsing because of Wall Street's errors. It was for these banks' boards to determine what action was taken as a result of the mistakes. Some CEOs lost their jobs, as you've heard."

The chairman passed the questions to a Republican I had not seen before, a boyish puritan with round glasses who looked as if he'd been bullied at school by jocks and was now taking it out on others. He had a reedlike, insinuating voice.

"From what we heard, Mr. Shapiro didn't know what was going on in his own bank. I bet you're glad he was fired."

"That was the board's decision, as I've said."

"They were right, though, weren't they?"

"I believe Seligman Brothers now has sound leadership in place," Henderson said coolly. "That's all I'd say."

Henderson's face filled the screen as I clicked off the video. Either he or Harry had not been honest. Harry had insisted to me on the beach that the Treasury had wanted his head, but the man in charge had just blithely denied it—it had been a decision of the Seligman board, and he had been a mere bystander.

I didn't trust Harry and this was the first time I had even caught a glimpse of Tom Henderson, but I looked at his bland, practiced expression of innocence and I thought: *You're lying.*

17

My job is to be nice to annoying people—people in strange states, who aren't acting right, who have problems that stop them from relating properly to others. There's no one so hard to be with as a depressed person locked within himself. We're like friends, but friends who don't get bored or frustrated and try to change the subject.

That's my way of looking at it, even if it's low-paid work by the standards of medicine. Spending forty-five minutes listening to someone for $400 sounds okay, but it isn't plastic surgery–style wealth. So my profession is drifting away from it, leaving it to psychologists with their happy-talk cognitive behavioral therapy, using checklists to persuade people that they worry too much. It's more efficient to practice genetic medicine and hand out pills in fifteen-minute sessions to alter people's brain chemistry. This patient has the short arm of the transporter gene, so she's got serotonin imbalance. Give her a re-uptake inhibitor and she'll be good to go. If that doesn't work, try another brand or combine it with a lithium booster. There's an entire algorithm of combinations to try before you have to admit defeat.

Some residents want to forget all about therapy, and there's not much evidence that it works, although no drug company will fund the research, so who knows? Should we leave people in misery because their moods can't be measured scientifically? It's a matter of personality—the psych's, I mean, not the patient's. Therapy suits me even if it's a fading form of medicine. I like sitting and listening, trying to reconcile the latest story I'm told by a familiar patient with what he's said before or probing the mask of a new one.

The afternoon sun was reflecting off the windows on a nearby block and I'd lowered the blinds behind me to shield Lauren's eyes.

"Tell me more about your work," I said.

"I'm a partner at a place you've probably never heard of, called Fleming Dupont. Before that I was with Seligman Brothers."

"I've heard of them."

She smiled, perfectly in control. "I'm sure you have. They've been in the news. You want to know about my work. What do you notice about me?"

"How do you mean?"

"What I'm wearing," she said impatiently. "How I look."

I allowed my gaze to travel from her face down her body to her leather shoes and up again. She was little changed from the first time: her makeup was immaculate, with her brown hair fastened a touch more severely at the side of her head, and she wore a similar suit. Her blouse had wide mother-of-pearl buttons and no ruffle. As before, her suit was well cut enough to be demure while giving off a hint of femininity.

"Professional," I said.

"What you mean is, I'm dressed like a man," she said, not hesitating before restating my summary. "A black pantsuit and pumps, no cleavage. I'm in uniform. I wear the same goddamn thing every day. One Armani suit after another."

"Is that to impress your clients?"

"I don't think they care. No, it's because of all the guys around me. I have to blend in. They're all fragile egos, men who measure their worth by what they earn. They can't stand the idea of a chick being better than them."

"*Are* you better than them?"

She looked at me coolly, as if weighing whether to be honest. "Yes, as a matter of fact, I am—most of them, anyway. I work harder, I hear more. They're so busy showing off, they don't listen to the client. I listen and I pick up anything that helps the deal. It's similar to your job, I guess."

"I know someone from Seligman," I said.

She paused and I could see her brain puzzling as she tried to work out if I was going to talk about Harry. I enjoyed the sensation of power, of being able to shock her. She was wondering how far I was willing to go, I could see. That was the same thing I wondered about her.

"Who?" she said.

"John Underwood. We met by chance."

She grimaced. "Underwood always hated me, thought I was a bitch. I used to call him the ice-cream guy."

"What do you mean?"

"When I started on Wall Street, all of the men told me the same story. If you're with the ice-cream seller, you love ice cream. You love vanilla, you love strawberry—whatever he's got. If you're with the frozen yogurt man, you hate ice cream."

She paused as if she had imparted a self-evident truth.

"I don't understand," I said.

She laughed. It was a nice sound, high and throaty, as if she liked my bluntness. The pristine contours of her face relaxed, giving a glimpse of a different woman, one who wasn't so constrained.

"I'll try again," she said. "I advise CEOs, tell them to sell companies or buy others, or restructure. Every time there's a deal, we get a fee. It could be $5 million, could be $20 million. It's a lot, anyway. The business is full of liars and egomaniacs. That's what they do—

buy ice cream. Tell the CEO they love whatever he's got. All deals are great."

"But they're not?"

"No, they're not. A few are disasters and it's our job to warn the CEO, to stop him from doing the wrong one. If you tell him not to do the deal, you won't get paid your fee, but it's the best advice you'll ever give."

So why didn't someone tell Harry not to buy Greene's bank? I thought. It was the first time I'd thought of that. I hadn't known how Wall Street worked until she'd told me. Harry had made the affair sound like a handshake between the two men. *Sure, Marcus, we'll take a look,* he'd told Greene. But if there had been something wrong with Greene's bank, why hadn't anyone found it? On the most important deal of all—the one involving Seligman itself—Harry had been stranded.

The thought distracted me for a minute, and when I looked up, Lauren had a strange expression, as if something were welling up inside her. Her lips were pursed and she was staring at me.

"Psychiatrists mustn't sleep with their patients, must they?" she said.

She looked at me inquiringly, as if it were an intriguing academic point rather than the most explosive issue in therapy. The relationship between a psych and a patient of the opposite sex involves the greatest intimacy there is short of a sexual one, albeit one-sided. The patient tells us things she wouldn't confess to anyone else but a lover. That makes it dangerous. We were schooled in the pitfalls as well as the uses of transference, the risk of therapy slipping into illicit intimacy.

"That's malpractice. It's an abuse of the therapeutic relationship and it would harm the patient."

"You'd lose your job?" She gazed directly at me, and I started to feel embarrassed, as if she were accusing me of misconduct.

"Any psychiatrist who did that would."

"So your job's like mine."

She wasn't talking about me, I realized—she meant herself. Her gaze had gone from me and was back in the middle distance. Her expression didn't change, but for the first time I sensed sadness in her, a lake of longing.

"I had an affair with Harry Shapiro," she said flatly. "It was so . . ." She paused, as if searching for a big enough word, and frowned with frustration and regret. "Stupid," she concluded.

"What happened?"

"Underwood did it, that's the crazy thing. I worked with him and he couldn't stand me showing him up. He was so keen to stop me making partner, to block me. He would shut me out of the credit on the deals I'd brought in, throw me off others. It happened so often, I decided I either had to leave, or go to Harry.

"I'd never really spoken to him, only in client meetings. I thought he was an animal, like people said. But he wasn't like that. He listened to me, he sympathized. He sorted it out so that Underwood backed off. I hadn't seen that side of him. I'd just separated, I was lonely."

I waited. It wasn't hard to contain my reaction since I'd known about her affair, but it was a relief. The tension I'd felt of waiting for her revelation to emerge had dissipated. We were back on the usual footing of a psych and his patient, with her holding the secrets rather than me. Yet I also felt a sense of foreboding. The door of confidentiality had slammed shut on the secret of Harry's affair, like that of a jail or a closed ward.

"Like I said, it was stupid. You're so vulnerable on Wall Street, all these men thinking you're just a woman so you don't deserve to have your job. If anyone had found out about us, that would've been it for my career—sleeping with my boss. I came to my senses one day and took another job. It was almost over by then."

"Why did it end?"

She half smiled, as if mocking my innocence. "It was just an affair, nothing more. We were both consenting adults. He didn't want to wreck his marriage and I had to move on. We shouldn't have got carried away."

"Are you still in touch with him?"

"We haven't seen each other since I left."

Her gaze was unblinking. If Anna hadn't told me about her visiting East Hampton and seeing them together with her holding his head in her hands, I don't think I'd have known that Lauren was lying. I didn't envy the bankers who had to negotiate with her—she didn't give anything away. Over her shoulder, my clock showed six p.m., and although I yearned to press her further, another patient was waiting.

"Our time's up, I think," I said.

At night, when I heard the sirens crossing the city and I'd turned from one side to the other in an effort to fall asleep, I thought about Anna. I'd called her several times since she'd walked away from me, leaving messages on her cellphone, but had gotten nothing in return.

I willed there to be an innocent explanation so we could return to the state in which we'd existed before, but I couldn't convince myself. I thought of what Nora had told me the first time I'd seen them together, with her arm draped around Anna's shoulders: *I can't tell you how much I rely on her.*

When I'd met Anna, she'd seemed young and innocent, hardly a part of the Shapiros' world. But she was Nora's confidante and Harry's protector. She'd said she didn't like him, but she'd driven Lauren to him and kept their rendezvous secret from Nora. She'd served him no matter what she'd thought of him. Now that the Shapiros were under threat, I wondered how far Anna would go—or had gone—to shield them.

My name's like me. One big muddle, she'd told me. That was the image she projected of herself, just a yoga waif picked up by Nora who would soon be on her way. It was an affectation, I'd come to realize. Anna was the organized one. Nora had been scared to enter her own kitchen, but Anna made sure there was food in the fridge. She'd arranged for their East Hampton house to be redecorated to cover up the killing. She knew everything about their lives, was privy to their secrets. I was Harry's psych, but she knew what he'd hidden.

That Friday, I drove out of the city toward her with an object sitting on my dashboard. It was the glove she'd left behind when she'd abandoned me. I took the I-495 through Queens, past the ruined remnants of the World's Fair, driving until the buildings by the road petered out into a line of trees. The only landmarks out there were the strange objects sticking out of the woods: two white water towers and a cellphone mast disguised as a gigantic tree. It hung above the green horizon, a white stick with dark metal branches spaced at unnaturally perfect intervals.

There was a truck outside the Shapiros' house, and when I walked to the rear and looked through the conservatory windows, I saw two workmen standing on ladders, roller-brushing the ceiling with white paint. Anna was at the far end, dressed in overalls with her hair pinned up, pointing something out. I watched for a minute before she looked up and saw me. As she did, her face stiffened and she stared at me as if I were an enemy who was about to invade. She walked into the kitchen, and as I came around the side of the house, she opened the door and stood silently.

"You left this behind," I said, holding out her glove.

She frowned at me. "If you've driven all this way, you can come in for a minute," she said, taking it from me.

Inside, she poured me coffee from a French press and perched on a chair as I sipped it, which seemed as far as she was prepared to go by way of hospitality. The silence lengthened and she glanced around distractedly, as if my presence made her jumpy. When I'd first come to the Shapiros' house, it had reminded me of a fairy-tale cottage, but now it felt like a sinister place, marked irrevocably by a murder that had sapped the energy of its occupants. Anna looked no better than Nora when I'd last visited—just as pale, with dull eyes.

"You know who attacked me, don't you," I said.

The question instantly enraged her, as if she were already on edge and it took only a small provocation to send her over the edge.

"How would I know? I told you to leave me alone," she shouted.

She threw her glove at my feet and walked into the living room, slamming the door closed. As I followed, the door handle struck my knuckles, making me shake my hand and cry out—an appeal for mercy that she ignored. As I emerged into the living room, the work-men had looked up at the commotion.

It was already hard to remember what the room had been like before. The sofas and furniture had gone the way of the geometric rug. Even the doors to the conservatory had been removed and re-placements fitted. The men had painted the walls in a delicate pale blue, erasing the previous colors. Anna wasn't there and one of the men shrugged at me, as if to indicate that he knew all about furious women. He pointed silently to a door on the far side of the room. I walked along the hallway and saw that the door to Nora's study was open. Anna was by the window overlooking the drive to the bay side, with her back to me.

"Remember in the car, when you drove me to the city, that first day?" I said. "You told me you were too honest for your own good. You said you'd always got into trouble for trying to tell the truth. What happened to that?"

She didn't speak, so I carried on talking. I felt my anger and bewil-derment at how she'd behaved toward me bubbling up, and my voice starting to crack. "You're so honest, are you? It doesn't seem like that to me. You just want to keep Harry's secrets."

I was shouting now, but her back was still facing me. I walked across and pulled at her shoulder, but she shrugged my hand off as if she couldn't bear my touch.

"Yeah, you know what?" she said. "I do my job, and my job means I know stuff about people who employ me, even if sometimes it's not nice. Why don't you do *your* job? Why pick on me?"

She paced across the room toward Nora's desk, and her words were spoken standing by it. As I looked at her, I was distracted from her face by the sight of a metal plate embedded into the wall by her left shoulder. It was Nora's safe, where she'd told me she had placed Harry's gun for safety. I stared until Anna glanced behind her.

"You know how to open it," I said. "Don't you?"

She stared at me contemptuously for a few seconds, then swiveled and put her hand up to the dial. She spun the wheel to the left and right four times, then placed her hand on the brass lever and pulled open the door. Inside were some jewelry boxes and a stack of papers. On top of them, I saw the glint of the nickel Beretta: Nora had told the truth.

"Satisfied? Happy now?" she said bitterly, then shut the safe door and walked out. When I got back to the living room, she was standing in the middle of the floor, beckoning to me. Her face was stiff and hostile.

"Come here," she said, and I walked slowly, one pace at a time, across the wooden boards toward her. "A little further. . . . Stop there."

I was close to her, and the man who'd given me directions was standing on a ladder a few feet to my left, painting a cornice silently, as if willing himself to be invisible. Anna ignored him as she spoke.

"That's where the body was," she said. "They had to sand Marcus's blood off the boards. It took a long time."

I remembered Pagonis handing me the photograph of Greene's body and seeing it lying in a pool of blood. I felt as if I was treading on sacred ground and I took a step backward as Anna walked off again. She strode through the half-painted doors of the conservatory and onto the lawn, halting by the edge of the pool. She was white and shivering, her arms wrapped under her breasts as if holding herself together. I stepped toward her, but she swayed back, keeping her distance. The sea breeze pushed aside the last of the thin clouds, and sunshine spread across the grass. The light changed so fast that if you blinked, everything changed.

"I realized something," she said.

She walked to the stairs leading down the dune, as Harry had done, and I saw her step down, her head sinking from view. I hurried after her, getting close enough to throw a final question.

"What was it? Tell me."

"Look around. Work it out for yourself," she said.

She ran down the steps to the beach, where waves cascaded into foam and were sucked back into the ocean, becoming nothing again. I struggled along behind her for a few yards, my feet sinking into the sand, but she easily outpaced me. Halting, I watched her walk furiously, head down, away to the west.

18

I wore a dark tie and my wedding suit—pale gray with a waistcoat—
to testify to the Suffolk County grand jury. It hadn't been my wedding: it had been my brother's two years earlier. The suit had already
outlasted the marriage. Maybe it was all of the traveling that Guy did
for his job or there'd been something he hadn't confessed to us, but
Marianne had steadily become more absent from our family get-
togethers until finally he'd admitted that we wouldn't see her anymore. They hadn't had children, so it had been a simple divorce.

I'd enjoyed the wedding. Rebecca had helped me choose the suit at
Bloomingdale's and had flown with me to London. They'd held the
ceremony in a tiny, ancient church in the City of London with a Henry
Moore sculpture—a huge block of white stone—in the middle, and
the choir had sung in Latin, I remembered. My father had behaved

himself and, remarkably, so had Jane. Rebecca and I had spent the Sunday walking round the West End and in Hyde Park. I remembered lying on the grass by the Serpentine with her, feeling as if I had no cares in the world.

This wasn't such a nice occasion, and the surroundings were a lot gloomier. I sat in a witness box in a drab windowless room in the Riverhead court building, with a grand jury spread out in front of me. Few of its members had made much of an effort to dress up. The men were in casual pants and sweatshirts except for two middle-aged guys in jackets, and the women weren't much smarter. They didn't seem to be taking the matter as seriously as I was—they had less at stake. Most of them seemed bored, and a man at the back was already yawning, although it was only ten thirty a.m. You'd have thought that the Shapiro case would have been more exciting than routine indictments, but it didn't appear to be.

The only other people in the room were a court reporter and Baer, who sat cozily with each other in another box; he shuffled through his papers and she stroked the keys of her transcription machine. The twenty-three members of the jury were sitting on two raked rows of chairs as if we were in an experimental Off-Broadway theater.

Joe had briefed me one last time on how it worked—urging me not to talk too much, just to answer questions briefly—and was cooling his heels in the hallway. As Pagonis had said, he wasn't allowed in the room. There was no judge to interrupt Baer, who'd walked us up to the jury room at his usual stately pace, and Joe's plea for me to halt proceedings and come out to consult him if I was worried felt like a poor substitute.

When I'd called Joe to tell him about Pagonis delivering the subpoena, he'd sounded gloomily unsurprised, like a man who wasn't disappointed by events because he always expected the worst. "I didn't want to worry you, but I thought he might do this. We should talk," he'd said.

The next day at his office, he'd told me how it worked. Mostly, grand juries were impaneled to arraign and indict suspects. They heard ADAs present preliminary evidence and rubber-stamped indictments. The hard work of proving that the suspect had committed the crime came later, in a full trial. But the grand jury could also investigate a case if the ADA had an unwilling witness he wanted to put under oath. That was what Baer had done to me—unless I took the Fifth Amendment, I had to testify.

"You first treated Mr. Shapiro in the psychiatric emergency room at Episcopal, is that correct?" Baer said.

Joe had told me to look at the jury and to try to be sympathetic, but when I glanced up, I wasn't encouraged. The foreman who had put me under oath, a chunky man with a gold chain and a chin bulging beneath a trimmed beard, was staring at me as if I were a defendant rather than a witness.

"Mr. Shapiro was brought to the hospital by his wife. I assessed him there and advised him to admit himself voluntarily, which he did."

"On what grounds?"

"I believed he was a danger to self—that he was at risk of suicide. He had a number of symptoms of depression. He'd lost his job and his wife was concerned about his mental state."

"Did he tell you he might kill himself?"

"He didn't say that directly."

"Why did you believe it, then?"

"His wife had found him earlier that day at their house in East Hampton with a gun on his desk. She'd been worried."

Mention of the gun brought the jury to life. A woman in the front row who had been glancing around as if not fully engaged sat up in her seat, and a man at the back gave a silent exclamation, his mouth shaped in an "O." I tried to maintain a blank, neutral expression, as if I were an expert witness, but my heart thudded as I waited for Baer's next question. If he asked me more about the gun, I'd have to say that Nora had brought it into the ER and I'd let her leave with it. There were too many witnesses to lie.

"So you knew he was dangerous?" Baer said, an edge in his voice.

It was his toughest question so far, but it wasn't what I had feared, and I relaxed a little. Joe had anticipated that question, and so far, we were within our prepared testimony. We had practiced in a long rectangular room at his office with blinds covering the windows to block out the sunshine. I'd sat at one end of a mahogany table and Joe had walked up and down, lobbing questions at me. He'd filmed my responses and afterward we'd watched my performance on a screen that covered an entire wall at the head of the table, observing each hesitation and note of anxiety. It was reverse therapy—an exercise in hiding my feelings.

"I was concerned that Mr. Shapiro might be a danger to himself. I never believed he was a danger to anyone else."

"Your diagnosis was wrong, then?"

I started to feel the absence of a judge in the room. *Surely he would object to this kind of questioning?* I thought. It wasn't just the foreman who seemed to regard me as the defendant. Taking my eyes off the jury, I looked across at Baer and the court reporter, who had her head bowed over the machine. He gazed back at me mildly but imperturbably, as if I'd brought this on myself by being uncooperative.

"Mr. Shapiro hasn't faced trial, so I can't say," I said.

Strictly speaking, I was pushing the truth since Harry had admitted killing Greene to me, but I was legally correct, as Baer conceded with a tight smile and a skeptical glance to the jury.

"He stayed in the hospital two days and then you discharged him, I believe. You let him out, just like that. The man you'd been so worried about only two days before, a man who had been found with a gun?"

"He'd admitted himself voluntarily and he expressed the wish to leave on Monday. We'd started treatment and I didn't think there was cause to convert him to involuntary status."

Baer's eyes glinted. "So Mr. Shapiro became your private patient. Until he was arrested one week later for killing Mr. Greene, that is. That must have felt good. He was a rich and powerful banker, Episcopal's biggest donor. Quite a catch."

I felt things slipping out of my control. Baer was right—that was

exactly the thought that had gone through my mind. Wanting to ac-
quire a rich patient wasn't such a crime; that was why Jim had relo-
cated to Park Avenue, for God's sake. But Greene's death had changed
everything, transformed human ambition into medical misconduct. I
hesitated, wondering whether I should insist on a pause in the hearing
and go out to the hallway to get Joe's advice, but it felt as if it would
be an open indication of guilt.

"I—I wanted to ensure that Mr. Shapiro was cared for properly,"
I stammered. "Just as I'd have done for any patient."

"How do you normally treat patients?"

"I don't understand."

"They come to your office, don't they? But Mr. Shapiro didn't do
that. You went to his house in East Hampton. And you got special
treatment in return. You'd helped him out, so he flew you to London
in his private jet, didn't he?"

One juror gasped when he said it, and another one scribbled a
note on paper. My mind went blank and I struggled to find a way to
explain why I'd taken that Gulfstream flight. *I had to protect Harry.
He should have been in hospital. I'd been told I had to discharge him.
I'm not to blame.* After a few interminable seconds, I refocused, with
everyone in the room staring at me, and forced out a reply.

"My father had taken ill and I had to visit him. Mrs. Shapiro offered the flight so I could see her husband promptly. I thought it
would be wise."

"You're saying Mr. Shapiro wasn't stable? You'd discharged him
but you were still worried about him?"

"I just wanted to be sure."

The half truth I'd just told about Harry's discharge made me sound
guilty of terrible misconduct—guilty alone. *That's it,* I thought as
Baer paused so that the jury could absorb my testimony. *Whatever
Duncan does, my career is finished.*

"You did everything Shapiro wanted because he'd bought you off.
He had you on a string, didn't he?"

"It wasn't like that," I muttered, unable to look at him. My face was flushed and two middle-aged women on the jury were gazing at me sympathetically, as if it were a one-sided boxing match that should be halted.

"Thank you, Doctor," Baer said, sensing the mood and bringing his questioning adeptly to an end.

I found Joe outside, sitting on a low bench by one window, doing correspondence on a BlackBerry. "Go okay?" he said brightly.

I couldn't bear to tell him what had gone on—my head was still reeling. We walked to Baer's office, where my tormentor had invited us for a post-hearing discussion. He had taken off his jacket and loosened a couple of buttons on his waistcoat by the time we got there and looked satisfied.

"I hope you didn't think I was too hard on you, Doctor. Just wanted to get some of the facts established," he said, shaking Joe's hand.

I saw Joe wince as he realized something nasty had occurred out of his sight. "What's next?" he asked Baer, moving to the critical point.

"We'll see. We can keep Dr. Cowper's grand jury testimony under seal for now, not hand it to the defense immediately. I don't want to cause him any trouble that I don't need to. But you and I should talk about how he might help us, whether he'll cooperate now. Shall we take a stroll?"

Sitting in Joe's car, I saw him and Baer through the windshield a hundred yards away, their shapes outlined against the gray prison walls. I couldn't hear what they were saying, but I got a sense of it from watching Baer's gestures and Joe's solemn, accommodating nods as they walked side by side.

They looked like what they were—two professionals who had abandoned the job's public showmanship and were striking a deal. I was still shaken from the trauma of giving evidence and I wanted to escape from that place, with all its nasty associations, as fast as I could, but Joe had asked me to wait. I thought of Harry playing cards or lifting weights in the jail that loomed above their heads. They talked for twenty minutes and then I saw them shaking hands. Baer headed toward the DA's offices and Joe turned back to me. He kept his head down as he walked, looking grim and pensive. As he approached the car, he looked up and smiled, but it required an effort.

"So?" I said as he climbed in beside me.

"Let's get a coffee," he said, starting the car.

There was a McDonald's on the traffic circle near the jail, its giant yellow "M" stuck on a pole above the chaletlike shack, and Joe turned into the parking lot without preamble. Whatever he had to say, he wasn't going to soften it by taking me somewhere fancier. We lined up for two bland, frothy approximations of cappuccino and took them to an empty booth, where Joe stirred the contents of his foam cup vigorously, as if he might find flavor in its depths. I imagined the inmates watching this place from across the highway, longing for Big Macs.

When Joe spoke, he was more solemn than I'd seen him before. His encounter with Baer had squashed his usual good cheer.

"I'm sorry about what happened in there," he said. "It sounded like it wasn't any fun. That guy's pretty tough. I'm glad I don't spend too much time out here. New York City's a playground compared with Suffolk County."

"It felt like that on the witness stand," I said

"I'll be honest, I didn't like the sound of the Gulfstream when your dad told me about it. It doesn't appeal to a jury, although you were doing your best to help the guy. The thing that worries me is that Baer knows a lot of stuff we don't want him to know. It sounds like he has more up his sleeve, too. Someone's been talking to that detective of his. Usually, I'd suspect the defense, but that doesn't make sense. They don't want it to look like Shapiro planned to kill Greene."

Joe stirred his cup a couple more times—he had not yet placed it to his lips—and looked at me closely.

"Who do you think talked?"

"I don't know."

He didn't say anything but kept gazing at me as he finally took a sip from the cup. He didn't bother to hide his disbelief. Beneath that southern charm, that sunny chatter, I knew then, was a lawyer who was used to spotting lies and whose patience with my half truths had run out.

"I'll tell you something that Roger said when he first asked me about you," he said. "He said: 'My son's a very bright young man, but he keeps secrets. You never know exactly what he's thinking. Maybe that's why he's good at his job.' I've got to say, Ben, I think he knows you pretty well. There's stuff you haven't told all the way through this affair. It was okay until now. I guessed you had your reasons. But maybe you don't know how serious it's becoming."

"I do know. I found out in there," I said, avoiding his main accusation.

"So I'll ask again. Who do you think it was?"

I looked out of the window. In the distance, I saw the jail and the woods that petered out a few miles south into flats and dunes. The Long Island settlers hadn't been able to cultivate the salty land by the sea and had sold their prime real estate to anyone who would take it. I thought of Anna abandoning me on my last visit, striding off along this beach. I'd done everything she had asked of me, and I couldn't keep faith with her anymore. The gash on my forehead was nearly healed, colors fading like old stains, and I touched it as I spoke.

"This," I said. "I wasn't mugged. Someone followed me in the park and attacked me. He ransacked my apartment, too."

"Go on," Joe said quietly.

"I'd been out that evening with a woman. She's called Anna Amundsen. I met her . . ." I paused for a few seconds before carrying on. It felt even worse to say it aloud. "When I saw Shapiro in East Hampton. She's his housekeeper."

"Shit," Joe said. He looked struck dumb, as if he'd expected me to confess to some minor misdemeanor but had uncovered a felony.

"She knows who attacked me, I think. She knows a lot about the Shapiros. I asked her—I saw her two weeks ago—but she wouldn't say."

"Shit," Joe repeated blankly.

He didn't look angry, more horrified at the expanse of legal liability that had opened before him. I struggled to force out the last part of my confession, feeling even worse than I had in front of the jury.

"Anna's . . . well, I was attracted to her. It was kind of a date. I shouldn't have done it, I know. It was stupid of me, you don't have to tell me that. She told me something about Mr. Shapiro, but I promised to keep it secret."

"This date," he said warily. "How far did things get?"

"Nothing. Well, she kissed me once. Briefly."

"Okay, I don't need all the details. Could be worse, I suppose. What was it that your pretty friend told you?"

I sighed and tried to look as apologetic as I could. Bad as I felt, I somehow felt worse for Joe that he had been landed with me. Those nights out with my father in Las Vegas had cost him dearly.

"I'm afraid I can't say because it's covered by doctor-patient privilege. It's not Anna and it's not Harry. I know that he's waived privilege," I said hurriedly. "It's another one of my patients."

Joe closed his eyes and rested his head in his hands. He remained in that posture for a full minute while I waited sheepishly. Then something happened that surprised me—his shoulders started shaking and I saw that he was laughing.

"I'll say this, Ben," he said when he stopped. "I don't think I've ever had a client like you. No offense, but I'm kind of hoping I never do again. You've done all this stuff that I can hardly credit and I'm sure a judge wouldn't. Amazingly, while you're doing it, you dig up new evidence and now you won't tell me what it is."

"I *can't,*" I said. "It would be malpractice."

"Right," he said, deadpan. "Like those malpractice charges you'll face when you're subpoenaed to testify at Shapiro's trial by Baer and your boss decides she's not going to protect you. That sort of malpractice?"

"Is that what Baer said he'd do?" I said dumbly.

"Pretty much. I'm your attorney, although just at the moment I'm wondering why, so let me lay out the options as simply as I can. Either you do what Baer wants, which is to tell him about what happened at the hospital and out there at Shapiro's house, or he's not only going to make you testify at the trial, but he's going to make you look as bad as you looked just now in front of the grand jury. Meanwhile, the only way you'll keep your job is if you tell Baer to take a hike. It's your choice."

He looked at me almost fondly as he said it, as if both exasperated and impressed by how I'd landed in such a mess. *That must have taken some doing,* his expression seemed to say. His mood was lighter, as if he'd progressed beyond despair into acceptance that his client was indefensible.

"As my lawyer, what would you advise?" I said.

"My advice?" Joe said. "Find another lawyer."

19

Joe's mood must have been infectious because I slept soundly, and when I woke in the morning, my subconscious had already decided for me. I was tired of keeping secrets, of covering things up out of duty and cowardice. I'd made a mistake with Harry, one that might cost me my job, but I wasn't prepared to shield him any longer, and nor would I protect Duncan. I'd go to Baer and tell him everything— the gun Nora had brought to the ER, the pressure Duncan had put on me, and what Harry had said to me on the beach. I'd tell him that Harry was a murderer.

As I stepped from the shower I felt relieved, as if a burden that I'd been carrying for weeks had just been lifted. My job was to keep people's secrets, but Harry had used it against me and I wouldn't let him anymore. I didn't know why he'd killed Greene, but that was

Baer's job to discover, not mine. *I'll be a whistle-blower,* I thought, and that sounded better than being a fraud. I hummed cheerfully over breakfast, and when it was done, I picked up the phone to make some appointments.

My first stop was the Shapiros' apartment, and as I rode in the elevator, I wondered if Anna was going to be there. *I don't care,* I thought. *She's Harry's servant and she can suffer the consequences.* When I arrived at the thirty-seventh floor, I composed my face for her—mimicking the glare she'd worn when I'd last seen her—but I softened my expression as the door opened on Nora. This was going to be the hardest meeting. I no longer cared about offending Harry, but I still felt for her. She hadn't done anything wrong, just tried to care for her husband, and she wasn't going to like what I was about to say.

"Anna's out at the house cleaning up, so it's just me here. Come through," she said, smiling. "Can I get you something?"

"I'm fine, thanks," I said briskly.

We walked to her study. It was a sunny morning and I caught a glimpse of Central Park through a window, the soft green blanket of the solid tops of trees stretching toward Harlem, with the line of Fifth Avenue on the far side. It was like sitting in an aircraft and seeing the clouds below—that lofty, detached sensation.

"There's something I want to ask," I said as we sat. "Steven Baer, the prosecutor in your husband's case, called me to testify before a grand jury yesterday. He asked me some difficult questions. He knew a lot about my treatment of Mr. Shapiro after I discharged him—that I'd been flown to East Hampton after visiting my father."

Nora looked puzzled. "There wasn't anything wrong with that, was there? I wanted to help."

"Of course, and I'm grateful, but it doesn't look good now. You didn't tell the detectives about it, did you?"

Her mouth opened in shock. If she had been the informant, she was doing as good a job of concealing the truth as Lauren.

"Absolutely not. That would be a terrible thing to do. You believe me, don't you?" she said, holding a hand to her mouth.

I nodded. "I'm sorry. I needed to be sure."

I believed her. It wasn't merely that she seemed innocent. It wouldn't be good for Harry's defense to make it look as if he'd manipulated me into letting him out of Episcopal in order to murder Greene. Their lawyer would have briefed her not to volunteer information, just as Joe had briefed me. Nora had done all she could to fulfill Harry's wishes and had landed me in trouble, but she'd had no reason to betray me.

"Did you speak to Sarah?" Nora said. "Will she help?"

She looked at me eagerly, and I was touched that she cared. She was already embroiled in a desperate effort to save Harry from the disasters into which he'd arrogantly plunged himself, from the failure of his bank to Greene's death. I wanted to reassure her, but I'd be helping her husband out if I did.

"I don't think that will make any difference now. I'm likely to lose my license no matter what she does."

"No!" Nora exclaimed, placing her hand on mine as she'd done in the psych ER at our first meeting. "That's terrible. After everything you did for Harry, it would be so wrong for you to suffer."

"Would it?" I said. "I let your husband go and he murdered Mr. Greene. I'd have said I didn't do my job."

The word *murdered* seemed to strike Nora like a body blow. She leaned forward in her chair and I saw the distress in her eyes as she stared at me. It was as if I'd spoken in a foreign tongue and she was struggling to understand.

"How can you say that?" she cried. "You treated him. You saw the state he was in. Harry didn't murder Marcus. He didn't know what he was doing."

I leaned forward in my chair and rested my elbows on my legs with my hands clasped. I didn't want to distress her further, but I believed she ought to listen for her own good. There were things I couldn't tell her about Harry's behavior—Lauren was now my patient—but I wouldn't lie about what I thought of him. If Harry went to jail for murder, I didn't want Nora to pine for the rest of her life.

"Mrs. Shapiro," I said slowly, "everything I've learned since the killing has convinced me I misdiagnosed him. I don't believe he was ever in danger of suicide. He'd always meant to kill Mr. Greene. That's why he had the gun."

"No. No. I don't believe that," she said, standing and gripping her right elbow with her left hand. "I'll never believe that. You're wrong, Doctor. I thought that you understood Harry, but you don't. You never will."

As she stood there, I felt ashamed. I'd rushed up there eager to tell her the truth, but the person I should have been confronting was Harry himself, not his wife. It wasn't her fault that he'd fooled her. What had come over me, acting like an avenger to a woman whose life was already shattered?

"I'm sorry," I said quietly. "You're right. I don't know your husband as well as you. I think I should leave now."

Her eyes were closed and she stood rigidly, her muscles tensed, as if still tortured by my outburst. Finally, she relaxed slightly and sat down again, looking more desolate than I'd ever known her, even in her study in East Hampton.

"Perhaps you should," she said.

She stayed seated as I walked out of the study and unlatched the front door to let myself out. The last sight I had of her was with her hands folded in her lap, gazing blankly at a bright acrylic, no doubt million-dollar, painting.

Once I'd endured the usual wait, Duncan appeared and beckoned me through. I'd never noticed personal touches in her office before, but as I sat down, I saw two photos framed by her desk. One was of a hulk holding an oar and the other of a teenager in braces.

"Yours?" I said, pointing at them.

"Louisa's mine. That big guy is my stepson. He's at Stanford," she said. "You haven't got children, have you?"

"Not even a wife, I'm afraid."

There was a pause as we both smiled formally. I realized that she knew that already from having read my personnel file. There was nothing I could tell her about myself in small talk that she didn't already know. That didn't bother me, because I'd kept other things from her and was about to bring her up to date. After my shame at the way I'd confronted Nora, this was light relief. I didn't care about upsetting Duncan.

"You asked to see me?" she said.

"I'did. I wanted to let you know that I've thought over what you suggested when we last met, and I have an answer."

"Which is?" she said icily, as if she didn't appreciate me playing games. She wanted only silent obedience.

"No," I said.

"No what?"

"No, I'm not going to keep quiet. It's too late for that. I've informed the Suffolk County ADA about what happened when Mr. Shapiro was admitted to Episcopal and why I came to discharge him. I testified yesterday to a grand jury."

"You did *what*?" Duncan said incredulously.

"Testified to a grand jury. In Riverhead."

"*What?*"

She was all but gasping. Her face had turned puce with shock, and I was happy to have stunned her, even temporarily. She walked to the window with a view of the Queensboro Bridge, standing motionless as if she needed time to think. Then she recovered her bearings, and the rush of surprise turned to a blast of anger.

"This is the first I've heard of a grand jury, and you testify without even telling me? What the hell did you say?"

I savored that moment, for I had her fate in my hands and she had to wait for me to tell her. The truth was that I hadn't told Baer about how she'd forced me to discharge Harry because he hadn't asked. But I'd already made up my mind that when he did that, I would. I'd ceased to care about Duncan—nothing she did could save me.

"I'm under oath to keep my evidence confidential."

That was childish, I admit—that's what the subpoena said, but I could easily have told her if I'd wanted to or if I'd trusted her. Duncan naturally believed I wasn't telling her because I'd implicated her.

"Dr. Cowper," she said, "we talked about the importance of sticking together, that the hospital would stand behind you. It seems you have betrayed my trust."

I'd done pretty well to keep my temper during all of our interactions, I thought, but that made me lose control.

"I didn't ask to treat Mr. Shapiro. You were the one who wanted me to do it. My mistake was obeying you."

"I don't know what you mean," she said firmly, looking down and pretending to smooth an invisible wrinkle in her skirt.

"Bullshit. You pressured me from the start to do what the Shapiros wanted and then you tried to keep it quiet."

She stared at me as if unable to understand why I could be behaving this way: *Why won't he do what I say? What's wrong with him?* I didn't fully understand that myself. All I knew was that I felt better for having defied her.

"All right, if you wish to destroy your career out of stubbornness, there is nothing I can do to prevent it. You may have relayed some fantasy to the grand jury about how you behaved and why. When the time comes, I will protect this institution by telling the truth."

The purest rage I've ever felt erupted inside me. How dared she lecture me about the truth when she'd blatantly lied?

"You've never told the truth. You don't even know the meaning of the word," I shouted at her.

Duncan ignored my outburst. She walked to her desk and flicked a file shut as if it wasn't any of my business anymore. In that moment, I knew that although I'd had some fun, I couldn't defeat her. She ran this place, and Nora wouldn't make her save me now that I'd turned on Harry. Episcopal would cast me aside just as Seligman had discarded him—the institution would protect itself.

"I await your resignation," she said.

I hadn't talked to Rebecca since she'd fixed my skull. I'd seen her in the distance in the hospital hallways, talking to someone or rushing somewhere, a blur of green scrubs and blue cap. Once I'd thought she'd noticed me from the corner of her eye and had turned to avoid a meeting. She finally turned up just after I'd left Duncan and was standing in my office, tallying how many boxes it would take to hold my possessions.

"Hey, you," she said.

I turned, scanning her face again. Memory is strange: When someone we love leaves for a while, the image fades. Only when they depart forever is it etched permanently in the mind. I can picture my mother's face more vividly than my father's.

"Hey," I said, half pondering a kiss on her cheek but not moving, a safe yard between us. The last time I'd seen her I'd been strapped to a gurney, but this time I had an awkward amount of freedom. "I'm sorting things out."

"I can see that. You're really shaking things up in here," she said, sounding amused. "How's that head of yours?"

"Pretty good, I think. You did a good job."

"Sit down. I'll take a look," she said firmly.

I lowered myself obediently into my patients' chair and felt her delicate fingers part my hairline to examine the skin closely. It felt comforting, like a tiny, unobtrusive massage, and my tight shoulder muscles unwound a little.

"Looks like the head's healing nicely. How's your mind doing? That's your specialty, isn't it?"

"Still in bad shape," I said.

She sat opposite, in the chair I used during therapy. I found it unnerving to be observed from there, especially by her.

"I heard a rumor that the psych department was upset with you. You're going to be okay, aren't you? You're not in trouble?"

For a split second, I thought of confessing the truth to her. It was the end of a long day, one on which I'd started out feeling resolved that I would tell the truth to power but had finished with power setting me straight. I felt alone, and she more than anyone else would understand. But I was lost in a maze of half truths and half secrets that Greene's death had uncovered, and I couldn't think of where to start.

"I'll be fine. Don't you worry about me. It's been a bit of a palaver,. but it's all okay now," I said. "It's nice to see you. We should have a drink."

"We should. Let's do that," she said as vaguely as I had proposed it, and slipped out of the room again.

I examined my shelves for a bit, pretending to be sorting out books, as if I could deceive myself with appearances in the same way I might fool someone else. Then I gave up and sat at my desk unhappily. Somewhere along the way, she'd let me go.

In the stygian gloom of the subway below Hunter College, I waited for the 6 train to carry me home. I could see the lights of one approaching along the tunnel, glowing dimly in the distance. It arrived with a rattling shudder, crammed with bodies, and I pushed myself on board. As the doors closed, I saw a man stick his arm through them farther down the carriage and lever them apart. As he struggled to gain access, the passengers by me groaned and the announcer cried hopelessly, "Stand clear of the closing doors."

Finally, he pushed his way through and I looked along the carriage at him. All I could see as he grabbed a pole and the passengers arranged themselves around him was his peaked cap—I couldn't glimpse his face. The train pulled away and we shot southward under Lexington Avenue. At Fourteenth Street, I escaped from the bodies onto the platform. It wasn't yet full summer, but the stations were already warm—it was a choice between the air-conditioned crush of the trains or the spacious heat of the platforms. A bundle of people burst out of the train, and the troublemaker hurried ahead to my exit.

I couldn't see him when I got to the surface. It was dusk, and as I walked down the street toward my apartment building, I glanced behind me twice—my experience in Central Park had made me wary. There was no one in sight. Bob was standing by the front desk and gave me a watchful nod as I entered. *Does he have something to tell me?* I wondered, but he stayed silent. As I got to the middle of the hallway on my floor, I saw a glint of light under my front door. I waited, with my heart racing, before edging forward.

The door was unlocked and I pushed it ajar, then stood listening. "Who's there?" I called.

There was no reply, and I took two paces inside, my heart beating, ready to turn and run. A man was sitting in an armchair, reading my copy of *The New York Times* with a glass of my whiskey at his side and listening to a Mahler symphony.

"Christ," I said. "You scared me half to death."

"I thought I'd surprise you," my father said.

20

I still had a job, at least temporarily, and I turned up to do it the following day, having fixed to meet my father that evening. He hadn't been forthcoming about why he'd arrived out of the blue, although he'd mentioned that Joe had called him. The day went by unremarkably, with nothing further from Duncan or Jim. It almost felt as if the Shapiro affair had been a dream. I nodded through forty-five minutes of Arthur Logue and then waited for Lauren.

The minute hand clicked around the wall clock. Five minutes after five, ten minutes after five. *She'll be getting out of the Town Car now,* I thought. *Walking through the lobby and showing her ID to the guards.* With two minutes to go, I started listening for the sound of her heels clicking down the hallway. I knew little of her beyond what she'd told me the previous week, but she was the only connection I had left to Harry. Everyone else—Anna, Nora, even Joe—had spurned me. I hadn't even heard from Felix in a while.

Only when the hand clicked past five fifteen and kept descending did I realize. She wasn't coming. That shocked me more than it should have. It wasn't unusual for patients to fail to show up and she'd hardly been entirely truthful with me, yet I'd been so sure that she'd come. *Why did I have such faith in her?* I wondered as I sat there, feeling spurned. It was because she seemed so unafraid. If she'd decided she didn't want to see me again, she'd have told me to my face. But when the hand reached five thirty, I knew there was no point in waiting. I gave her two minutes' grace and then called her cellphone on the off chance she'd been in an accident. She wouldn't have forgotten.

"Ms. Faulkner, this is Dr. Cowper. I was expecting you for our appointment. I hope nothing is wrong," I told her voice mail.

I sat for another few minutes, feeling abandoned. "Fuck," I said softly. I had no one left to talk to except Baer and Pagonis. The previous day, I'd felt elated by my decision to tell the truth about Harry, but now I was desolate. This was it—the end of the line. My last patient of the day was on vacation so that was the end of my duties. I unclipped my red-and-white badge and went to find my father.

He was at a table in a corner of the King Cole Bar at the St. Regis Hotel, with a large martini in front of him. Behind the bar, the Maxfield Parrish mural of the monarch grinned as inscrutably as Harry in Riverhead. *It's fine for you, with your pipe and your slippers, and your fiddlers three,* I thought. *If I had your job, I'd be merry, too.* The waiter brought a glass of wine and my father clinked his own, brimming with bulbous green olives, against it.

"Here we are again. Cheers," he said.

I studied his face as he sipped. It was sallow in the soft bar light, and the lines around his eyes were deeper. The heart attack had aged him—he looked older than the undaunted image I carried in my head. He'd lost some weight and his legs had looked stick thin as he'd padded around my apartment in a dressing gown in the morning. I'd given up my bed for him and slept on a couch. In the early hours of the morning, I'd woken to hear his raspy snores from the bedroom, like a foghorn in the night.

"What are you doing here, Dad?" I said.

"Joe's worried about you. He says you've been under a lot of strain and you haven't been telling him everything. He thinks you could be in trouble. I'm due in D.C. later in the week so I thought I'd take a detour, see if I could help."

I looked around the bar, which was filling with an early evening throng. Waiters passed among tables with trays bearing drinks and silver bowls of nuts and snacks. Opposite, a white-haired tycoon sat alongside a pale-faced beauty—perhaps his daughter, perhaps his mistress. I should have been grateful to my father for flying on this mission, but it irritated me—I was too exhausted to be angry. Why play the concerned parent now, when he'd never bothered to do it before? He'd arrived at the exact moment when it was too late.

"You told Joe I was secretive," I said.

My father sucked one of the olives off his cocktail stick and munched it. He looked at me warily, trying to gauge my mood.

"Even as a kid, you were always a mystery to me," he said.

"So you'll remember the secret I kept for you."

He widened his eyes, taken aback. I routinely confronted my patients with awkward questions about things they had suppressed from their past, but I had never summoned the nerve to do it to him. I could be grateful to Harry for that, at least—he'd battered me into a condition in which I didn't care anymore.

"I'll have another. What about you?" he said, signaling to the waiter.

"Is that a good idea?" I said. Then I decided against acting as his heart doctor as well as his psych. "Oh, hell. I'll join you."

My father sat silently with his head tipped back as the waiter tidied up the table and brought over new drinks. He gazed at the ceiling of the bar, as if seeking divine inspiration for what to say. By now, the tycoon was resting his hand in a position on his companion's leg that proved she wasn't his daughter.

"The thing with Jane," my father finally said. "When you found us that day. It's so long ago, isn't it? I'm surprised you remember."

"Are you really? It's not the kind of thing you forget. I was only a child. How could you have done that?"

I forced myself to look at him—not wanting him to escape the force of my outrage—and to my surprise saw weakness and shame. It hadn't occurred to me that he was capable of feeling guilty. He'd always seemed so adept at moving on rapidly from his emotional failures, leaving others with the aftereffects.

"I know," he said quietly. "I hurt your mother and I hurt you. I fucked it all up, that's the truth. I wish I'd never done it."

"Done what? Made me lie for you?"

He sighed. "Not just that, the whole thing. The affair, breaking up the family like that. I know you think I'm just a selfish bastard, but it crushed me when your mother died. It felt like I was being punished for what I'd done. It hurt Jane, how long it took me to get over it, but she'd been my wife. You don't forget that."

"And Jane?"

"Benny, you think what you like about me—God knows I deserve it—but don't keep blaming her. It's not her fault."

He took a gulp and sighed again. I didn't know what to feel. Part of me thought it was a masterful performance from a man who was good at getting others to pity him—another of his manipulative ploys. But there was a kernel of something genuine in it. Even if it was just a show, I was grateful he'd cared enough to fly here to put it on. An awful lot of people fall apart and end up in therapy or in the psych ER, but thousands of others carry on with their lives. They just bear their burden of guilt or unhappiness as privately as they can. Maybe he'd been one and I hadn't noticed. What kind of psychiatrist was I?

"You're right. She doesn't," I said.

"Could we talk about something else now?" he said plaintively. "And don't tell Jane what I just said, will you? Please?"

I put a hand on his shoulder and squeezed it. I felt better that I'd at least managed to voice the resentment I'd bottled up against him for years—it was as if I'd managed to seize back some power over our relationship.

"I'm glad you came, Dad," I said.

"Of course," he said, waving his hand magnanimously. "Tell me about this case of yours. What do you think happened?"

"Honestly?" I said. "I think Shapiro planned to kill Greene before I even saw him the first time. He played along with his wife when she found him with the gun because he knew he'd have an excuse if he looked crazy. Then he got himself discharged and did what he'd always planned to do. So now I'm his defense."

"That's clever, I've got to admit," my father said, easing seamlessly back into the role of lawyer. "Why did he want to kill the guy in the first place?"

"I don't know exactly. Something happened between them that I don't understand, before Seligman got into trouble. It's not just Greene he blamed. He had a thing about the Treasury and Rosenthal. Greene had worked there and so did Henderson, the Treasury secretary."

"Those Rosenthal people do stick together. I've dealt with one or two of them in London. They're like the Moonies. What'll you do now?"

"I'm going to tell the Suffolk County ADA what Shapiro said to me and let him deal with it. There's nothing else I can do."

"You can't give up like that," my father cried, so loudly that the couple at the next table glanced worriedly at us. "You can't just sit there. You have to find out what happened, why he did it. That's your only hope."

He sounded outraged. All the talk about Harry seemed to have revived him—either that or the two martinis. The color had returned to his cheeks and he talked as animatedly as if it were his own case. *He must be tough to face on the stand,* I thought. He was just as relentless as Baer.

"That's not my job, Dad."

"What the hell is your job, Ben?" he said indignantly. "You sit and listen to what people tell you, but if they feel like lying to you, you let them get away with it? That doesn't sound very smart. Joe said you wouldn't even tell him what you know because of a patient."

"I can't. You're a lawyer. You know the rules."

"I know rules are sometimes made to be broken."

He drained his martini and glared at me as if only a coward would disagree. I didn't reply because I was thinking of Anna and how similar their complaints about my profession had been. *She didn't have much faith in me,* I thought. I remembered her final words as she'd walked away on the beach: *Work it out for yourself.* She had flung that at me not believing that I would.

It was time to prove her wrong.

Lauren's house was beautiful. It must have been mid–nineteenth century, flat-fronted in red brick with what looked like the original brass knocker on a black-painted wooden door. It was off West Fourth Street in the middle of the West Village.

Peering through the windows, I saw wide-planked floors and marble fireplaces that stood out against the chalky walls. All of the furniture and fittings, from the chandeliers to the chairs, looked selected for the space. There was a yard at the back with a crab apple tree, from which a copper lantern hung. It looked almost too perfect— nothing was out of place. It reminded me of the way Nora had decorated the house in East Hampton. They had something of the same aura. Was that why Harry had fallen for both women? I wondered. They both provided some haven from his uncontrollable rage.

Lauren wasn't home, and I retreated along the street to a café to await her return. I knew she'd be back—it was a warm Saturday morning and a copy of *The Wall Street Journal* rested on a table in the living room, still in its wrapper. She must have retrieved it before going out earlier. I'd called her once more since she'd failed to arrive for her session earlier that week, but there'd been no reply. Whatever she'd wanted from me had taken only two meetings and I knew I'd have to seek her out if I wanted to discover more. Her address was in my records, but I'd had to steel myself to follow my father's advice.

It was four hours later, after lunchtime, when I saw her walk down the street in a pale overcoat. I let her go inside and gave her five minutes' grace. Only when I'd climbed her stoop and was at the top about to knock did I have a feeling of hopelessness. I was once again chasing one of Harry's women, knocking on a closed door. I'd already gone to Nora and Anna and gotten nowhere. It was a hopeless mission—Harry was the only one who knew why he had done it. I'd had one chance to get it from him, and I'd failed. *Why am I here?* I wondered. I felt like a stalker who can't forget the object of his obsession.

When Lauren opened the door, something had changed. It wasn't just her shock at seeing me and her frown of displeasure. It was something else. She wasn't the same controlled woman who'd come to my office and told her story: she looked despairing and adrift. Her face was blank, like that of a distressed starlet caught by surprise in a paparazzi flashlight, and she hesitated before she could articulate her words.

"Dr. Cowper," she said.

"Can we talk for a minute? It won't take long."

She paused, as if trying to reconcile my presence with what she'd been thinking of before, and looked dazed. Then she stood aside and ushered me through. She led me along the hallway into a living room dominated by a long oak table. Sunshine streamed through the rear windows, with frames that bowed at the top. I could hear the faint sound of traffic from the street outside, but it was a peaceful refuge.

"You've got something to say?" she asked.

We were still standing, since she hadn't offered me a seat and showed no sign of doing so. She gave the impression that she wanted to get me out of there as fast as she could and resume pondering whatever had been on her mind.

"You didn't keep our appointment," I said.

"I decided I didn't want to," she said crisply, regaining some of her former poise. "I'm sorry I haven't returned your call. I was intending to. Do you always chase your patients like this?"

"I don't, but you're an unusual patient."

She arched her eyebrows. "How so?"

"You know what I mean. You didn't pick me out of a list in a magazine. You came to me because I'd treated Mr. Shapiro. You wanted to make sure I couldn't tell anyone about your relationship."

"That sounds too clever for me," she said.

"You're an intelligent woman."

"What do you want from me?" she said.

"You told me that you didn't see Mr. Shapiro after you left Seligman, but that wasn't true. You visited him in East Hampton only a week before he killed Marcus Greene. Why was that?"

Lauren trailed one hand on the table and then tapped it a couple of times, as if coming to a decision. She looked purposeful again, more like the woman I'd known before. She stepped forward and put her hand on my arm, as if trying to ensure that I listened to her, and her eyes were fierce.

"I want you to leave now. You shouldn't be asking questions like that. It's not a good idea, believe me. You've already been attacked once. Do you want to put yourself in more danger?"

She had started to guide me out of the room and back toward her door, but her question stunned me. How did she know about my assailant in the park? I had only just told Joe of my suspicions.

"What do you mean? Tell me," I said. I grabbed her arm. "Tell me."

"I mean what I say. You should take care," she said.

My father had left for Washington and I was alone in my apartment, thinking of my final glimpse of Lauren as she'd opened her door to usher me out. The moment when she'd warned me not to ask questions had been shocking, but it wasn't what I remembered most vividly.

The image printed on my mind was her arm reaching past me in the last moments before I'd stepped onto her stoop and walked away. As she'd turned the bolt, I'd noticed a mark on the back of her hand. It was a green circle, faint against her skin, and I might not have seen it if it hadn't been familiar. It was the same ultraviolet stamp with which I'd been marked before the officer let me through the cage at Riverhead.

We don't want the wrong guy leaving, he'd told me, training a flashlight on it to light it up. Then they'd slid open the bars and I'd walked through to find Harry waiting for me in the corner. That was where Lauren had been before she'd come down the street looking ashen—in Suffolk County with her lover. Five minutes later, I'd blundered to her door to press her about the secret she'd shared with him, days before he'd killed Greene. That circle worried me more than her warning, for it told me that Harry was still close to her. They'd never been out of touch—not before the killing and not since. I'd believed all along that Nora was Harry's confidante, but I'd been wrong.

Should I take her words to heart, I wondered, and keep myself from further harm by abandoning this quixotic effort to discover the truth about Harry? My father had left town and no one else was speaking to me, so it would be simpler and less risky to call a halt. But momentum had taken me, and Lauren's words echoed in my brain as a provocation, not a deterrent. I might have lost my job, but I wouldn't let Harry use me.

If she wouldn't tell me what had gone on between them, I'd find out in the place where it had all begun.

21

Seligman Brothers took up a block of Broadway, and it was hard to discern, looking down the avenue toward Times Square, the border between the worlds of finance and entertainment. The bright screens in Times Square outdid the spring sunshine with ads for movies and electronics, while the Seligman building was lined with strips of pulsing colors, blaring out stock prices from around the world.

One strip was a ticker of prices from the New York Stock Exchange, the stock symbols racing sideways with red or green numbers next to each one—BRK, ABK, TCI, GS, USX. I had no idea what they meant, but I knew they signified a lot to others. Buried in them were fortunes rising and falling.

I was sitting in a street garden, a collection of white metal chairs arranged around a courtyard space, with a waterfall running down a wall. The sun fell on a sliver of the square, the rest thrown into shadow by the canyon of skyscrapers around me. I tilted my head back to gaze up the forty floors of the Seligman building, its blank wall of glass and metal. A small jet passed way above the tower, streaming a faint white wisp into the blue and making me dizzy. Near me, a couple of office workers—a man and a woman—were lingering over a pair of torn-up croissants, heads down in whispered conversation. I wondered if they were doing a deal or having an assignation.

As I strained to hear, a man walked up to my table and asked me for change. I'd seen him on the street before—a tall Robinson Crusoe figure with a straggly gray beard and his rambling story written on a cardboard sign. He had to be schizophrenic, I guessed. I often felt as if I saw more mental illness on the way to work than when I arrived. I briefly considered trying to talk to him but gave him a dollar instead.

Then I saw Underwood coming out of the doors of the Seligman building, dressed in his banker's uniform—an Italian suit and mustard yellow Hermès tie. He smoothed his hair with his right palm as a gust of wind lifted a lock, then walked over the road and up to me.

"Hello, Doctor," he said, enclosing my hand in a lean grip. "It's good to see you again. A lot of water under the bridge. Isn't that the expression?"

There was sardonic amusement in his eyes, suggesting that I'd conceded something by coming to see him.

"A lot," I said.

He took a newspaper someone had left on my table before and used it to swipe some invisible dirt off the chair opposite me, then sat down, looking over at the dealmakers, or lovebirds, near us. The man nodded to him furtively.

"Do we need to be out here?" Underwood said distastefully. "We might get more privacy inside."

"I didn't know what you'd prefer," I lied.

I'd suggested meeting there because I'd felt afraid of going inside. I feared bumping into Felix in the building, not wanting to put him in the awkward position of seeing me. I also wondered whether it would be safe to confide in him. He'd made it clear that his loyalties were still with Harry, and enough information had already found its way to Riverhead.

"Okay then," Underwood said, looking around again with the air of a celebrity who attracts attention if he lingers too long. "Let's go."

We walked back over the road and through the doors into the Seligman lobby. It was marble-floored, with a wide desk facing the entrance, behind which a line of women in uniform was handing out visitors' passes. Underwood ignored them and strode toward the barriers to one side, glaring at the guard who stepped forward to try to impede my progress. The man stepped back obediently and instead waved a card at a barrier, making it part for me.

I expected us to rise far up the tower, but Underwood stepped out of the elevator on the fourth floor, leading me through some glass doors with a swipe of his card. We stepped onto a trading floor, with long lines of desks covered in multiple screens stacked beside and on top of one another as if they'd been dividing and multiplying like cells.

I'd never been in such a place before, and I had always imagined it would be a hive of noisy activity, like those they show on television, with young men in bright jackets waving and calling to one another. Instead it had a detached air, like a station that was monitoring the action on some far-off planet. There must have been a thousand people on the floor and a few were typing on keyboards, but most seemed to be doing nothing. They leaned back in their seats, gazing half-attentively into the digital void or chatting to others nearby. None looked especially happy or sad, just intrigued by the numbers on the screens.

A woman in a suit like Lauren's sat on a desk, talking with three men gathered by her. They all nodded deferentially at Underwood as he passed by, walking between lines of desks toward a corner of the floor. I walked beside him, seeing the tilt of heads as we passed. Everyone was sitting in plain view, with none of the usual trappings of status—individual offices with assistants—yet I knew that all of these people probably earned more than me.

As we reached the corner, Underwood led me into a glass box office with windows looking out over Broadway and panels giving onto the trading floor to the interior. A blind was pulled down one of the four panels, but the others remained open, so he could watch everything that was going on outside and those who were interested could observe us, like animals in a zoo. There were photographs of his family on one ledge, but the room was otherwise free of personal touches, as if he were a short-term tenant who might be evicted at any moment.

He waved me to an armchair on the side with a vista of the open floor. A woman walked in and gave him a pile of papers that he perused with a frown before handing it back. Then he came and sat by me, grinning.

"So, Ben. How can I help?" he said.

I didn't like Underwood any more than the first time we'd met. He was like a primate in expensive clothes that might tear me limb from limb. He emanated barely contained aggression and contempt for the mortals who didn't exist in his elite world of corporate wheeler-dealing. I wondered if it was an act to intimidate opponents or if he really was like that. There was something of that quality about the whole place. He was the leader now, but I could imagine a pack of those traders crashing through the door at his first sign of vulnerability.

"When we talked before, by the plane, I remember you saying it was Mr. Shapiro's fault, everything that had happened to him, before Mr. Greene's death. I wanted to know what you meant," I said.

Underwood let out a breath and laughed flatly. "That's a long time ago. I don't know what I might or might not have said back then, when Marcus was still alive. I don't remember you telling me much, Ben. Not even your name, as I recall."

"I didn't. Things were different then." I didn't see any reason to apologize for that, to him of all people. "Look. Mr. Underwood. John. Could I ask you something? How much do you know of my involvement?"

"I've seen the documents and I've talked to the Greene family. It's not a happy story, is it? There are accusations against this bank as well as you, and I need to be careful what I say. I don't know if we should be talking. Margaret is a good friend of my wife's."

I leaned forward in my seat. If I was to get anything from him, he had to believe I wasn't a threat. Despite his familial references to the Greenes, I suspected that he didn't care too much about them now that Marcus, his boss and patron—the man who could influence his career—was dead. I'd adapted my pitch from something Lauren had said.

"When we met before, Mr. Shapiro was my patient, as you know. I couldn't say anything about him. You'll understand that as a banker. You can't talk about the clients you're working for. I can't tell you anything that was said to me in confidence, and I'm not asking you to do it either. But my career is in jeopardy and I'm trying to understand why Mr. Shapiro killed Mr. Greene. Can you help me?"

Underwood nodded as if I'd made some sense. "I would have thought that was obvious," he said, wrinkling his nose. "The merger went wrong. Harry was unstable and blamed his own failure on Marcus. He shot him. End of story."

"But why did it go wrong? That's the part I don't yet understand. I'm not a financier. All this"—I waved my hand at the glass panels giving onto the vast, hushed trading floor—"mystifies me. It's your world."

I wondered whether the flattery had been too obvious as Underwood gazed at me. But it turned out that Lauren had been right about something else: male investment bankers have big egos. He stood and beckoned to me.

"You want to know how Harry fucked up? I'll show you," he said.

Underwood and I left the elevator on the thirty-fifth floor. It led to a softly furnished lobby like an English drawing room, with a grandfather clock in a corner, its mechanical ticks echoing in the empty space. There was little sign of life, nobody sitting at the oak reception desk near the elevator. After the glass-and-steel floor, it felt as if I'd stepped into a Walt Disney version of the nineteenth century. There were no doors or electronic panels to impede us here, just a long, dimly lit corridor, visible through a mahogany arch. As we walked, I saw dark rectangles marked on the walls, each illuminated by a brass wall lamp.

"Harry kept the Old Masters from the art collection up here. They're in storage now. I don't want them," Underwood said.

He opened a wooden door at the end of the hallway and led me into a small space, with two empty desks next to each other, then through another into an enormous office. It was a shock to enter after the gloomy hallway, for it was filled with light from two sides. It was on the corner of the building, facing south toward Times Square to one side and Rockefeller Center and the East River to the other.

I looked around the room. There was a wooden desk bearing two neat piles of paper and a computer with a twin screen. It was still blinking figures and graphs, although it looked as though it hadn't been used for a long time. On the side by the hallway, there was a recessed alcove lined with books, like a kind of tiny library with a sofa and chairs, where the occupant had received guests. A Persian rug, an antique by the look of its muted threads, dominated the floor.

I walked behind the desk to look out at the room from that angle. Two framed photographs stood on the desk—one of a boy, a college student, perhaps, wearing the bulky pads and bright purple shirt of a hockey player. Other players had flanked him, you could see, but they had been cropped out to leave only his face, staring out cheerfully from under a helmet. The other was a portrait of Nora, looking happier than I'd known her.

It had been Harry's desk.

Underwood was standing on the rug, waiting for recognition of where we were to dawn on me. "What can you see from there?" he said.

I looked around me, casting my eyes across the empty office and then out of one window. "Rockefeller Center?"

He snorted. "Nothing. That's what you can see. Fuck all."

"What do you mean?"

"The guy was in his own world, cut off from what was happening, just his few cronies up here with him. The first thing Marcus did was to move down to the trading floor, get a proper grasp of what was going on."

"Where you are now?"

"Someone's got to keep the place going. Maybe I'll keep the job—they'll give it to me if they've got any sense. Marcus wanted to gut this whole floor, put some real revenue earners up here, but he hadn't gotten around to it."

I walked toward the window to look out at the view, a glittering panorama of the lower wedge of Manhattan. Underwood took my place behind the desk, pushing the chair back and planting his polished shoes on the surface. One of his heels grazed Nora's photo, shifting it by an inch.

"So you're saying he shouldn't have agreed to the merger? He should have known there'd be problems?"

He shrugged. "Sure looks like it to me. Harry had got too grand. He thought he'd be able to lord it over Marcus. He was a fool—that guy knew more about making money than anyone I'd ever met. He was a great salesman, one of the best."

"He wasn't honest with Mr. Shapiro, though, was he? Didn't tell him everything he should have."

Underwood laughed out loud. "What should he have told him, Ben? This is Wall Street, for God's sake. Harry wasn't a widow or orphan. He was paid $45 million, he had a Gulfstream. There were bankers being paid millions of dollars to advise him. If you want me to feel sorry for him, you're out of luck."

"I suppose so," I said doubtfully.

"Listen, what's the biggest deal you've ever done? You've sold a house, haven't you? So did you tell the buyers everything or did you cover up a few cracks? I bet you did. It's *their* job to find them. That's why they have an engineer."

That wasn't far from the truth, in fact. My mother's house had some dampness, but we'd replastered it smoothly enough not to be obvious when we'd sold it after her death. That had allowed me to buy my apartment in New York.

"Caveat emptor," I said.

"Right. Buyer beware. I was Marcus's banker, and Harry got his own people to advise him, a woman he should have known wasn't very good. She didn't work hard enough or ask the right questions. That wasn't our fault."

I tried to look amused at his and Greene's achievement in having deceived Harry and his female banker.

"Does she still work here?" I said.

He grinned. "No, she decided to leave, before we got rid of her. That was smart. She wouldn't have lasted long."

As he spoke, he reached into his pocket and pulled out his Black-Berry, the same one I'd seen him using on the Gulfstream.

"Okay, I'll be there soon," he said, and tucked it away again. "Well, Ben, I think that our excursion is over. I hope you learned something."

I once witnessed an accident, a hit-and-run in which a car went through a red light and struck a woman before accelerating away. After she'd been taken away in an ambulance, the cops at the scene interviewed me and another passerby. The thing I remember best was that although we had no reason to lie and wanted to tell them exactly what had gone on, my version was completely at odds with his.

I told them the driver had ignored a red light. He said it was amber. The driver was a woman. No, it was a man. The cops who took it all down weren't riled. They looked as if they expected a mixed-up version of the event. It was bad enough when we were doing the best we could to be honest. When people want to bend the truth, it's a wonder anyone agrees on anything.

The scene that Anna had witnessed from the dune in East Hampton fit Underwood's story. If Lauren had messed up the deal, had failed to realize that Grayridge was in much worse trouble than Greene admitted, that accounted for Harry's distress.

Although Underwood was the type to lie for his own advantage, I didn't see what his motive would be here. He hadn't had to tell me about Lauren, and his contempt had looked genuine in the moment. He hadn't even mentioned her name, just gloated about her in passing. If his rival had been male, I wouldn't have known whom he'd meant. Yet one thing he'd said—she hadn't worked hard enough and hadn't noticed the flaw in Greene's bank—made no sense to me. I didn't think she'd told me the whole truth, but I believed she'd been honest about how she worked.

I'd seen the contempt in her face for Underwood and the men with whom she competed. Lauren had ascended Seligman on sheer merit— doing her job relentlessly, sweating the details, and leaving nothing to chance. *I work harder, I hear more,* she'd told me. I knew she'd have dug up every scrap of information before signing off on the deal. The woman who'd warned me not to ask difficult questions was not lazy, or vague, or willing to let things slide. If she hadn't foretold the looming disaster, she'd had a reason.

22

After stashing my things in the locker at Riverhead, I was led inside without needing to have my hand stamped. This time, an officer guided me down a hallway into a wedge-shaped area lined with cubicle-like rooms just large enough for two people to sit. It was the place where lawyers came to meet prisoners, and they'd allowed me in as a psych. A guard sitting at a desk pointed me to a room with two chairs and a table squeezed inside. Once I'd waited a couple of minutes, I heard the guard greet someone and Harry came in, dressed in a dark green jumpsuit rather than the yellow for the visiting room. He stared at me as if I were a bug he'd tried to squash that was still buzzing around.

"You're back," he said.

"I am."

I felt uneasy, although the officer sat just on the other side of the door. It looked as if he'd kept up his visits to the gym. His face was leaner and his arms were muscled under the short-sleeved jumpsuit. Wherever he ended up after this—a psychiatric hospital or a prison— he'd be able to take care of himself. After everything that I'd been through since I'd come to Riverhead the first time, it was disorienting to see him again. On my first visit, I'd gotten some inkling that something was wrong with his version of events, but I hadn't known what it could be. Now I could feel myself getting close to the truth.

"What do you want?" he said disdainfully.

I'd come for a reason—to gain an introduction. I needed him to say something to me, but I couldn't let him know what it was or why it mattered. The idea had come to me as I'd thought about what Lauren had told me. She'd told me I was in danger and that I should take care. It had struck me later that I wasn't the only one at risk. The man in front of me had killed someone—he was dangerous. That had its uses, for it released me from some of the duties that constrained me. The only thing it required was to get him to lose his temper, which I didn't think would be hard.

"Tell me why you killed Mr. Greene," I said.

"I can't remember what happened. I told you that."

"I don't think it had anything to do with the settlement or the plane. You were angry that Greene had deceived you before the merger. He'd hidden the truth about his bank. He'd made a fool of you."

Harry didn't move, but I felt something alter inside him, like the click of a thermostat just before the boiler fires up. There was a faint glow in his eyes now, the same ember I'd seen in the psych ER. I attempted to fan it into flames.

"You weren't the only one he screwed," I said.

Harry's eyes narrowed as if he could hardly believe what I'd just said. Then he levered himself to his feet, leaning over me with his eyes a few inches from mine. I was shocked by their animal intensity. This was the Harry I'd always known was there: the ferocious one that Greene must have seen in his last seconds. I glanced through the glass panel in the door for help, but the guard was still absorbed in his paper.

"What the fuck do you mean by that? You should mind your own business. Why don't you listen?" he hissed.

I tried to hold his gaze, but it wasn't easy. Lauren had warned me to take care, and I knew then she was right. I'd always thought that Harry fell into another category from schizophrenics who were dangerous, but now I wasn't sure. *He really is violent,* I thought—*he didn't just put it on in the* Wall Street *jungle.* He stood over me for thirty seconds with his hands planted firmly on the table. Then his stare softened and he sat down, breathing unevenly.

"You don't know what you're talking about. You don't know anything," he said, as if reassuring himself.

"Tell me, then. What went wrong?" I said. "When we spoke in East Hampton, you said it was to do with mortgage bonds."

His jaw was still clenched, but the question seemed to settle him, as if it were comforting to be back on finance and not fencing off hints about Lauren.

"Interested in Wall Street, are we?" he said, his voice like battery acid. "You wouldn't understand that stuff even if I told you."

"Try me." I'd given up trying to be polite.

He gazed pointedly at me, as if I'd forced him to show that I was out of my depth, but he started talking. I wasn't really interested in mortgages—I wanted to talk him down from his fury for a while before we got to the subject I was there for—but I tried to keep up with him as he spoke.

"Grayridge was into mortgage securitization. They took subprime mortgages from Texas and California and they bundled the paper into CDOs. They made money with that, so they got into synthetic CDOs, built from credit default swaps. I'm not going to try explaining that to you. They had a bunch named after elements. Cobalt, Gallium, Radon."

"Elements?" I said.

"Yeah. Don't ask me why. The guy who ran the origination desk was into chemistry." He laughed grimly. "It was like alchemy in reverse. The substance the Elements turned into was shit."

"So if the Elements were Mr. Greene's responsibility, why didn't the bank fire him when they went wrong? Why you?" I asked innocently.

Harry stared at me. "Now that *is* a good question. You're asking the wrong guy, though. I mean, look." He waved expansively at the tiny room. "Does this look like the Federal Reserve? Or the Treasury?"

"Who should I ask? Tom Henderson?"

Harry's eyes registered that I knew something. "Maybe."

"You told me you wanted your bank to be like Rosenthal but they wouldn't allow it. I thought that was a strange thing to say, but I did some research. I found out that Henderson was at Rosenthal before the Treasury. You told me that Greene worked there, too. That's a coincidence, isn't it?"

Harry laughed bitterly. "Is it? That's all you need to know about Wall Street, not the math about CDOs. Rosenthal runs the place, it always has. Why do you think Henderson is Treasury secretary? Count how many Treasury secretaries they've had. They've got Washington stitched up."

I'd heard lots of people say Wall Street was a cabal. To hear one of its own saying that, even in jail, was different. Was Harry paranoid? I wondered again. There was something almost possessed about him, but perhaps he'd been driven to obsession. I thought of Henderson on the C-SPAN video, his quality of controlled calm.

"I went to my board, told them all the problems we'd had with Grayridge, how he'd landed us with all that crap. I didn't know the full story then. I . . . ." He paused and seemed to think better of what he'd been about to tell me. "They didn't listen. They'd all had calls from Henderson saying he wanted me out."

"Could he do that?"

"He could do whatever the hell he wanted. They needed the Treasury's money. They were cowards."

We'd reached the moment for which I'd come to Riverhead.

"So Mr. Greene's dead but Mr. Henderson's doing just fine, isn't he? What does that make you feel?" I said.

Harry grimaced, then got up and walked a couple of paces to the door, looking through the pane of glass set into it to check on the guard outside. Then he turned to face me with his back to it, his face fervent.

"You know what I *feel*, Doctor?" he said contemptuously. "I feel like doing to him what I did to Greene."

He'd given me what I'd come for—a threat to Henderson. It was all I needed and I didn't want to spend any more time there, although I'd learned some other useful things. I signaled to the guard and got up, leaving Harry staring bitterly after me. The road was clear when I drove out of the lot, but I stayed well below the speed limit until I was a long way clear of Suffolk County. I didn't want to be hauled off to Yaphank again.

Somewhere on the journey from New York to Washington, D.C., maybe around Chesapeake Bay, you cross the border into the South. The air turns softer, the humidity rises, and you are deposited off the Acela at Union Station into another country entirely, with its slow cabs and steadier, more baroque manners than its Yankee cousin.

It was a bright June day, with all of the city's monuments shining in the sun, and I stood for a few minutes gathering my thoughts on the paved section of Pennsylvania Avenue, where tourists massed in groups next to the White House railings. I was at the edge of the strip opposite the eight Greek columns of the Treasury, its granite façade drab and gray next to its iridescent neighbor.

I'd arrived early, having caught the early train out of New York, and I pulled a dollar bill from my pocket to look at it. On it were the crumpled face of George Washington, the Treasury seal in green, and Tom Henderson's scrawled signature. To the left, over the *B* on the Federal Reserve Bank of New York seal, was a promise in uppercase letters: THIS NOTE IS LEGAL TENDER FOR ALL DEBTS, PUBLIC AND PRIVATE. I'd come to ask about a fatal debt.

Having climbed the steps and passed security, I was directed up a stone staircase to the third floor. I set out along a dim corridor, checking a piece of paper on which I had scrawled the number of the room. When I looked up, I saw to my surprise the man I'd come to visit. He was standing by himself about fifty yards down the corridor, gazing at me kindly. On the C-SPAN video, I'd seen senators melt in his presence, but I hadn't grasped why until that moment. He stood in socks with a gentle smile on his face as if he had all the time in the world. He looked completely relaxed, his shoulders at ease and his face soft and knowing, like a beneficent monarch. As I reached him, he stepped forward one pace to squeeze my hand.

"Dr. Cowper, I presume," he said, pronouncing my name correctly and smiling wryly at his own Victorian reference.

He led me into a high-ceilinged room with ornate plasterwork and a chandelier that looked as if it could do with a dust. It was a drawing room, I guessed, with drapes that hung in folds and Louis XV–style chairs arranged by a mahogany table. As we entered it, a young man appeared. He was plump, with a bland smile and rimless glasses—impossible to pick out in a crowd. Henderson waved me to an armchair and sat opposite, while his new companion perched a few feet behind him like a stage prompt.

Sitting there, with the weight of history and authority bearing down on me, I felt sweat on my forehead. Some impulse had brought me there, a determination not to let Greene's deception die with him, but my pretext for coming felt awfully thin.

"You wanted to see me," Henderson said.

"Thanks for sparing the time."

He nodded self-deprecatingly, as if half an hour of his time were an expensive gift he'd decided to bestow on me. The other man looked on silently.

"As I mentioned when I called, I'm a psychiatrist in New York and Harry Shapiro was one of my patients. He told me a number of things that may come out in evidence at a trial, but there is one matter that I don't think can wait."

Henderson said nothing, but cocked his head slightly to one side, his Buddha-like smile unchanged. *I've no idea where you're going with this, but I'm fascinated to see how you'll finish,* said the smile.

"I've just seen Mr. Shapiro in the Riverhead Correctional Facility, where he is being held on murder charges. He told me that he wishes you harm because he blames you as well as Mr. Greene for his predicament. Given that he's already confessed to one killing, I must take that seriously. Have you heard of the Tarasoff case?"

Henderson pursed his lips and shook his head a couple of times as if he'd not only not heard of it, but saw no reason to care.

"It involved a woman called Tarasoff who was killed by a therapy patient after he'd told his psychiatrist that he intended to do it," I said. "The courts held that therapists have a duty to protect anyone they suspect might be harmed by their patients. The normal rules of confidentiality are waived. That's why I'm here."

It wasn't really the reason, of course. Harry was no immediate danger to Henderson. But it had given me a plausible excuse to demand to see him and to watch how he reacted to the other things I wanted to say.

Henderson nodded. "Thank you, Doctor. However, I'm not sure what the rush was. Shapiro's in jail, isn't he? He doesn't present much of a threat to anyone at the moment, does he?"

"I still felt that I should come. Mr. Shapiro told me a number of things about what he thinks happened as a result of the merger between his bank and Mr. Greene's. He believes that he was deceived."

Henderson gazed at me, looking innocently bemused. He had an intimidating quality that had nothing to do with threats or with overt aggression, like Harry. It was subtler than that: a benign puzzlement that anyone could question his version of the truth unless they were misguided or malign.

"Really? I suppose there was a rivalry between the two of them. That's now evident. I'm not sure how it affects me."

I took a deep breath. "Mr. Shapiro claims that you placed pressure on the board to fire him because you and Mr. Greene were close as a result of having worked together at Rosenthal. He thinks Rosenthal was behind the whole thing."

Henderson hardly moved, and his expression was unchanged, but he coughed once and then deflected his face slightly to the left to address the man behind him. "Andrew, I think Dr. Cowper has some things to say in private. Would you mind?"

The man replaced the cap on his pen, folded his notebook, and left the room without a word. When he'd gone, Henderson smiled at me again, just as broadly but this time with the warmth turned down to a low simmer.

"Dr. Cowper, forgive me, but I'm going to ask a question. Why are you here?"

"I was curious."

That answer seemed to amuse him, and the skin crinkled around his eyes. Then his face turned watchful again. "I'm told that you're no longer Mr. Shapiro's physician and your job at Episcopal is in doubt," he said, tapping a finger on his chair.

"You're right," I said. I didn't know how he knew, but I supposed he was in a position to find out, and there was no point in lying.

"So I surmise that you don't feel you have a lot to lose. If you'll forgive the description, you're a loose cannon. Correct?"

I saw that beneath his veneer of calm, I had him worried. Maybe he believed I was losing control and was ready to denounce him.

"Perhaps," I said, nodding.

"I'm going to indulge you for a few minutes, between the two of us, to satisfy your curiosity. You tell me why you think Marcus died."

"I think that Grayridge was in trouble and Greene needed a white knight. Something was wrong with these mortgage bonds—the Elements. You were at Rosenthal and he trusted you. Maybe you told him to merge with Seligman to cripple a competitor. By the time Seligman got into trouble, you were here. You bailed out the bank and then you ensured that Greene took over."

"And his death?"

"Mr. Shapiro found out what had happened, I don't know how exactly. It made him so angry that he killed Greene. He couldn't get to you."

Henderson tapped his finger contemplatively as he thought it over and then smiled again. He didn't seem particularly upset by me accusing him of conspiracy to defraud Seligman and the U.S. government.

"It's a gripping theory. You think there was some kind of plot involving Rosenthal, do you? You're not the only one. It's a fine institution and it produces a great many people who go into public service. They sometimes face this kind of accusation, which is long on gossip and short on evidence. We are, sadly, used to it."

As he spoke, his voice rose and there was a flash of passion in his eyes for the first time. He looked more upset by my doubting Rosenthal than by my accusation against him, as if the bank were like a country and came before self. *We,* he'd said.

"When the president appointed me," he went on, "I shed all my ties to Rosenthal and sold my stock in the firm, which was not a good investment decision, let me assure you. There are many conflicts of interest on Wall Street, and if people don't deal with them in the appropriate manner, they're out of business. Mr. Greene and I once worked at the same firm. Is that all you've got?"

"I think it's more than that."

"Not from what you've said. You don't have any evidence, merely the imaginings of a psychiatric patient. As I told the Senate, the board chose Marcus without consulting me. But you know what, Dr. Cowper? I'd have done exactly the same thing in their shoes. He was a great banker and a fine leader. Shapiro . . ."

He paused as if he had a lot of thoughts on the subject of Harry that he didn't want to go into. There was a contemptuous glint in his eye, and he stood to end our meeting as he finished his sentence.

"Was never stable."

It was the "never" that stayed with me. As the Acela looped northward to New York after I'd been shown off the premises by a still-silent Andrew, I sat by the window wondering what it had signified.

The Maryland coast gave way to the boarded-up row houses of Baltimore and North Philadelphia while it rattled in my brain. Except for that word, I might have accepted defeat, but something bugged me about it. I was certain Henderson had ejected Harry and put Greene in the job, but he wouldn't have done it just because Greene was an old colleague at Rosenthal. That would have been crude, and Henderson was subtle.

He'd known Harry for a long time, though. That was what his final words told me. There was history there—an echo of the past.

23

A quotation from John D. Rockefeller, inscribed on a long panel, greeted me as I walked into the New York Public Library's business branch on Madison Avenue the following morning: *Next to knowing all about your own business, the best thing to know is all about the other fellow's business.* That was what I'd come for. I'd thought of Harry talking about Greene that day on the beach, scraping sand from a seashell as he spoke. *I knew a guy who'd run private equity in Europe for Rosenthal. Marcus Greene,* he'd said.

I went downstairs to the electronic center and located a free terminal. The first place I looked was the Rosenthal & Co. site, looking back at its past annual reports for a biography of Henderson. There was his meteoric career at Rosenthal, joining the bank in New York in the 1970s, rising to run its fixed-income division and then becom-

ing chief executive. Along the way, one foreign job: chairman of
Rosenthal International, 1990 to 1994. Henderson had been Greene's
boss in London at the same time that Harry had been posted there by
Seligman. *The City of London's a small place,* I thought. *Even more
of a club than Wall Street.* It looked as though they had all been there
for the same purpose—to prove themselves overseas before returning
to New York in glory.

I started reading old copies of *Euromoney* for anything that linked
them further. It was like the *Vanity Fair* of the City of London, with
admiring interviews with bankers in odd corners of financial markets,
adorned with heroic photos. As I read about the 1990 property crash,
some of the material became familiar. *Euromoney*'s idols had been
the vulture funds that had picked through the wreckage of the banks'
lending mistakes. I'd been a teenager then, and the only crash I'd noticed was my parents' divorce. But even I could observe, in the tale of
burst bubbles and real estate blunders, that history had repeated
itself.

I found two articles in which Greene was quoted—one a description of the Canary Wharf bankruptcy in which Rosenthal was involved along with almost every other bank I'd heard of. Later on,
things got more cheerful, with talk of recovery and the writing back
of Latin American debt. There was some excitement about the new
credit derivatives market in London.

I soon got bored and flicked through photos of bankers dressed in
black ties to receive prizes at risible award ceremonies—Bank of the
Year, Asset-Backed Issue of the Year. I saw the younger Henderson,
shaking a hand or standing in a group of bankers, wearing his smug
smile, his hair a mottled gray. As I flicked through the pages, I came
across a photo of another prize awarded to Rosenthal and Seligman
jointly. On the left were Henderson and Greene and their people, and
on the right was the Seligman crew, led by Harry. Harry looked like
another man, not just in age but also in his beaming pleasure—you
could tell that this silly award had meant a lot to him.

And nearby, Harry, by Henderson's shoulder, dark-haired and
youthful yet unmistakable, stood Felix.

———

Even now, as I look back at the mistakes I made—the way I had misunderstood Harry when he'd first come to the ER, the way I'd slipped easily into the world of wealth—the thing I'll always regret is what I did next. *Primum non nocere,* we were taught in medical school: First, do no harm. Even in psychiatry, where nothing is so obviously mistaken as a surgeon cutting out the wrong body part or leaving a patient bleeding, some things are dangerous.

The worst is to push a patient past his limits, confront him with something so painful that he can't cope. I don't know if it made a difference—maybe the events were rolling inexorably toward their end. If it had all happened without me, though, I wouldn't blame myself. I should examine my motives, but I've done it many times and I've come up short.

Every job has rules—barriers stopping abuse or even an appearance of it. They become wired into you, so you don't have to think when you get close to the border. You hold back like a dog with an electric collar that gives it a shock if it passes across a buried wire. I've seen them standing there, barking wildly yet constrained from pursuit. I think of myself having crossed that border anyway, unable to hold back, only to find out what happens when you transgress. I'm more circumspect now—careful not to go past the line or even to approach it. I stay at a safe distance, warning those who pass me by but staying inside the wire. If we'd all stuck inside our limits, I'd still be a psych at Episcopal and Harry would still be a rich guy with his name on a plaque.

When I called, Felix picked up almost immediately, as if he'd expected it, and made no protest. If I'd thought more, I'd have realized that was a sign in itself. I told Felix about the people I'd met and what I'd discovered, and he listened silently.

"What are you doing later?" was all he asked.

———

Felix's apartment was on Riverside Drive at the end of a street in the nineties that sloped down from West End Avenue. It ended on a quiet spot along the drive above the Hudson, illuminated when I arrived by a full moon. That moon picked out the buildings in New Jersey and a tanker riding low in the river, leaving a glittering wake. The night was quiet apart from the moan of cars and roar of trucks on the parkway. I gazed down at Riverside Park for a while, taking in the view and wondering if I should head back home. Having come so far, I was frightened by the prospect of at last finding out what had been hidden within Seligman—not just the financial deceptions, but also the broken relationships.

Then I saw Felix. He was standing a hundred yards away, his hands in the pockets. He hadn't seen me and I walked toward him, waiting for him to look up, but I was within three yards before he showed any sign of noticing. At the last minute, he looked at me and nodded in acknowledgment.

"Shall we go inside?" he said quietly.

We walked across to his building, passing a Latino deliveryman wobbling the wrong way up the drive on a bicycle with no lights. It was the first time I'd known Felix to be quiet, and it felt alien, as if he'd had a stroke and lost the use of his larynx. He still hadn't spoken by the time we got to his apartment, which was decorated in an ornate, gloomy way, with heavy curtains and furniture. He went into the kitchen and took a whiskey bottle from a cupboard.

"Single malt?" he said joylessly, as if it were medicine.

After he'd sloshed out two measures, he led me to his living room, where he lounged in an armchair with a knee across one of the arms. With his sweater riding up above his pants, he looked thinner than when I'd last seen him in my apartment. I wondered if he'd been eating properly or if drink had become his diet. I remember worrying briefly for him. I'd seen too many people dose their anxieties with drink, and it only made them worse. But I had always imagined Felix as so capable, so good at navigating a world of powerful people, that I wasn't as concerned as I should have been. I didn't think of him as in need of help: I'd relied upon him to help me. He raised his glass and the ice tinkled.

"Faithful servants," he toasted.

"Your family's away?"

"Yes, the wife decided to extend her stay there, put the kids in school for a while. It's for the best, I'd say."

He looked down at his glass, the rims of his eyes red, trying half-heartedly to make his life's disintegration sound like a strategy.

"I saw a photo of you together in London—Harry, Marcus, Tom Henderson," I said. "You worked at Rosenthal. You never told me that."

"I didn't realize you wanted my CV. Next time I'll know." He smiled flatly. "I guess Harry underestimated you. Unusual methods for a doctor, I've got to say."

"What is it about Rosenthal, Felix? Why is everyone so obsessed with the place?" I said. "Henderson seems to love it."

He smiled. "It's hard to describe. So much of Wall Street is dog-eat-dog. We looked out for each other. If someone got in our way we were brutal, but there was camaraderie to it. We didn't think we were the best. We knew it. Once you've been there you're always part of it. I guess I've worked at Seligman twenty years now. If you cut me open, it would still say Rosenthal inside."

"Why did you leave, then? You told me you were at Seligman when Harry came over from New York."

"Not exactly. It was a mission Tom gave me. Rosenthal was a smaller place then, a partnership without a lot of capital. We'd got involved in Canary Wharf with Seligman and we were overextended. A lot had to be fixed. Then Harry came to town, swaggering about and making threats. Tom didn't want him to blow it all up. They needed someone to watch him. Harry had taken a shine to me and he offered me a job. He adored the idea of stealing from Rosenthal."

"You said you liked him," I said.

"Rosenthal can be a cold place and Harry was warm. Tom laughed, thought it was a great idea. That's the kind of thing that amuses him.

Someone else thinking they're getting a bargain when they're doing what he wants. 'Come back when we're done,' he said. I wish I had, but I never did. We fixed the deal. We even got a prize. I got Harry to go along with some things they needed and he never realized. His time in London worked out well and he got the top job with Seligman. I thought it was over, but Tom thought Harry owed them."

"Even twenty years later?"

"They're patient—they wait a long time to get a return. When Marcus got into trouble, Tom thought it was time for Harry to repay the debt. He called me, made it sound like it was my duty to help Marcus. Patriotic duty, duty to Rosenthal, I don't think he sees a distinction. Harry was hot to trot, loved the idea. The only problem was Marcus's balance sheet."

"The Elements," I said.

Felix's eyes widened. He had been talking in a confessional, far-away tone, but as I spoke the words he became alert.

"Who told you about that? Lauren, I suppose."

"Who?" I said as blankly as I could.

"Harry's girlfriend," he said reproachfully. "You know that, Ben. So did I."

"How did you know?"

Felix rose a little unsteadily, picked up our glasses, and made his way back to the kitchen to refill them. I heard him twist off the cap of the whiskey bottle and the icemaker spit chips. Looking around the apartment with him gone, I saw a door leading to one of the bedrooms. It was ajar, and through the gap I saw a child's bed with a line of stuffed animals on one pillow, blankly awaiting her return. She must have left without them, trusting she'd be back. He came back into the room, handed me my glass as he walked by, and sat down again.

"Harry told me one night when we'd had a few drinks," he said. "We were in China to beg from a state-owned bank with a pile of money. We'd flown in on the Gulfstream and had dinner, just the two of us. We went to a bar that was full of Korean call girls and Russians in tracksuits, the usual Silk Road crap. We sat and drank moonshine. He was bursting with it. He had to tell someone. Next thing I knew, he'd put Lauren on the Grayridge deal. Love's blind."

"She wasn't, though."

"Nope. There were huge losses on the Elements already—running into the billions. Greene tried to hide it from Harry, but she spotted it. She's a smart cookie, that woman. I couldn't have figured it out, I'll tell you."

I'd known that Underwood's story couldn't be correct. Lauren wouldn't have missed it. If she'd been Harry's adviser, it would only have been a matter of time before she found the weakness at the heart of Greene's bank.

"How would you hide billions of dollars? I don't understand."

"Beats me. I'm no rocket scientist. Anyway, Greene was on to her before she could tell Harry. They keep the documents for mergers on computers these days. There used to be a data room in the lawyers' offices, but it's all online now. The bankers on the buy side have a security key and they download what they want. Most of it's deadly dull, but you're supposed to look at everything just in case.

"Trouble is, it leaves a footprint. The sellers know what you're interested in. Underwood knew Lauren was suspicious about the Elements from the amount of material she'd downloaded, and he told Greene. Greene came here one night. He said the merger was at risk and I had to fix Lauren somehow. He was sitting right where you are. 'We've got to screw the bitch,' he said. Charming man."

"So you told him."

It all made sense, suddenly—it reconciled the kind of person Lauren was with what she'd done. She hadn't drifted off at the end of an affair or failed to notice what was wrong. She'd known everything, but Greene had blackmailed her.

Felix nodded, his head down. His face looked red and swollen, as if something were welling up inside. "Tom talked me into it. Marcus told Lauren he'd make the affair public if she didn't keep quiet and leave. That's what she did. She didn't tell Harry about the Elements and he only found out after it was too late."

I thought of Lauren telling me how her career would have been ruined if others knew of her relationship with Harry. *Stupid,* she'd called it, but the word hardly described the disaster it had caused. Then I remembered what Anna had witnessed—the two of them together in East Hampton, his head in her hands. Lauren must have just told Harry what Greene had done and why she'd abandoned him. It wasn't hard to understand what happened next.

Of all the lies I'd heard, I found this one the most shocking. Felix was Harry's friend, but he'd abandoned him. "Why did you do it, Felix?" I said.

"Because Tom was right," he said slowly. "Harry thought he could match Rosenthal, but I didn't believe him. He'd been fine for Seligman in the good times, but it wasn't like that anymore. The markets were falling and I was frightened. I'd been there before. If Marcus was in charge of the place, Rosenthal would be behind him and Treasury, too. I had all my money tied up in the stock. I couldn't afford to lose it."

"You betrayed him for money?"

It was a harsh thing to say, tougher than I should have been, and I think about it still. I wish I could take those words back. My excuse is that I was angry, not only that he'd deceived me but that he'd broken Harry's trust in a heartbeat, hardly thinking about it. I felt as if I'd struggled to keep other people's secrets and had suffered for it, while he'd just looked after himself.

"Oh, Ben," he said reproachfully, "what do you think we are, you and I? We're helpers and servants. They say 'whistle' and we pucker up our lips and blow. Harry was in Tom's way and I moved him for his own good. What would you expect me to do? I tried to make it up to Harry afterwards."

"What did you do?"

Felix gazed into his whiskey, his eyes as cloudy as the spirits, and gulped it down. "That's a story for another night," he said.

"Take care of yourself, Felix," I said, getting up.

"Too late for that."

When I reached Riverside Drive, I walked toward the George

Washington Bridge in the clear night. I'd traveled as far as I could and found out all I could about Greene's death. For a long time, I'd kept some hope alive that it might save me, but I'd abandoned it now. Greene had deceived Harry and blackmailed Lauren, but he was in the ground and beyond justice. There was no evidence of Henderson doing wrong: in fact, there wasn't evidence of anything unless Lauren and Harry talked. She'd gone out of her way to hide her actions, and he wouldn't admit to murder.

It was time to find myself another job.

24

My first reaction when I heard Joe's voice was relief. I thought he had abandoned me, but he didn't sound annoyed. His voice was friendly, but low and sober, as if he didn't want to startle me. It was two days after my encounter with Felix, and I'd thought a lot since then about how he'd betrayed Harry. I'd wanted to despise him, but the feeling hadn't stuck—his excuse about us being servants rang uncomfortably true.

"Hey, Joe," I said lightly. "I thought you'd fired me."

"Hell, no. I'm still here. I just thought you'd want a lawyer who could do a better job for you, that's all. I spoke to your father. He told me you guys had talked and I didn't want to get in the way. Have you seen the news?"

"What news?" I said.

I think I knew immediately. I'd stepped irretrievably beyond the psych's frame and I'd feared what could result, although I'd tried to block it out.

"Turn on the television. Try CNN." His voice sounded strained and I hurried across the room to obey him.

It felt like being transported back to my gym that Sunday morning. There was no helicopter this time, but the anchors were babbling just as incoherently about a death, and the scene was similar as well—a street in a Long Island beach town where a reporter stood, her back to a cordon. There was a ticker at the bottom of the screen, this time with the headline SELIGMAN TRAGEDY. I sat down unthinkingly and found I was still holding the phone. My brain couldn't make sense of it.

"What happened? What's going on?"

"Have you heard of this guy? Felix Lustgarten," he said, pronouncing the second half of the name with a soft *t*, like garden. "He worked with Shapiro, they say he was a friend. He just killed himself, walked into the sea off Southampton. They just fished him out. I got a call at dawn from Baer. He's gone crazy."

"Oh God," I said weakly.

"Ben? . . . Are you there?"

I'd slumped forward with my head in one hand and the phone in my left, and I heard his voice only faintly. It felt as if someone had blown a dog whistle nearby, sending a high-pitched whine through my brain. *I should have known it. I should have stopped him,* I thought. *He was close to suicide. Of course he was.* I remembered how I'd walked out of his apartment in a fit of pique because of what he'd done, without stopping to help as my profession required. Why hadn't I stayed to save him? He'd sat in front of me, drinking, confessing. How much louder could he have cried for help? Then I had another thought. *Suicide? Last time, it was a murder. I went through this with Harry and he came back to life.* I tried to believe that Felix would rise again, too.

"Ben!" It was the distant voice of Joe in the receiver, yelling so loudly that he finally broke through.

"I'm fine," I said, struggling to pull myself around. "It's a bit of a shock. I knew him. He was the one who came with me in the Gulf-stream. I saw him a couple of days ago. He was a decent man."

"Where did you see him?" Joe said, sounding tense. His estimation of me as a client had clearly tumbled farther, if that were possible.

"In his apartment on the Upper West Side. He asked me over for a drink."

"Do you know why he did this? Did he tell you anything?"

As he asked the question, I saw from the corner of my eye the television screen turning another color, and I looked up to see them playing the tape of the hearing in Washington. Felix's face had been circled in red to identify him as he sat behind Harry and Greene. *That's how he'll be remembered,* I thought—the man in the background. I recalled his defeated expression as he'd raised his glass to me. *Faithful servants,* he'd said.

I wondered if I should tell the truth, but I excused myself with the thought that it would defile Felix's memory without doing me any good.

"Nothing important," I lied. "He seemed okay."

That might have been it but for Gabriel, who was waiting for me when I left my office for lunch three days later. He sat on the sofa by the elevators, under a notice board on which some guides to mood disorders were pinned. He drew my attention because he was loung-ing easily—not like an anxious patient or a parent who was waiting for a child in treatment—and because I vaguely recognized him. As I walked by, I saw him scan my badge and look at my face, appraising me with narrow eyes. Then he got to his feet.

"Dr. Cowper? My name is Gabriel Cardoso. We had a friend in common, I think. Felix Lustgarten."

He spoke unhurriedly, in a rich voice with an accent I wasn't sure about—it sounded Spanish. *Gabriel, that's it.* I remembered him standing on the balcony of his TriBeCa apartment at his party on the night of Greene's death. I'd been talking to Lucia before we'd left together, and she'd pointed him out. I recalled his air of detachment, as if he didn't know most of the guests but enjoyed having them fill the place.

"I was saddened by his death," he went on. "We were not close friends, I would say, but we were once colleagues. He was a man I liked." He gave the impression that he didn't say it lightly: he had standards.

"I'm sorry, too. I'd just gotten to know him. Shall we?"

I gestured at the sofa and took a seat—I didn't know how long I would want to stay. Gabriel reached into a jacket pocket and pulled out an envelope with his name and, I assumed, address scrawled on the front. Inside were two sheets of paper, well thumbed, and a small metal block: a computer flash drive.

"I got this in the mail yesterday," he said, frowning. "It's a letter from Felix, and he'd enclosed this." He held the drive between thumb and finger. "There are a bunch of documents on it. I looked at them last night and found them interesting. Disturbing, in fact. Felix asked me to show them to you. Just you, no one else."

I looked at the drive, now nestling in Gabriel's hand. Felix had given no indication of having this in mind, and I couldn't understand why he had sent an emissary from beyond the grave.

"If he wanted me to see them, why did he send them to you?" I said.

"Ah, well . . . They require some explanation."

It dawned on me then. When Felix had talked of Greene trying to hide the losses in the Elements, he'd said they were hard to grasp. He'd sent Gabriel to help me, I realized. I was touched by his posthumous gesture: he hadn't just written me off after I'd walked out on him. Yet it worried me to be entrusted with this legacy.

"You're a rocket scientist?" I said, remembering Felix's words.

"I am indeed," he said, beaming. "Do you have some time to talk? Maybe somewhere private. I will need a computer for this."

I hesitated for a few seconds, but I didn't really have a choice. I owed it to Felix in death, no matter what he'd done in life.

I could have wasted hours in Gabriel's apartment just looking around. Maybe that's how he spent his time, since he seemed to have plenty to spare. In the sunlight, with the view of Manhattan I'd seen from his balcony only at night, it was captivating. It was long and wide, with a dovetailing maze of rooms into which light spilled from high windows. A couple of rooms seemed devoted entirely to art, with blinds drawn to protect his collection of drawings. There was no sign that he shared it with anyone: it was just him in his monument to Wall Street wealth.

"You have an unusual name, Mr. Cardoso," I said, making small talk as he slotted the flash drive into a computer in his study and tapped at the keyboard, manipulating a baffling array of numbers.

"It's Portuguese," he said, smiling. "I am originally from Brazil, you see. I came here to teach mathematics at NYU. Wall Street headhunters kept calling me. Trading is all mathematics now, based on models. Traders don't understand it properly, so they need people like me. Rocket scientists, like you said. Most traders don't have a clue what they're doing."

He sounded pleasantly amused by the idea rather than outraged. I began to realize why he looked so bemused by his surroundings and his wealth. They had been handed to him through a twist of educational fate.

"You worked at Seligman?"

"Used to. I was pushed out last year by Marcus Greene, before Harry killed him." He chuckled as if Harry had meted out retribution for him. "I wasn't in Greene's clique, eh? And I said some things he didn't like, too loudly. But I was there long enough to be comfortable," he said, waving to his apartment. "That's how I know Felix, and Lauren Faulkner as well. Felix mentioned her, I think?"

I didn't reply, but my silence didn't seem to bother him because he kept talking as if he hadn't noticed.

"You want to know how we became friends? I had a nice office off the floor at Seligman. Just a glass box, but I had a very comfortable chair in there, a leather armchair. You couldn't see who was in it from outside, and Lauren would come by to take a nap. They work stupid hours, bankers. They don't get enough sleep."

"That's funny," I said. I tried to imagine the ever-alert Lauren curled up on Gabriel's chair. It would have been a more relaxing time, I imagined, when she hadn't been under such strain. It made her seem human—not the woman who'd threatened me.

"I remember us talking one evening, before the merger. She said she was looking at the Grayridge books. I told her to be very careful. Things were becoming difficult in the markets and I'd heard rumors. It was very complex stuff, you know. I offered to take a look with her, make sure it was all okay. I had the feeling something might not be right. A couple of days later, she was gone."

"Didn't you find that odd?"

"No one gets much warning on Wall Street, you know. They put a trash bag on your desk for your stuff and escort you from the building in case you steal something. It's like you've been executed. The same thing happened to me. I didn't know how bad things had been at Grayridge until I saw this."

"These are the Elements?" I said, looking over his shoulder at the screen. I could see what Felix had meant: it was just a blur of numbers to me.

"This is Radon. Let me explain."

Grayridge had sold the Elements through the Cayman Islands to investors trying to make money from the housing boom before it fell apart, Gabriel said. The mortgages had been bundled together and then divided into securities with differing amounts of risk in them. It wasn't even that simple, because they were synthetic CDOs, built out of credit default swaps based on mortgages. They'd been a crazy mash-up of financial risk.

"There were nine deals like this one structured by the CDO desk," Gabriel said. "They did the same thing each time. Sold the equity and mezzanine to hedge funds and kept hold of the triple-A tranches. They issued the risky paper, the bonds that paid the most, to other investors. But the yield was very low on the super-senior tranches they kept, so they levered them up to make a return. They held about $120 billion, yielding $160 million a year."

His explanation reminded me of what Harry had told me on the beach at East Hampton and in Riverhead, and I hadn't understood that, either. I wasn't treating Gabriel for depression, though, so I could ask him what I wanted.

"A hundred and twenty billion *dollars*?"

"That's right. What's your question, Ben?"

"It sounds like a lot of money."

"It was, but the paper was supposed to be risk-free, like a government bond. There wasn't going to be a default even if the mortgage holders stopped paying. They'd built it to take a hundred-year storm. Take a look here. This is the loss on all of the Element deals at the date of the merger. What does it say?" he asked.

I looked at the screen and there were hundreds of figures on it, a grid of numbers. I shook my head as if baffled, which I was, and Gabriel gave me a clue by wiggling the mouse to make the onscreen arrow jiggle by one box.

"Three hundred and twenty-four," I read.

"A $324 million loss. When the merger went through, Harry thought there wasn't much of a problem. It seemed like Marcus needed a bit of help, but it would be okay. You want to know how much they'd already lost? The whole $21 billion."

I frowned at him and looked back at the screen to scan the numbers again. "I can't see anything like that here," I said.

Gabriel smiled. "Felix knew I would understand. Marcus told the traders to alter the model, shift the correlations. That altered the figures for long enough for the merger to be approved. He hid the entire thing."

"Correlations?" I repeated dumbly. "What are they?"

"You're a doctor. Do you know about broken heart syndrome?"

Gabriel's question was so unexpected that it took a few seconds for me to respond. I hadn't expected to be an expert on anything amid this deluge of mathematical finance, but he'd at last mentioned something familiar. I'd been taught about the condition in medical school, and a widowed patient of Rebecca's had died from it.

"I have," I said. "Stress cardiomyopathy. Heart failure caused by chemicals released into the bloodstream after an emotional trauma. It can happen to people whose wives or husbands have died. What's that got to do with it?"

"It's a correlation. The first death makes the second more likely. It affects the price of life insurance. It's the same with mortgages. If some borrowers stop paying, there will be a loss, but you need to know the chance of the defaults being followed by others. If the correlation is low, the loss will be, too. If it's high, the loss will be, too."

"So the correlation was high on the Elements?"

"Incredibly high. Like nothing I've ever seen. It's like you have a hundred people outside in a storm. What's the chance of all of them being struck by lightning?"

"Pretty small, I guess," I said.

"Unless they're all together—they're tightly correlated. Then if one gets hit, they're all hit. A vast number of mortgage borrowers stopped repaying all at once. The triple-A paper was going to be wiped out. Three months before the deal, Greene found out. He couldn't admit to it because his bank would have been bust. He got the desk to lower the correlations so the model showed the losses not reaching the triple-A. He knew he couldn't hide it for long, but he didn't have to. Just long enough to fool Harry."

"How do you know it was him? Couldn't the traders have done it themselves?"

"There was one thing Greene didn't want anyone to find, a document Lauren discovered in the data room. It was buried in here. I only found it at three a.m."

He clicked the mouse and a printer whirred to life on the shelf by me, spooling out a sheet of paper. It was an email message to Greene with a brief opening line—"Here are the metrics we discussed"—and below a list of the Elements.

"When Greene found out, he got Rosenthal to run the numbers on the models. They gave him the right assumptions, all the volatilities and the correlations. It predicted what was going to happen very pre-cisely. Those guys are smart, I must say."

I examined the paper. At the bottom of the email was a piece of legal boilerplate saying it had been sent from a Rosenthal employee and warning against disclosure. There was a list of five email recipients at the top, led by Marcus Greene. The final three names were all from Rosenthal, and the bottom one was Tom Henderson.

Henderson's calm disdain as he'd reviewed my feeble efforts to pin him down came back to me: *You don't have any evidence, merely the imaginings of a psychiatric patient.* He had given me a long enough hearing to discover if I did, though. He hadn't just been indulging a runaway psych bearing an unconvincing threat.

I've got evidence now, I thought.

"You enter these numbers in the model and guess what comes out?" Gabriel asked.

"I don't have to," I said, knowing already what Lauren had found.

"Negative $21 billion. Marcus already knew."

25

We gathered at Green-Wood Cemetery, a grand affair spread out on a hillside in a scrappy neighborhood of Brooklyn, with a view over the docks, the harbor, and the Statue of Liberty glowing copper green in the distance. It was a wet spring day, but the clouds parted as I got there and the sun emerged on the blossom trees and mausoleums on the slopes. *Felix couldn't have asked for more,* I thought. Maybe he'd chosen it: I wouldn't have been surprised.

I walked up the hill to the cemetery through a stone arch on which was a bas-relief of Jesus being laid to rest following the Crucifixion. Unlike Christ, or even Harry, Felix wasn't coming back. He had drowned off Southampton and washed up on the long, broad beach among the seashells. He'd left a note for his wife and children, I'd been told, which was brief, remorseful, and blessedly vague.

To my left was a field with low gravestones set into it and a multitude of tiny Stars and Stripes fluttering in the breeze. A pair of Canada geese was waddling defiantly past, and when I bent down to scan a couple of stones, they turned out to be the graves of Civil War veterans. In death, Felix had transcended obscurity and was being sent to the afterlife accompanied by high technology and higher security. I passed a dozen or so huge trucks with satellite dishes on their roofs and burly technicians watching over a cardiovascular array of cords.

A couple of reporters leaned by them, take-out coffees in hand. One of them was my friend Bruce Bradley, who'd led me astray on Fox News about Harry. He was wearing either the same blazer or another like it and was laughing overheartily at his producer's joke. Higher up the slope, near the arch, were five or six black Lincoln Navigators and Chevy Suburbans with another group of burly men clustered by them, these in suits rather than casual gear. They had translucent wires stuck into their ears, carrying Secret Service radio chatter. Someone important had turned up for Felix. Finally, there were three Suffolk County sheriff's cars filled with uniformed officers trying not to be overawed by the Feds.

All in all, it was quite a show. Felix would have liked it, or found it entertaining. My feelings were still raw, but I'd found that despite everything he'd done, I'd come to miss him. Although he'd betrayed Harry, he'd been the nearest I'd found to a kindred spirit, at least until our last meeting. I didn't count Anna—she came under miscellaneous.

A familiar vehicle was parked under a tree beyond the arch, which marked the border between the gawkers and the mourners—Nora's stone gray Range Rover. I felt odd seeing it, and I peered into a window as I walked past to check if she or Anna was inside. It was empty, but I saw Nora as I looked up again. She was standing on a hill thirty yards away by a pink blossom tree, dressed in black with a small cap fixed to her hair. I watched her turn away from the scene to walk farther into the cemetery.

I'd entered a minefield of encounters by being there, but I hadn't felt able to avoid it. I hadn't done much for Felix, so I could at least attend his send-off. Walking after Nora, I came over the brow and looked into a bowl-shaped arena with a chapel at the bottom like a bonsai version of Christ Church in Oxford, in the same limestone with ornate carvings leading up to its dome. It was overlooked by rows of mausoleums and graves set along pathways.

As I got there, I saw an encounter unfold below me. Two vehicles were parked near the steps by the chapel. One was a heavy black limousine from which Tom Henderson had emerged and was shaking hands with two men I didn't recognize. The other was a Suffolk County sheriff's truck holding Harry. As Harry emerged, wearing a dark suit and handcuffs, they gazed at each other, but I couldn't see their expressions from a hundred yards away. A Secret Service man stepped in front of Henderson, as if to protect him from a felon, and he sprang up the steps while Harry was held behind. Finally, Harry was allowed to proceed and he walked slowly through the wooden doors of the chapel.

By the time I arrived, most people were in place on the seven rows of benches in front of the altar, under a brass ring of blazing electric lights. It suited me, for it allowed me to slip into a backseat and scan the mourners. Nora was in the same row as Harry but a few seats down from him, as if jail protocol had to be observed, and Henderson was on the far side. Gabriel was on the same bench and gave me a nod. There was no organ, so we sat there in silence until the doors opened and a minister in white robes led a procession into the chapel: first the coffin and behind it Felix's wife, black-haired with an ashen gray face, and their two children. The little boy had Felix's molelike nose.

When the priest spoke, I realized he was reading from the Book of Common Prayer, as if we'd been taken back to an English church. *It's Episcopal,* I thought—my brand. It was the first time I'd seen the religion in action, rather than treating patients in its name.

"I am the resurrection and the life, saith the Lord," he intoned. "He that believeth in me, though he were dead, yet shall he live."

I looked across at a stained-glass window that was backlit by the sun and attempted to ignore the sound of Felix's wife weeping. It wasn't easy; she had a low-pitched, agonized gulp that sounded as if she were dying herself, the body's last effort to fill the lungs. I wanted to place my hands over my ears to block the sounds of pain, but it was impermissible. The first psalm was a relief—it was a cue for her to blow her nose and for the rest of us to cough and shuffle before the reading started. It was De Profundis, and I listened unthinkingly.

I look for the Lord; my soul doth wait for him;
in his word is my trust.
My soul fleeth unto the Lord before the morning watch
I say, before the morning watch.

We spilled out into the sunshine at the end of the service, and I drifted to one side so as not to intrude. The coffin was put back in the hearse and the priest led the mourners up a path to a lawn with a view over warehouses and docks. By the grave, I caught a glimpse of the little girl whose toys I must have seen in their apartment, holding her mother's hand while the minister read the committal.

The priest hesitated fractionally on the last lines of the committal: "Suffer us not, at our last hour, through any pains of death, to fall from thee." The widow started to weep again; the sound of her gulps mingled with those of clods of earth falling on the coffin.

I had gotten about fifty yards back down the path toward the arch, my duty to Felix done, when I heard footsteps behind and two Secret Service agents fell in beside me, making me jump with alarm.

"Dr. Cowper?" The agent who spoke had a shaved head and wore aviator sunglasses, making it impossible to see any impression of humanity in his eyes. "Secretary Henderson would like to speak with you."

The pair led me back toward Felix's grave, where a clump of mourners was still gathered, including Harry, who was talking to the priest and seemed to be making the most of his day out from jail. Halfway there, they deviated toward a concrete-and-glass building surrounded by water. The aviator led me across a bridge, while his companion hung back.

At first, I didn't know what the building was. It was like a library, with rows of floor-to-ceiling stacks lining a corridor and chairs in the empty spaces. But instead of shelves, the stacks held rows of boxlike cubicles, each with a glass door. Then I realized—it was a columbarium. There were urns in each cubicle, with the remains of a dead person in each one. Some were brass and others were jade. Most of the names were Chinese or Asian, and I saw small portrait photographs propped by some of them, with artificial flowers on the other side.

Henderson stood by a padded bench next to one of these walls of ashes. Opposite the stack was a glass wall that overlooked the lawn where Felix had just been buried. I could see the mourners still lingering by the graveside, but I knew we were invisible to them.

"Hello again, Dr. Cowper. Look at all these names." Henderson was tracing a finger over the glass face to the cubicles that lined the stack. "Pui Wah Choi. An Ying Qu. Chinese mainland or Taiwan, I wonder? A fascinating place, Green-Wood. My wife insisted on us taking a trolley-bus tour once. All the mausoleums for the well-to-do of the nineteenth century. Now it's the Chinese from Sunset Park in vases."

"It's very striking," I said, unsure of where all this was leading.

"And now one Englishman, too. Although Felix had become an American citizen, I think." He sat on the bench and crossed his legs. One of his pants legs rode up and I saw a long sock, the touch of a gentleman. "I wrote a testimonial letter for him a couple of years back, when the Rosenthal name helped. Homeland Security would probably deport you now."

He lapsed into silence, seemingly in no hurry to get to the point. Something had gone out of him—the menacing authority I'd witnessed in Washington. He looked deflated and unhappy.

"It's a tragedy," I prompted.

"A terrible one. I always liked Felix. We were together in London, you know, a long while back. Why did he . . . do this?"

I looked at him, trying to discern if there was an accusation there, but the question seemed guileless.

"Perhaps he felt remorse for betraying Harry," I said.

I didn't say what I meant, but Henderson nodded as if there were no need for us to pretend with each other.

"He'd told you about that, did he? He must have been unhappy. I want you to believe one thing. Whatever was done . . ." He grimaced, as if the habit of deflecting responsibility had become so deeply ingrained in him that he had to force himself out of it. "Whatever *I* did, was meant for the best."

Who gave you the right to choose Harry's fate? I thought. It angered me, his halfhearted regret. He'd played with people, and he'd believed he was allowed to do it because his bank ruled Wall Street.

"You told me how great Rosenthal was—what a fine institution— but you didn't save Seligman, you used it," I said. "Greene's dead and now Felix is, too. Harry could be in jail for the rest of his life. You can't justify that."

He frowned and the lines in his forehead were deep and heavy—it was an old man's face. "Not with two deaths, no. I've talked to the president. I've told him it's time for me to step down. I hope that's enough for you."

It was an appeal for clemency. He knew what Felix had disclosed, and he didn't want me to publish it. I hadn't decided what to do with the document that had been bequeathed to me, but I wasn't willing to let him rest easy.

"Not really," I said.

"You think about that. I have to go now," he said, offering me his hand to shake. "Be well, Dr. Cowper."

He went out of a far entrance toward Felix's grave, and I retraced my steps along the path to the cemetery entrance, pausing at a stone cross in memory of a Scottish woman who'd died in the 1800s. As I crested the brow of the hill, I looked down to see Nora standing by her car with Harry. The prison officer had let him approach her, and he was leaning down to meet her lips briefly with his. Then he was led away and she stood alone for a few seconds, dabbing her eyes, before she climbed into her car and drove away.

As she did, I saw a driver open the door of a limousine parked near the arch for a woman to get out. She was in her fifties, tall and imposing, with a gaunt face and thin, upturned nose, and she was bearing a bouquet of purple and white flowers, arrayed in matching colored paper tied with twine. It looked like the kind of casually expensive arrangement you found in Manhattan. She'd timed her entrance so that the Shapiros were no longer around, and she walked up the path into the cemetery. After she'd passed me by, I turned to follow, for I'd recognized her. She was the woman in the Senate video who'd placed her hand on Anna's arm.

We walked in lockstep, me twenty yards behind her, toward Felix's grave. The path was hard underfoot, and I heard the scrunch of her heels striking the ground as she walked. The place was emptying and a group of workmen was getting ready to start an excavator and tip the earth back into Felix's grave. It felt too exposed to follow her all the way there, so I sat on a bench nearby and watched from a distance. As she approached, she squatted briefly to examine the flowers by the grave and then put her own bouquet by the others. She straightened up again and I examined her face. It was blank and unmoving, as if it had been an act of duty or she were an envoy. Then she started the trek back along the path. I hid my face from her by looking at my phone as she passed, letting her walk out of sight.

I sat for a while to make sure that no one else was coming. The workmen were standing talking near the grave, a couple of them smoking. In the distance, I heard cars starting up and the buzz of electronic chatter—either the Secret Service readying to leave or the television crews spreading the news. Then I walked across the grass. My heart was thudding and my mouth was dry, although no one seemed to be watching. I reached the border to the grave, where the grass had been pounded by feet into mud, and bent to look at the flowers she'd left. There was a mauve envelope pinned to the bouquet, and I slipped the card from inside.

"To Felix," it read. "In memory. Margaret Greene."

———

The temperature had risen in the previous few days, the heat of Washington moving north and bringing hints of a humid summer to come. The nights were warmer, and that evening I went to a window that led onto the fire escape that snaked down the side of my apartment building. Sitting on the sill, I thrust my legs over and rested them on the platform. I could hear sirens course through Union Square and the nighttime buzz of the city.

I had poured myself a glass of bourbon, and as I'd added ice, I'd thought of Felix on our last night. *Faithful servants,* had been his toast, but now I wondered if he'd been faithful to anyone at all. I'd trusted him, but so had everyone else: Harry, Nora, Henderson, the Greenes. Seeing Margaret Greene's note had made me wonder if he'd told me the truth, even at the end. Felix had betrayed Harry because he'd believed in Henderson—or the bank he personified—but he'd tried to compensate. That's what he'd told me.

They'd come to mark his passing. Margaret Greene had cared enough to be driven there and place her memento on his grave. Everyone was willing to forgive him, so why had he killed himself? His sin didn't seem enough to warrant despair. The only absentee had been Anna. She'd left Nora to drive her car herself. On the subway ride back to Manhattan—Felix had thoughtfully chosen to get buried near the N line—I remembered the line in the psalm: "My soul fleeth unto the Lord before the morning watch." That was the last sight I'd had of her, walking along the beach. Now I realized what she'd hidden from me.

I'd never bothered to find out about the Greenes before. All the stories I'd heard about them had made them seem impersonal, hostile forces rather than people. But I had rectified that when I'd returned home, reading the newspaper stories around the time of his death that I'd ignored before. Greene hadn't been a nice man—almost no one I'd talked to had much good to say about him. He was singlehandedly breaching the motto that you shouldn't speak ill of the dead. But outside of Wall Street he'd been human. He'd married a woman and had a family. They had brought up children together.

Holding my phone, I climbed out onto the fire escape platform and punched in Anna's number, then placed it to my ear to hear the tone. It went on for six rings and then switched to voice mail. Her voice invited me to leave a message and I vacillated for what felt like several seconds but was only a fraction of one before pressing the icon to end the call. I couldn't confront her on voice mail: it had to be done in the flesh.

26

It was a pristine day with a blue bowl of sky as I drove out from the city with the afternoon sun behind me. The temperature was in the seventies and it had been like walking into a refrigerator when I'd entered the air-conditioned hospital earlier in the day. Independence Day was near but the traffic was sparse on the Long Island Expressway once I'd made it out of the city. There weren't many cars, which was why I noticed the one behind me.

It was a dark Mercedes crossover, but I couldn't see enough in my rearview mirror to know who was driving. It was trailing me about two hundred yards back, staying in position as I passed trucks. I eased my speed up and down a few times to see whether I might leave it behind or trigger it into passing, but it stuck there. After a while, with nothing happening and no sign of it catching up, I wondered if

I was being paranoid. It couldn't be Pagonis—not in a Mercedes—and who else was interested in me? But Lauren's threat lingered in my mind.

After a while, I decided I had to discover if I was imagining the whole thing. I had plenty of gas, but I joined the exit lane at a refueling stop. I looked in my mirror to see the Mercedes still following me at the same distance. As I stopped by a pump and climbed out, it parked about fifty yards from me in the lot. There was no movement from inside, and the sunlight glinting off the windshield prevented me from seeing the driver. I went into the gas station to pay and to use the restroom, hoping vaguely that when I came back out it would have gone. It hadn't, and I saw it ease out after me as I drove away, getting caught briefly behind another car as we rejoined the express-way but reappearing in the same place as before.

I knew then who the driver was—and that he wasn't going to stop. He would trail me all the way to East Hampton, right to the Shapiros' house. Unless I confronted him, he'd follow me to Anna and I'd have to face them together. I knew he wasn't acting rationally, that he'd lost all self-control since I'd first encountered him. He wasn't a danger to others, just to me. The miles went by accompanied by the steady thump-thump of the tarmac, and nothing altered except for the air, which became sweeter. With my window open, I smelled the heather by the side of the road and a hint of ocean air. We slowed together off the expressway and joined the single-lane road for the last few miles to our destination.

We drove past Bridgehampton without any break in the invisible link between us, although he was farther back now—it was too obvious out here in the potato fields and woods to be as close as he'd been before. I had no idea how to shake him off, but I didn't want to lead him to her. My opportunity came before I'd had a chance to plan anything, or even to think about it. The highway bent in an S curve, first right and then left, and as I came around the second bend, I saw roadworks ahead of me and a man letting a line of cars through a single-lane gap. He signaled for me to stop, but I spurted through the small gap instead.

I saw the Mercedes being forced to halt behind me. The driver had no choice because the man had blocked his path. He flashed his lights with annoyance, but the man wouldn't give way. I had a minute before he'd be after me again, and I accelerated around another curve through a forest. I needed a hiding place, but I didn't see anything that would work until I passed an old Sherman tank on the side of the road, its barrel trained uselessly toward the sea. It was a war memorial, and just beyond it was a lane into the woods.

Glancing in my mirror, I saw nothing, so I swung left and sped around a bend that hid me from the main road. There was nothing to do but keep going, and I drove as fast as I could through thick woods, with the plain brown trunks of trees poking through hilly outcrops. There was nothing there—just a few houses in patches of land cut into the woods—and I wondered if the road would lead anywhere. After five minutes, the woods thinned out on my left into a field leading to an airstrip, with three small jets near a clapboard building.

There was a parking lot between the building and me. It was empty apart from a single vehicle, a Lexus SUV parked by the entrance. I checked ahead of me to where the road thinned further and turned into a track leading through fields. I didn't have time to think, and on instinct I swung the wheel and headed toward the airstrip. My plan, such as it was, was to find someone to be with—preferably a group with whom I could mingle to protect me from my follower—but the Lexus was empty. As I got out of my car, I remembered seeing Anna here, standing by the Shapiros' Range Rover. It was the airport where I'd landed in Harry's Gulfstream, before it jetted away without me. That felt like a very long time ago.

I headed at a trot into the building to discover only an empty atrium with a flight of model aircraft hanging decoratively from its rafters. "Hello?" I shouted, walking to the side of the building nearest the strip. There was no reply, and I couldn't see anyone in the offices by the hallway. I walked onto the tarmac and looked around. The aircraft I'd observed from the road had been parked and left for their owners' eventual return. There was no sign of life on the runway.

Then I saw a dot in the distance above the fields and woods, and as it grew, I realized it was a helicopter approaching. I stood watching as it descended about thirty yards from me and settled on the ground. It was a dark green Sikorsky—a solid-looking beast—with two uniformed pilots. They waited for the blades to slow and then one took off his headphones, climbed out, and walked to the side of the aircraft, where he stood as a door opened and some steps folded down. An odd group emerged: a tall man, wearing a suit as if he'd come straight from the office, and two children—a girl and a boy, both maybe seven or eight years old. They were in tartan school uniforms and the boy had a tennis racket over his shoulder. The man waved briefly to the pilot and then the trio strolled across the tarmac toward me.

The pilot walked around the aircraft, his ceremonial duty done, and climbed back into the cockpit to start the engine again. By the time the party had reached me, the helicopter had lifted off into the sky, its passengers safely deposited.

"Excuse me," I said as the man approached. "Could I speak to you?"

"What is it?" he said, slowing his walk slightly but not stopping as the children ran ahead into the building.

"I need help."

I could see his eyes glaze over as he glanced at me, still moving, as if I were a loser whom he had to shake off.

"Sorry, buddy. Next time," he said.

Before I could say anything else, he'd walked past me and through the building with the children. I trailed after him helplessly, as if drawn in his wake, and saw him raise the back gate of the Lexus to put the boy's tennis racket inside before driving away. I stood there feeling dazed and humiliated. He'd just treated me as if I were some beggar in the street with a sob story about losing his MetroCard and needing a fare home. I suppose when you're rich enough to commute to the Hamptons in a helicopter, every passerby looks like a panhandler.

Humiliation, however, wasn't my biggest problem. As I looked up the hill after him, I saw another vehicle come through the trees and halt on the slope above me—the Mercedes. The driver paused, and I imagined him scanning the scene as I had done and then seeing my car—now the only one in the parking lot. I was still inside the building, so I probably wasn't visible to him, but I soon would be.

I thought about my options and realized I didn't have many. He was parked on top of the slope, cutting off the road down to the highway, and there was no one in the building to shield me. My car was a beacon signaling where I was. If I tried to get back in it and drive, I'd have to head either straight toward him or to the left along the dirt track and into the trees. He could easily seal the path behind me if I did that. Jogging back to the airstrip, I looked around for some means of escape. I couldn't run on the tarmac, for I would be starkly visible on the flat landscape and he could catch me in his car. I looked to my right and saw a ditch by the side of the field that ran toward the trees. That ditch was the only cover I had.

I started up the hill, half running with my head down, hoping that he wouldn't spot me. It was muddy and stony and I stumbled and half fell a few times, but I was making progress when I glanced over my right shoulder to see the Mercedes roar into life, speeding up the hill parallel with me. When it reached the brow, the door opened and a man in his twenties tumbled out and sprinted across the field toward me. My pursuer was tall and blond, and he covered ground very rapidly. He was solidly built, with wide shoulders and a thick waist, and stared at me as he ran as if he had plans to crush me. The good news was that he didn't seem to be carrying a weapon. The bad news was that he didn't look as though he needed one.

All I could think of was to keep going, to reach the woods. Maybe I'd lose him in the forest, where his size would give him trouble. I coughed and choked as I scrambled to make cover, but it was useless. He tackled me five yards from the trees. I felt his weight on me, as I had in Central Park, and we toppled into the undergrowth. He grabbed me in a headlock and dragged me roughly across the ground. The pressure on my neck was brutal; I thrashed wildly to force myself free.

He was hauling me into the forest, out of reach of rescue. I tried to shout, but only gurgles emerged from my mouth. Then we were in the trees and I felt one of my feet catch in a root. It only made him yank my shoulders harder, and I felt a shooting pain in my ankle as my foot sprang free. He dragged me ten yards into a clearing covered in leaves and twigs, and I felt the pressure slacken on my neck as he let me drop to the ground. I bent over, reaching for my neck, and as I did so, he kicked me in the ribs, as if finishing his assault. I shuddered with the pain of it and looked up at my assailant.

The last time I'd come across him, it had been dark and I hadn't caught sight of his face. Now I saw him. He had blue eyes and a lean face with his mother's nose. His blond hair was streaked and tousled as if he didn't bother to keep it trimmed. *He and Anna would have made a nice couple,* I thought as he stood above me, panting with the effort he had put into pummeling me. It had come to me the night before, as I'd read about the Greene family. Their son, who worked at a hedge fund in New York after being shunted through the Ivy League, was called Nathan. It was just uncommon enough a name that I could remember the last time I'd heard it—from Anna, as she'd talked of her old boyfriend.

He was borderline, my therapist reckoned. He hooked me, and then made me suffer for loving him, she'd said.

Having witnessed the intimacy between her and Margaret Greene, I knew that was who it was. It had to be. Who else would have followed me after my meeting with Anna and trashed my apartment? It had to be someone with a grudge, and Nathan Greene had several. He had not only seen his old girlfriend kissing me, but he knew me as the psych who'd let Harry out of the hospital to kill his father. I'd remembered Rebecca's old dress, slashed through from shoulders to waist. He must have believed it was Anna's.

I had just enough time for the thoughts to pass through my head before Nathan dropped onto me, his knees pinning my shoulders to the ground and his body knocking away my breath. He put his hands around my neck in a throttle grip and squeezed. I was immobilized—

his weight was enough to eliminate any thought of being able to struggle free—and I strained for breath.

"Murderer!" he shouted.

On his tortured face, I saw something that gave me hope. He was weeping. Tears were running out of his eyes and down his nose, and a couple dripped on the ground. *He doesn't want to kill me,* I thought. *He doesn't know what he's doing.* I was only barely conscious, and I knew I didn't have much time left. I summoned what energy I had and thrust my head sharply to one side while pushing up with my shoulders to release his grip.

"Nathan!" I cried weakly. "Nathan. Stop."

He reached forward and reengaged his grip on my throat. He started to squeeze again, but then his hands went slack and he seemed to pull back. He was still sitting on me, but as I turned my face upward, his hands were covering his face and he was shuddering with emotion, the hostility leaking out of him like his tears.

"I'm sorry, Nathan," I said, spluttering and trying to spit a piece of twig out of my mouth. "I didn't kill your father. I'm sorry."

He cuffed my head with one hand, but there was no force in the blow—the assault was over. Then I felt his weight lift off me and he sat on the forest floor with his knees up and his arms wrapped around his legs and sobbed to himself without speaking. I got my breath back and then sat up myself. My ankle still hurt badly and my throat felt sore, but I was otherwise all right. We stayed like that in those woods, the two of us, for fifteen minutes, not talking, letting the panic subside, and then we walked to his car—me limping on my damaged ankle.

It took a little while for him to start talking about why he'd fixated on me as the cause of everything that had gone wrong in his life. When he did, the truth spilled out unchecked for over an hour. I sat there listening as I'd been trained to do, interjecting occasionally to try to convince him I was innocent—although I wasn't sure I was. He was only a few years younger than me, but he seemed like a child. I felt sorry for him. He'd been exploited to hide the truth about Greene's death. I almost liked him, although he had inherited his father's arrogance. He needed therapy, but I wasn't going to volunteer. The best I could offer was to forget about his twin assaults and having trashed my apartment.

It was quiet there—there wasn't anybody around. Once I heard the sound of an engine from the airfield, and I looked over to see a small plane landing in the distance. Otherwise, we were by ourselves. If he'd really meant to kill me, I'd taken him to a perfect spot.

After we'd finished, I made him promise to drive back to the city and wait for my call. The resistance had gone out of him, and I trusted him to do what I advised. My ankle was hurting and he drove me to where my car was parked, still alone in the lot. I steered it down through the woods to the highway and headed toward the woman who'd made me his target.

27

When I reached the entrance to the lane, I halted the car and got out, standing where Bruce Bradley had stood that day. To my left was the road to the sea, with surf now being blown from green waves. The beach was empty, as usual. The hedges and flowers along the lane were verdant, and blossoms had cascaded from a sculpted tree in the front yard of a home nearby, carpeting the lawn and drive.

Halfway along the lane, a line of contractors' vehicles were parked outside a house at which someone was having work done. Mostly, there was silence—interrupted only by the wind whistling in the tele-phone wires and the distant roar of the sea. I squinted along the lane at the Shapiros' house but couldn't see any sign of life. I tried to imag-ine the view as it would have been that Sunday, the lane jammed with police vehicles. Pagonis and Hodge would be picking up Harry to take him to Yaphank.

I thought of what Nathan had just told me and tried to piece it together with the rest of what I'd learned. I'd taken it on trust for so long that Harry had killed Greene—everyone had. He'd confessed to the crime, not just to the police but also to my face. But what if he'd been lying? Anna's complaint about psychs not checking on whether their patients were telling the truth had stuck with me since she'd said it. To us, truth is something to be found inside a patient, and only he can dig it out from his subconscious. We assume they are trying to be truthful, apart from the things they don't even know about themselves. That was why they have paid us money to talk.

Yet most of what I'd found since I'd met Harry were half truths and deceptions—not the distortions with which people comfort themselves, but blatant lies. I'd found that out only when I'd broken my profession's rules. The biggest deception of all was the one thing I'd never thought to doubt—that Harry was the boss. He had been the CEO, the banker who'd ruled Wall Street. Those around him were, as Felix had insisted, helpers and servants. I hadn't realized that one of them was in charge.

I got back in the car and drove down the lane, on alert for any human presence, but the white gates and the trees did their work, screening the lawns and houses from scrutiny. At the foot of the Shapiros' drive, I halted the car and looked from my side window at the property. Still nothing. I eased the car up the drive, this time taking the slope at a steady speed, and halted on the square of gravel by the house. A few yards past the SERVICE sign, I tapped on the kitchen door and put up my hand to shelter my eyes from the glare coming off the sea, peering through the glass into the empty room. Then I stepped onto the lawn at the rear to gaze through the conservatory windows at the living room. The contractors had done their work well, and the scene of the death shone in fresh colors, like a frosted cake.

I heard a whirring sound behind and turned sharply, but it was only a bird washing itself in the pool and shaking off the water in a spray. My ankle was bothering me and I limped around the house, emerging next to my car. I rested a hand on its roof and gazed down at the gravel beneath my feet, as if I might see all past tire marks if I looked hard enough.

Squatting, I passed a hand over the surface, feeling a prickle from the sharp stones as they rubbed across my palm. I looked down the slope toward a row of flowers. As I did it, I noticed from the corner of my eye the curtains move in a window of the single-story house across the lane: the Shapiros' guesthouse. When I looked again, the fabric was still, but I knew I hadn't been mistaken. I made my way slowly down the drive, leaving my car behind and gazing at the window. At the bottom, I crossed the lane and opened the small wooden gate guarding the entrance. It was a white clapboard cottage, not as intricate as their house but pretty all the same. The lawn was neatly trimmed and rhododendron bushes were set into oval beds, wood chips scattered around their roots.

As I paused, with the top of the gate still in my hand, the cottage door opened and Anna stood there. She was wearing a pink dress, with mother-of-pearl buttons on scalloped material running to the waist between her breasts, and the same black flip-flops in which I'd met her. There were five yards between us and we both stood in place, looking at each other. Her neck and cheeks were flushed and she twisted the strap of one flip-flop between the toes of one red-nailed foot.

"Why are you limping?" she said.

"Your boyfriend caught up with me. He talked to me, after he stopped throttling me. He told me a lot of things."

"That bastard," she said. "Don't believe a word he says."

We both stayed where we were, still frozen.

"Why did you run away?" I said.

"I was scared." Her lip trembled and she pinched one side between her teeth, the top ones shining white in the light.

"You told me to work it out myself. I've done that."

I walked along the path toward her. She was only five or six paces away, but they went very slowly and the gap hardly seemed to close until I was right by her. I took in her scent and felt the warmth of her body under the thin cotton. I reached through her dense hair, my fingers searching for the back of her head, and as I pulled her toward me, she stood on her toes so that our lips touched. Her tongue brushed against mine and I felt the softness of her mouth. We stayed together for several seconds and then she pulled back, looking up at me.

"This isn't very professional," she said.

"Fuck my profession," I said.

I pulled her to me, and as we kissed again, I could feel her draw back. She kept her arms slung around my shoulders as she moved, leading me back toward the open door. I walked along with her and caught her by the small of her back as she almost stumbled passing over the threshold. She pulled me to my right, her back against the hallway wall, as we got inside and reached under my arm to push the door closed. It swung toward the latch but failed to click and I kicked backward with my heel. My foot missed, tipping me to one side and making her giggle. She ducked under my arm and shoved the door with both hands, ramming it closed, then turned to face me again.

I took her face in my hands and kissed her slowly, and then I reached down to the top of her dress and felt for the first of the mother-of-pearl buttons. It was small and thick and I could not catch it at first, wrapped against a scallop of cloth. Then I pushed at it with my thumb and felt it slip through the buttonhole. The next five went faster, and as I got to the last, she pulled away from me, glancing down.

"Keep going," she said.

"Shut up," I said.

I pushed her dress off one shoulder and then slipped one bra strap after it and bent my head to kiss her shoulder. Squeezing her body between my hips and the door, I reached down to gather her dress up her legs. I could feel the tiny hairs on her thigh brush past my palm as she wriggled to free herself from the fabric.

She gazed at me, her eyes alight. "Don't stop," she said, and I pushed myself into her, hoisting her up the door. She raised one leg to hook it around my hips and moved with me until I came, feeling her quiver and, as she did, all of my pent-up bitterness and sorrow evaporated. We stayed like that, not moving, for a minute and then she lifted her other leg off the ground with a screech, toppling us over. We slid together down the crevice of door and wall and landed in a heap on the floorboards, banging my bad ankle.

"Oww. Why'd you do that?" I said.

"Didn't want to let you go."

After a few minutes, we gathered ourselves together and shuffled to a bedroom at the back of the house, dragging our discarded clothes with us. Anna stretched out on the bed and I lay next to her—she was so beautiful, I couldn't keep my eyes from her. She looked at me, both amused and affectionate, as I ran my fingertips down the slope of her body. There was a lot to be said between us, but in the aftershock of our coupling, it could wait.

The room was sparsely furnished, like a ship's cabin, with a glass full of white seashells on a table next to the bed and a tapestry hung on a wall. Her yoga mat was unrolled at the foot of the bed, and some of her clothes were gathered in a neat pile on a chest. Through the window, I could see a field of rushes bordering a pond that stretched out to the bay side of the lane. The sky glowed as the sun faded over the water, purples and reds mixing with the dark blue of dusk. I wanted never to move.

"Is this your Goldilocks bed?" I said.

"This is the one." She reached to brush a strand of hair from my forehead.

"Let's just stay here."

We had to get up eventually to wash, to eat. It was night when we did, and Anna took a bath while I hunted around the kitchen for food. I found some spaghetti and chopped up onions and garlic for the base of a tomato sauce while I listened to her soap herself. I found candles in one cupboard and I took one to the bathroom and set it beside her. In the kitchen, I placed others on the table and dimmed the lights so that they glowed next to the plates and glasses. I kept the curtains facing the main house closed but raised a blind on a window at the end of the room to let in a square of night sky. The stars glittered and I could see the wash of the Milky Way.

When Anna came out of the bathroom, she was wearing a silk robe and her hair was bundled in a twisted towel above her head, like a turban. She walked over to the saucepan and tasted the sauce.

"Mmm," she said. "You can move in."

She sat and I served the food, looping the pasta into a bowl and pouring some wine. Then I sat opposite her and we ate happily. I was reaching for the wine bottle to refill her glass when I saw a light shining over her shoulder through the open blind. It was far away in the distance, and at first I thought it might be the reflection of the moon from a house. But as I watched the beam snaking from side to side, I saw it was a car's headlights tracing the road along the coast. Anna kept on eating, her back to it, so I followed its progress alone, waiting for it to turn down a side road and leave us in peace. But it didn't. It kept on coming until it disappeared for ten seconds behind a house and reemerged, this time near enough that the single light had split into two, driving straight toward us along the lane.

"Anna," I said.

"What?" she said, looking up with a smear of sauce on her chin, then seeing my face and turning around.

I pinched out the candles between my finger and thumb, darkening the room so the driver would not see us. Then we stared from the window in dumb amazement, trapped at the end of this cul-de-sac far from the safety of the city. Anna rose without speaking and walked to the far side of the room, as if she could evade it by hiding, while I sat frozen, watching its movement like that of an arrow with the two of us as its target. As I got to my feet, it went over a bump and the headlights jumped upward, shining into the room and illuminating me. I ducked, but it was too late.

The lights went past the open window and we heard the sound of the vehicle for the first time as it came to a halt by the foot of the Shapiros' lane, the hum of its engine idling. I reached for Anna's hand and she held mine as we stood there half-naked. The glow penetrated the gap in the curtains near us and shone across the room. Then it faded and turned a fainter red as the car moved again, turning left up the drive to the Shapiros' house. I could hear it take the hill rapidly and the crunch of the gravel spurted out from its tires, as if the driver weren't familiar with the slope. *My car,* I thought. *I left it by the house.* We walked to the room adjoining the kitchen at the front. There was a sofa by the window and we knelt on it, her robe slithering with a silken hiss.

I reached to part the curtains for us to peer through, hearing her soft breath and feeling her warmth next to my face. She was panting slightly—now out of fear rather than desire. She placed her face beneath mine to look through the parting and we gazed up along the drive, past the split-rail fence and the weeping trees. The car had halted next to mine and the driver was climbing out. I still half wondered if it might be Nathan, having ignored our agreement for him to return to the city. *What if he catches us together like this?* I thought. *He's going to strangle me properly this time.* I didn't believe it, though. I knew it hadn't been a man behind the wheel of the car. It was a woman—the one who'd controlled this affair all along and who had fooled everyone but Harry.

As she extinguished the headlights and stepped out of the car, her face was shrouded by dark. A cloud covered the moon and only her outline was visible against the still-glowing sky. She stood by her car, then walked to mine and stepped around it at a slow, deliberate pace, as if inspecting it for damage. She bent to look through one window, then straightened and stepped onto the lawn, disappearing from sight.

"Where's she going?" Anna whispered.

"I don't know. I can't—"

I stopped speaking as the woman reappeared from behind the house and walked up to the kitchen door. She reached into her handbag for a key and unlocked it. As she walked inside, I expected her to turn on the lights, but the room remained in darkness. We had a vista of the front of the house, but it was useless without light. Then the moon emerged from behind the clouds. It shone through the conservatory and cast a glow in the living room. It was empty for a minute or two, until the woman entered the room from the hallway. She walked across the room and then halted in the middle on the spot where Greene had died.

I glanced briefly down at Anna, her lips open and her breasts uncovered by the robe, before the woman regained my attention. She moved toward the kitchen and flicked on the lights as she entered, clearly visible for the first time. She stopped at the brushed-steel intercom by the door and pressed a button, as I'd seen Anna do the first time I'd been in that room. As she did, there was an electronic crackle in the room, and I remembered Anna telling me that the whole estate was wired.

"Dr. Cowper?" said a disembodied voice.

We both flinched, and Anna's face, pale with panic, gazed at mine. She shook her head, imploring me not to answer.

"I know you're there," the voice said matter-of-factly.

Anna looked at me again and I shrugged. There was no way out of the cottage except through the front door, straight into our tormentor's line of sight. The rear of the building led to ponds and reeds, and I could hardly walk, let alone climb out of a window and swim. The only shred of privacy we had left was that Anna hadn't been caught in the headlights with me. I couldn't sacrifice that.

"Yes, Mrs. Shapiro?" I said.

"Come here," Nora said.

28

I stepped through the front door of the cottage into the night air. It was cool to the skin, the last warmth of the afternoon gone, and I walked down the path where I'd stood with Anna a few hours before. Then I crossed the lane to the bottom of the Shapiros' drive. The moon was full in the sky, and the night was silent: no sirens, no city hubbub, nothing but the hiss of the sea. As I started to walk up the drive, the crunch of my feet on the gravel echoed in the night.

Passing this way by car, concentrating on taking the turn up the hill in the daylight, I hadn't noticed that the drooping trees formed a tunnel, blocking the house from view until the last minute, like the long drive to a country mansion. It was more artful than I'd taken the time to realize. I looked up at the house as I walked but couldn't see anything through the trees except the glow of lights. I rounded the

last curve and there in front of me were two cars: my own and Nora's
Range Rover.

I walked the last few steps to my car and pulled open the front
passenger door as softly as I could. The car wasn't locked because I
hadn't bothered when I'd arrived, but things were different now. Nathan had caught me defenseless out by the airfield and I needed a
means of protecting myself. Leaning into the car, I pulled open the
compartment in front of the passenger seat. I removed a small package and placed it in my pocket.

The kitchen door gave to my touch. I stepped inside to see Nora's
leather bag on the counter, the one from which she'd extracted Harry's gun as I'd sat with her in the waiting room of the ER. The kitchen
was bare: the cutlery was put away, the plates stacked. Dust from the
renovation had been wiped from the kitchen surfaces so thoroughly
that I doubted if there were fingerprints left. The door on the far side
of the room was half-ajar, displaying a glow from the living room. I
paused for a second, thinking of watching Nora and Anna together in
this kitchen on my first visit. Her arm had hung around Anna's shoulders as if in casual friendship, but the gesture felt freighted now—
a display of dominance.

"Come through," Nora called from the next room.

I walked to the steel intercom and pressed a button on its façade,
making a light on it glow red. Then I opened the door and went
through to the living room. The room was bathed in a soft light from
the moon and a lamp next to an armchair at the far end of the room.
It was dim where I stood, looking across the room.

Nora was thirty feet from me. She was sitting in the seat under the
lamp and her face was pale, immobile. She held a gun in her right
hand, trained on me. It was the Beretta that she'd retrieved from the
safe. I'd seen that weapon before and even handled it, but I'd never
observed it from that angle. I stared helplessly into the tiny hole of the
muzzle, the sight notched above it on the barrel. She waved the gun
in the direction of the sofa opposite her, like a short wand. I hesitated,
but there was nothing I could do. I walked to the sofa obediently and
sat down where she'd indicated. We were about ten feet apart, slightly

farther than a psych and his patient, with her looking at me and me gazing back. There was no question about who was in charge.

From close up, I could see that her face was a mask of exhaustion. She'd never resorted to Botox or the knife, and her makeup was no longer doing its job. All of the softness I'd seen in her before had disappeared, leaving only an intimidating blank.

"You don't need a gun, Mrs. Shapiro," I said.

"You tell me what I've got to lose," she said, keeping the weapon pointing at me as she spoke. "The Episcopal sticker on your car let me know I'd find you in here. But where's Anna? Pretty little Anna."

I'd never heard such awful, dead cynicism in her voice before. Of all those who'd fooled me, she done it most adroitly. The woman in front of me felt completely different from the one I'd believed I'd known.

"I told her to leave. She's gone somewhere safer," I said, trying to control the quiver in my voice.

"You *told* her, did you?" Nora said in a tone of ridicule. "She used to take her orders from me, but I can see things have changed."

She scared me, but the sting of her betrayal hurt worse. I'd had a few hours to become accustomed to the truth, but it would take a lot longer than that to get over it. Why had I placed such faith in her from the first moment we'd met? She hadn't needed to work hard to deceive me because she had been my fantasy—the calm, devoted wife of an aggressive, selfish man. I'd rushed to help her without pausing to examine her story.

That was my failure, I knew now. It wasn't Harry I'd misdiagnosed in the psych ER—it was Nora. She'd been able to play me because I'd yearned to believe in her. She'd become the mother I still missed, and I'd rushed to take vengeance on the man I thought had betrayed her. My life was spent disentangling the psychological traps into which people fell, yet she'd lured me into the oldest one of all.

"The first time we met," I said, "did you know then what you were going to do? I believed everything you told me."

Nora smiled faintly, but the blank look in her eyes didn't alter.

"I didn't lie to you. Not then. I found him with the gun that afternoon. Just through there." She pointed to the wall behind which Harry's study was located. "He looked so haunted, as if he'd lost everything. I was scared for him. Then I held him and he broke down. He told me about that *woman*."

She pronounced the word with distaste and then paused for a few seconds, purging the memory again. Then she went on talking in a low, steady voice with her eyes blank. It was a kind of therapy for her, I realized, and I tried to encourage her by saying little, not even looking at the gun. It was some sort of redemption to be able to use the skills she'd abused to keep her from killing me.

"You must have felt hurt," I prompted her.

"Hurt?" she said contemptuously. "I didn't care about *her*. She thought she knew him, but he'd already forgotten her. It was Greene who'd taken him away from me. Harry was going to kill himself, but Greene had pulled the trigger. I'd only just caught Harry in time. If I hadn't, Marcus would have finished him."

"When did you decide what to do?"

"It was after you'd admitted him to the hospital. He was in a wheelchair and you'd taken his clothes away. He'd been stripped bare and humiliated. He was being wheeled away from me and this rage started to boil up inside of me. It wasn't Harry who deserved to die, I thought. It was the man who'd done that to him."

I remembered that scene. I'd witnessed it myself from another angle, in the hallway of the psych ER—Harry in the wheelchair with his notes on his lap, Pete O'Meara pushing him to the elevator silently, and Nora watching them. I'd believed she was just looking on sadly, with love for her shattered husband, not realizing the fantasy that was taking shape in her mind.

Nora looked at me with resolute, still eyes. She wasn't caught up in passion and self-pity as Harry had been—she was capable of murder. She gestured with her gun as she spoke, but it swung back to me as if drawn by magnetism.

"After I'd left Harry, I went home and thought. I knew I had a choice. Either I left it to you and you'd give him pills and talk to him, get him to accept defeat, or we could fight. That was the only way I'd get my Harry back and not a shadow. I realized that you'd given him an alibi. He couldn't be convicted of murder if we acted fast."

"Why did you choose me?" I said, remembering the moment I'd arrived at Episcopal on Monday morning to be told by Jim Whitehead that Harry had refused to be treated by anyone else. He'd come in on Saturday to see Harry, he'd told me, but the Shapiros had wanted their privacy. Now I knew why.

"You'd been kind in the emergency room and you were young. Whitehead was older and more obstinate. I thought you'd be, I don't know . . ."

"Malleable?" I suggested.

"Oh, dear. That sounds bad," she said, as if it mattered anymore what word I used. "I just thought you wouldn't ask questions. Sarah was so eager to help."

She certainly was, I thought. When I looked back on it, Nora had expertly ambushed me. Duncan and Harry had appeared to be forcing me to do what he wanted, but Nora had fixed the whole thing. The image of her sitting on the bed in Harry's room in York East as we had discussed him came back to me—both mother and seductress.

"You went to all that trouble and he still wouldn't do what you wanted. How did you feel about that?" I said.

It was the harshest question I'd asked, but I was already tired of playing along with her narrative. It had a weird logic, killing Greene in order to save her husband. Yet kill him Nora had. Harry's confession to the crime had been a concoction.

"You can take the credit for that," Nora said, regarding me coldly. "You were too good at your job. You got him talking on the beach and he told you things he shouldn't have. After you'd left, he told me he was thinking of therapy."

She laughed as if my profession were absurd, and for the first time since I'd known her, I started to hate her. All the kindness she'd shown me—how she'd flown me on their jet to London and asked after my father—had been calculated. She hadn't wanted to lose me as Harry's doctor because she'd thought I'd be compliant.

"By Saturday, I got tired of waiting," she said. "I called Felix and he came over to the apartment. I said I knew what he'd done to Harry and he was a spineless coward. He said he'd try to make it up, so I told him what to do."

That was what Felix meant, I thought. He had walked into the sea and drowned himself. Was that the act of a man who'd merely been indiscreet about Harry's affair to his old friends at Rosenthal? That shouldn't have been enough to prompt suicide. Felix had been far more involved in Greene's murder than he'd confessed, and he'd known that his deception was unraveling. Nora had made him pay dearly for his betrayal of Harry.

"Felix called Marcus and told him he should contact us that afternoon. When he called, I said Harry wanted to see him in East Hampton later. Harry was in a bad way, not coherent. The pills hadn't helped, they'd made it worse. He was lying on his bed, really depressed. I took him to the car and I drove him out there. We left Felix in the apartment. I thought he might be needed.

"When we arrived, I gave Harry the Beretta and told him what to do. He was shaking and sweating, very ill. I was so sad for him. I went to the study and I waited. I heard the whole thing on the intercom. Harry brought Greene in here. He'd just walked from Sagaponack, he said. It was such a nice day. Harry told him he knew everything he'd done, and Greene just laughed. 'Too late now, Harry,' he said.

"I waited for Harry to do it, but he was too far gone. It was like Greene had cast a spell over him. I wasn't thinking straight. My head felt jammed and I couldn't hear myself breathe. I'd brought a gun from New York. I walked out of the study and along the back of the house. I saw Marcus with his back to me. I came through the conservatory. He didn't notice me until I was inside."

"You killed him?" I asked.

"He turned toward me. He looked shocked, like he couldn't grasp it, when he saw the gun, I remember. Then he smiled. I don't think he thought I could do it. He was stupid. When Harry bought that gun for me, there was something I didn't tell you. I learned to use it on a range."

As she said it, she swung the Beretta up with both hands, one wrapped over the other around the stock, and pointed it directly at me. Her arms briefly locked in position and my heart raced. Then she lowered it, the demonstration over.

"I didn't say anything, I just shot him in the chest. He went down and lay on the ground twitching. There was a lot of blood right away. I knew he was dying."

I thought of the photo of Greene lying on the floor that Pagonis had pushed in front of me at Yaphank, and I glanced at the spot on the floor where Anna had made me stand to punish me. I'd had no idea what she'd really meant.

"Did you try to save him?"

"Why would I have done that?" she said, as if the idea were stupid. "I wanted him out of our lives forever. I wanted Harry back."

"You got what you wanted, then?"

She looked happy for the first time, remembering it. "I did. It was as if the sound of the gun woke Harry up. He took charge. I was standing here, shocked at what I'd done. He took the gun from me and said, 'You have to leave.' He wiped off my prints and he fired it again out of the window."

Nora waved the gun toward the ocean, as if indicating the path of the bullet. "That's what saved Harry," she said. "Not pills. Not a *talk* about it."

She kept saying that word—*talk, talk, talk*—and every time she did, she sounded more scathing. I wondered if she hated me as much as my profession, and if that was why she was holding a gun on me. I'd defied the rules of psychiatry, but I'd found her by asking questions. Asking questions had its uses. It occurred to me as I listened that Pagonis had a lot to answer for. She'd taken Nora at her word and instead tried to bully me into undermining Harry's defense. The fingerprints on the gun, the powder burns on Harry's hands, the call to New York from East Hampton—she'd fallen for everything that Nora had faked to throw her off the trail. I'd been naïve, but her performance had been terrible.

"I called Felix in New York to tell him to come for me," she went on. "I knew I couldn't leave in the Range Rover. Harry had to have driven it there. There was only one way to escape. On foot."

I nodded, for I knew where she'd gone. *Look around,* Anna had called to me. Nora had killed Greene in the room where we sat, yards from their lawn and beyond that the steps down the dune to their private wilderness. It was labeled public, but it wasn't really. No stranger could make it there without approval. Greene had died in a cottage with a ready-made escape route—that's where Nora had lured him.

"I walked along the beach until I got close to Water Mill. There's a road that leads down to the dunes there and I waited for Felix to come and pick me up. He had a place near there. I went to shower and clean myself off. Then we drove back to the house."

She stopped talking, exhausted, and I tried to work out what to do next. The talk had delayed the moment of confrontation, but she'd soon either have to put the gun down or use it—we couldn't stay in this standoff forever. Whenever I was caught with patients who could turn violent, I retreated. That wasn't an option here. Her eyes looked slightly softer, some of the steeliness gone.

"I think you should give me that, Mrs. Shapiro," I said, holding out a hand toward her and trying not to look threatening.

Nora looked at me blankly as I reached forward. I still remember her expression, its utter lack of emotion, because of what happened next. She said nothing at all. She simply pulled the trigger of the automatic. There was a deafening roar and I can picture a flash from the muzzle, but I may be imagining it. I lurched backward with shock, but she stayed in the same position, with the gun still pointed at me. The surge of adrenaline made me quiver, but after a few seconds, I realized that she'd fired over my shoulder.

"Get up," she said, and the blankness in her face was matched by the monotone of her voice. There was nothing I could engage with in her—the affect of the truly dangerous—so I obeyed.

"Walk backward. Keep facing me," she said.

When I'd got to where Greene had died, she told me to halt. She was now fifteen feet away—an impossible gap for me to cover safely, but probably close enough for her to shoot me. She'd killed Greene at that distance. Time was moving very slowly, or the adrenaline made it seem like that. Every move felt as if it took an age to complete.

Then, over her shoulder, I saw something glint. It was the conservatory door opening in the moonlight as Anna stepped through. I couldn't let my eyes linger for fear of being noticed, so I kept them on Nora's face and half monitored the blurred shape growing behind her like a ghost. The room was silent. Even knowing that Anna was there, I couldn't hear her walking. She trod lightly and the sound of the gunshot had been so loud that my hearing was muffled, so Nora's probably was, too. It felt like a surreal reconstruction of the story that Nora had told me, with Anna in Nora's place, walking through the room unnoticed. Nora drew up her left hand to grip the gun, wrapping her fingers around her right hand again.

"Don't do this, Mrs. Shapiro," I said, trying to make my voice sound soothing rather than challenging. "We can sort it out."

"I don't believe you," she said. Her arms shifted slightly and stiffened as if readying herself to fire. As they did, Anna called from behind her.

"Nora," she said. "Put it down."

She spoke gently, but the sound broke the silence in the room as completely as the gunshot and Nora flinched. She swung around, the gun turning with her, and I launched myself forward, reaching into my pocket.

I had a half-conscious fear that it would be like my dream, when my feet had slipped on the wooden floor as I'd tried to reach the stricken Harry, but the nightmare didn't come true. My shoes gripped the floor and I ran as fast as I could. Mortal fear and adrenaline do amazing things. I reached Nora in five long strides with my right hand high in the air, holding a syringe of Haldol and Ativan.

Nora started to turn back as she heard my steps behind her, but it was too late. I flung my elbow around her neck, hitting her arm to push the gun away from Anna, and toppled her forward. As we fell, I slammed my right hand down and plunged the syringe into her thigh, as close as I could to her gluteus maximus, where the big muscles would absorb the chemicals into her blood fastest. The gun fell from her hand, skittering across the floor as I squeezed the plunger. The drugs overwhelmed her within fifteen seconds.

I rolled off her body, now slumped facedown; she was unconscious. We had an hour or more before she came around—I'd loaded the dose for a grown man just in case. I sat there dazed, hardly taking anything in and only half-aware of Anna. Then I felt her arms reach around me and I started to shake with relief.

"Are you hurt? Are you hurt?" she cried.

"You're a complete idiot," I said, holding one of her hands in mine. "You could have been killed. What possessed you?"

"I heard what she was saying on the intercom. She was going to kill you. I heard the shot and I ran. I didn't want to lose you."

I turned around and kissed her, and then we stayed half-slumped on the floor, with Nora's body next to us, until we'd settled down. Then I got up and fished the card out of my top pocket that bore Pagonis's cellphone number. From this point onward, I was going to play by the rules.

We sat side by side on the sofa. Anna was in a tracksuit, a T-shirt, and white socks stained green by the lawn.

"She was *wulnerable* from the south," I said, nodding at Nora's inert body.

Anna gave a weak laugh and slapped my hand.

"When did you know?" I said.

"She went to see Margaret Greene. I think it had something to do with you. That's what she said. But Nathan was there and he told her about seeing you with me. When she came back, she was in a terrible temper. I'd never seen her like that before. She told me I had to drop you. I'd regret it if I didn't, she said."

"I remember that," I said, thinking of finding Anna in Le Pain Quotidien and how her manner had changed.

"She sent me out here, like I was in exile, and it gave me time to think. I wondered if I'd got Nora wrong—that thing about us being best friends. The more I thought, the more frightened I was. I realized her story didn't make sense."

Anna hadn't been the only one to experience Nora's other side. As I'd sat by the woods with Nathan, he'd recalled how she'd played on his jealousy of me. After I'd told her that I was deserting Harry, she'd called Nathan again. *He's been with your girlfriend again and he's going to get away with murder. I can't stop him without your help,* she'd said to him. He'd been easy for her to manipulate—in despair about his father's death and angry with me. He had never been stable, as Anna had said. Anna had confessed to Nora as well as her therapist about how he'd cycled between charm and cruelty, like his dead father.

Nora had sent Nathan to get rid of me, counting on him being so out of control that he'd tear me apart the way he'd slashed Rebecca's dress. But Nathan was more emotional than his father and less polished. He lacked focus. He'd rushed after me again before he'd even known what he'd do if he caught up. Instead of coming for me with a knife or a gun, as she'd counted on, he'd used his hands. She hadn't been able to correct Nathan's mistakes the way she'd corrected Harry's. So I'd survived.

I held Anna's hand. "Poor you," I said.

"Then you rescued me."

"You rescued *me*."

She put her head on my shoulder and we stayed like that for five minutes, next to Nora's body. Then I heard sirens along the lane and watched the conservatory windows flashing blue and red.

29

Pagonis burst through the door first, with Hodge right behind her. She had her gun drawn in front of her, but when she saw us sitting together on the sofa and Nora immobilized on the floor, she placed it back in her holster.

The fact that no one was firing at her didn't seem to make her any happier. She had a dark, glowering expression on her face as she looked at me. She walked over to Nora and bent down to check her pulse as if unable to credit the story I'd told her on the phone. Finally, she called in the uniforms behind her. They came into the room in force—the village police, a paramedic crew, and others I couldn't place.

Pagonis approached us and spoke to me alone, treating Anna as if she weren't beside me—as if she really had been a ghost.

"Bag his hands," she said to Hodge.

"What?" I said indignantly.

"There's been gunfire here and there's a woman on the ground. I want to know who fired the weapon. I'm testing you for powder," she said.

"Maybe you should have tested her for powder the first time round. You might have saved a lot of trouble," I said, pointing at Nora.

I felt that one strike home. Despite all her bluster, she'd missed Greene's killer at the start, not even submitting Nora to an examination when she'd arrived back on the murder scene later that night. It was understandable, given that the obvious suspect had already confessed, but it didn't look very good. Hodge reached into a case and produced two plastic bags, which he ceremoniously placed over my hands and taped at the wrists. Anna silently held out her hands, too, but Hodge ignored her.

"She fired the gun at me. There's probably a bullet in the woodwork over there," I said. "You're wasting your time."

Pagonis sighed heavily, as if feeling the weight of every frustration and misdirection she'd faced during the investigation. I could see it dawning on her that the only charge she could bring against me was assaulting Greene's killer. The paramedics had now turned Nora on her back and were checking her reflexes and her blood pressure.

"I subdued her with an intramuscular shot. Five milligrams of Haldol and two of Ativan. The syringe is over there," I called across to them, pointing to the middle of the floor where I'd dropped it.

"Okay, let's find somewhere to talk," Pagonis said. She beckoned to us, acknowledging Anna for the first time. "Mike, you go with her to the hospital. Don't let her go."

She gestured at Nora, who was being lifted onto a gurney by the medics and was about to be wheeled away to an ambulance. Hodge gave me one last hostile look before following. Anna and I followed Pagonis out of the living room, looking faintly ridiculous—Anna in socks and me with plastic bags taped over my hands. I wasn't worried, though. We weren't the ones who would come out of this looking stupid. As we left the room, it was filling up with white-overalled technicians preparing for another round of swabbing and sampling.

We walked into Nora's study and sat near the window.

"So what the hell's been going on?" Pagonis said.

"Shouldn't you read me my rights?" I said.

"Forget it," she said wearily. "You're not under arrest. You're not going to be under arrest. You're just a witness. Okay?"

I should have refused to talk to her and called Joe, but I wasn't too worried anymore and I felt a bit sorry for her. So I started to talk and explained the story as best I could, with Anna interjecting the odd supportive comment from beside me. Pagonis looked more and more unhappy as we talked.

It was a small thing that had made me first question Nora's story: the image of her by the Range Rover in Green-Wood Cemetery. It was the vehicle in which Anna had driven me to New York, the one I'd seen in the Fox News helicopter shot in my gym that Sunday. Nora and Felix had both told me that Harry had disappeared from his apartment in New York that Saturday and driven to East Hampton from the Shapiros' building. Once I'd stopped to consider, that made no sense. For years, Harry's life had been one chauffeured Town Car and piloted Gulfstream after another. Even the old Harry wouldn't have thought of driving himself there: it was out of the question for the man I'd known. Only Nora could have done it.

The Range Rover had meant nothing to Pagonis. The Shapiros inhabited a world with so many houses, so many cars, even a jet, that they wouldn't have wondered at the use of one vehicle. But to anyone who knew Nora, it jarred. She hadn't been infantilized by wealth like Harry: she knew her way around the world.

"Oh, shit," Pagonis said finally. "I don't know how we're going to clean this up. You'll have to provide a statement. Doctor, I don't understand you. One minute you won't tell us anything about Shapiro, the next you're tackling his wife."

"She wasn't my patient," I said.

———

After living through Joe's diminishing faith in my prospects of survival, I enjoyed seeing his face when I told him what I'd been doing the previous day. I'd got back from Yaphank with Anna at two a.m. after Pagonis had let us go.

"You're kidding me, right?" he said.

"It's all true."

We were sitting in his office on a sunny Manhattan morning, light reflecting off the skyscrapers through his broad windows. He was at his desk, checking a couple of law books and looking up cases on his computer screen. He seemed less disheveled than I'd seen him before, with his shirt buttoned up and his hair brushed neatly. Perhaps it was later in the day, when the vagaries of law and oddities of his clients had agitated him too much, that his body burst out of its confines. His smile broadened steadily as he looked at the screen, and when he turned to me to summarize, it was a full-blown grin.

"It's over," he said. "Finito, kaput."

Coming from a professional pessimist, that was surprisingly categorical. I'd worked out that Harry not having killed Greene had to be good for me, but I wasn't sure if my responsibility transferred wholesale to Nora. It turned out, however, that my retort to Pagonis about Nora was the crucial legal point.

"There's no wrongful death here, not for Episcopal, anyway, and no misconduct. You weren't treating Mrs. Shapiro and you didn't discharge her, so you're not responsible for what she did. It's got nothing to do with you."

"Pagonis said they'd want to interview me again."

Joe dismissed that with a wave of the hand. "Sure, they might want to find out what happened. You seem to know a lot more about it than they do. But there's no civil case and the grand jury testimony's irrelevant. Baer will have to put that in the trash. You made a judgment that Shapiro was safe to be discharged, and guess what? You were right. You could have flown around the world in their Gulfstream and it wouldn't matter. The wrongful death is on Mrs. Shapiro, and they can wrestle it out with Mrs. Greene."

I gave Joe the treat of calling my father with the news, since he deserved it for what I'd put him through. While he did that, chuckling happily over legal points that appeared to amuse them both, I sat with my coffee and the buzz of Anna's desire for me and gazed at the thicket of the Manhattan skyline, the view granted only to the city's leviathans and power brokers. From this vantage point, it was tempting to believe you could do anything—that an underling would spring out to fulfill any wish. That had been Harry's life until it had been taken from him, and he had never adjusted to losing it. He'd needed Nora to do everything.

Joe showed me to the elevator in an expansive mood, putting his hand up to my shoulder as we waited for its arrival.

"Take care of your father. I'll see you soon."

"I'll tell you the whole story one day."

He had a gleam in his eye as he held back the elevator door for me. "Ben, as your attorney, I don't want to know."

"Can I show you something?" Lauren asked.

We were in the parlor floor of her house and she led me to a table in the corner, on which stood a maroon instrument case. She snapped open the latches with her long fingers and lifted out a violin. I could tell that it was valuable even though I knew little about them. It had a faded golden patina, and the pattern on the back as she swiveled it over was striped like a tiger's fur. Near the edge, where the chin rest was clipped to the body, the polish was worn away.

"It's lovely," I said.

"Isn't it? It's a Guadagnini, made in 1773. I never thought I'd ever own a violin like this—I bought it at Sotheby's in London two years ago. It cost me £340,000."

"That's a lot of money."

"It is. I learned the violin when I was young, but I was never quite good enough to play professionally. I became a banker, and you know what? It meant no one had to lend me this. I could buy it for myself. That's what money means to me—this violin, and this house. My husband said the money would do better in Treasuries."

She laughed and stroked the instrument. Lauren seemed to have made the opposite transition in personality to Nora. Her sharpness and wariness had eased, replaced by someone I could imagine having a nap in Gabriel's chair—or even being a friend in another life. When I'd called, she'd invited me to visit her as if our last encounter were forgotten. She made coffee and we sat under the crab apple tree in her yard.

"I wasn't sure about you for a while," I said. "You lied to me about not having seen Harry. You'd been to Riverhead. That stamp was on your hand."

I prodded a finger on the back of my left hand to indicate the circular mark that had been on hers, and she shook her head ruefully.

"I wasn't thinking straight that afternoon."

"You threatened me, Lauren," I said gently.

"I'm sorry. It wasn't meant as a threat. Things were falling apart and I didn't know what you'd do. I'd just found out from Harry about what Nathan Greene had done to you. You'd broken the rules by coming to my house. You frightened me."

Reaching out of the frame of therapy had been more effective than I'd known at the time. That was what Henderson had said as he'd heard my story in Washington: *If you'll forgive the description, you're a loose cannon.*

"I wouldn't have betrayed your confidence," I said. "I knew you'd come for treatment to shield yourself but I did take an oath. I'd have honored it."

"You got pretty badly treated, didn't you?" Lauren said, looking at me sympathetically. "Underwood's such a reptile."

"What do you mean?" I asked. I thought I'd known everything, but there was one more layer of deception.

"You didn't know?" she said. "He blabbed to the detectives about you flying on Harry's jet. I saw Peter Freeman the other day. He's a decent guy. He told me he'd been on that trip. He said Underwood had laughed about it. He thought you deserved it, Peter said."

Felix had been annoyed when Underwood had pushed his way onto our flight, but I was the one who'd ended up suffering. I thought of the nasty smirk on Underwood's face as he had given me his tour of Seligman Brothers.

"God," I said. "That man really is a jerk."

"He'd sell his mother for a bonus," she said. "He was the one who told Greene about me. I'd found the whole thing—the Elements, Rosenthal, everything. I was about to tell Harry when Greene trapped me. It wasn't just that he blackmailed me; it was the way he did it, the pleasure he took in humiliating me." She shuddered briefly. "You think Underwood's a jerk? He's got nothing on Greene."

"And Mr. Shapiro?"

"I did love Harry. I told you it was nothing, but I lied. That's over now, though. I went to see him in East Hampton. Anna drove me. I felt so terrible about it—the way I'd let him down to save my skin. He said it wasn't my fault."

Her voice trailed away and she looked across her yard to where a patch of sunlight had settled on a weathered brick wall.

"When I saw you, he'd let me visit him in Riverhead at last. All he could talk about was her, how great she was. I knew I'd lost him, but I hadn't realized why until then. That's the irony. I wanted them to separate and now they'll be apart for life. Too late, though."

It was a cold-blooded thing to say, but I was beyond shock. Nora had killed Greene to get Harry back. Lauren wasn't violent, but she was ruthless in her way. Whatever Harry's flaws, he had the knack of being wanted. I sipped my coffee and looked up into the branches of the tree. There was a red cardinal hidden in the leaves. Nature was so weirdly bright and exotic in New York when it poked through the concrete and skyscrapers.

After we'd finished, she opened her front door to let me out onto the street. I left her alone on her stoop, clearing the scattered flyers.

Sarah Duncan had survival instincts that I'd come to appreciate: she didn't look back. The past was another country to her, one that she had no intention of visiting given its dangerous reputation.

By the time I sauntered into her office the following day, still en-

joying the sensations of love and professional salvation, the news had
reached her that the hospital's legal liability in the Shapiro case had
been lifted and a member of her board was being interrogated in
Yaphank for murder. It hadn't yet made the evening news, so there
was a curious lull for those who knew about Nora before bedlam
struck again, and Duncan didn't hang around. Seconds after my arrival, a summons came.

"This is shocking news," she said after I'd been speeded into her
sanctum in a record-breaking five minutes. "I'd come to regard Nora
as a friend."

She didn't look in the least perturbed, and her slightly more distant way of phrasing their relationship felt as if it would be the first
in a series of downgrades. This time, she'd come to sit by me on the
sofa and had rustled up a bottle of sparkling water. Lots of people
seemed to have regained their respect for me suddenly.

"Tell me about you," she said. "How do you feel? It must be a
relief."

"Do you still want my resignation?"

"Resignation?" she said, frowning. "I don't know why you'd resign, Dr. Cowper. You are a valued member of our team. We have
great hopes for you."

With that, as far as Episcopal was concerned, the affair was filed
and forgotten. Within months, she'd found a way to remove Nora's
and Harry's names from the pavilion and from the plaque above the
FDR Drive. A hedge fund manager who'd made billions by shorting
mortgage-backed securities came forward and the Shapiros disappeared into the recesses of the hospital's history.

I saw Harry once after that, when they'd indicted Nora and had let
him out of the Riverhead jail. There was talk of charging him as an
accomplice, but Baer needed Nora to testify against him. She wouldn't
do it voluntarily, and as Harry's wife, she couldn't be compelled.

It was August by then, in the full gridlock of a Long Island summer, with cars jamming the Long Island Expressway and crawling

down Route 27. East Hampton was one long line of vacationers, and I felt a proprietary sense of resentment at having to squeeze past a pickup truck with surfboards in the back that had halted by the village pond. *I've come to visit a resident,* I thought. *Why are you here?* Not just any resident, it turned out. The Shapiros' house had become a draw on the tourist circuit, and when I reached the end of the lane, there was a security guard checking credentials. The sign saying PRIVATE ROAD was bigger than before. He waved me past and I drove slowly down the lane, trying to spot the bump that Nora's Range Rover had hit that night, catching my face in its headlights.

A middle-aged man wearing a white jacket like a chef's opened the door to my knock. He regarded me sternly, as if I were being overfamiliar by coming to the kitchen rather than the main entrance, which I'd never used. Once I'd announced my business, he softened a little and led me through to Harry's study, where the ex-jailbird sat with a book. Harry rose and clasped my hand, taking off his glasses and resting them on the desk.

"Come on, let's take a walk," he said.

We strolled through the conservatory, which had been redecorated yet again, and crossed the lawn to the dunes. Harry was still thinner than when I'd first met him, and there was some hesitation in his stride. He took the steps gingerly, as if they might give way.

"You've got new staff," I said conversationally.

"Thomas is here now. He runs the place. That girl had to go after what she did. Oh yes, she's . . . Nora told me," he said.

He grinned as if, whatever he thought of Anna, he could appreciate man-to-man my having fallen for her. It was the first time he'd ever shown any interest in my life, and I found it endearing.

"How are you feeling?" I said as we reached the beach and walked by the sea.

"I'm okay. It's Nora I worry about."

I stopped walking at the mention of his wife's name. We were about two hundred yards along the sand to the west—the same route taken by Nora on the night of the killing, and by Anna, too. Far in the distance, I saw a lone figure walking down the beach. The wind was blowing off the sea and Harry shielded his eyes as he looked at me.

"I won't apologize for what I did, Mr. Shapiro, because I'd be lying. But I am sorry you're apart from your wife."

"You had a right to defend yourself," he said sadly.

We walked on for two minutes in silence before Harry spoke again.

"You know about Lauren, don't you? She came to see me in Riverhead, and I told her we couldn't see each other again. I don't blame her for running away, but Nora stuck with me. My wife's an amazing woman, isn't she?"

"Remarkable," I replied.

30

Unlike Duncan, I found it hard to write off what happened to experience, the kind of character-forming incident you recall happily in age, marveling at your innocence. I did think of staying at Episcopal. It would have been easy enough, once Jim Whitehead had extended an olive branch, but I couldn't bring myself to do it.

The past means something to shrinks—we can't dismiss it as Duncan wanted me to. I'd escaped punishment and my reputation had been restored, but I felt guilty. Harry had been my patient and I'd let him down. If I'd kept him in there for a while longer, Nora's plan would have fallen apart. Felix had been my companion in distress, and I should have saved him. The joy had gone out of my time in New York when Harry had walked into the psych ER, and it wasn't going to return.

The climate is different here: damper, softer, and less brazen than New York's. It has its pleasures, though they're subtle. I miss the pure skies, the monsoonlike storms—they have the city's bluntness. I swapped my apartment off Gramercy Park for a house in Kew, a cottage next to the towpath, tucked near a concrete wall they'd built to stop the river from flooding. "It used to get quite damp," an old man who's lived here forever told me when I arrived. Sometimes at night I hear the groan of the river flowing out to the estuary.

Anna loves it, and I hope she doesn't fall out of love. I bought her a rainproof jacket and Wellington boots as preparation for the English mud and rain, and she is sweetly enveloped in them as she strides along by the water's edge. It was a crazy way to start a relationship, but none of them are fully rational. If they were, I'd be out of business. She's been here twice and we are still tentative—neither of us wants to push our luck.

There's plenty of work for a psych in London, with everyone getting in touch with the feelings they used to hide away. There is the same proportion of madness, too, although I haven't settled at this hospital as I did at Episcopal. There are more rules; there is more drudgery. It isn't easy to combine private practice with my day job. I hear an unspoken note of disapproval, see the raised eyebrows, at my mixing of the two.

It would be easiest simply to forget the National Health Service and devote myself to private therapy. London has the same rich pastures as New York of financiers and professionals who've turned their neuroses into professional success and now want to talk about it at great expense. Yet something holds me back. Perhaps it is idealism about public service, but I could talk myself out of that if I wanted. Deeper than any idealism is fear—a fear of exposing myself fully to the gravitational pull of money, of placing myself at the whims of the people who are wealthy enough to afford me.

I remember Harry's face when I first saw him. He had lost his job and all that it meant to him—the power it gave him to control others, without even having to think about it. I wonder, if he had gone into therapy, whether I might have helped him. It was probably too late, for his wife had her own way of coping with loss—by revenging it with blood. Nora had never believed in my profession, although she realized when she came across me that I'd have my uses. Her cure for Harry's loss was not to sit in a chair and discuss his plight, but to take down the man who'd put him there. I think of the contempt in her voice when she talked of pills and therapy, and the curious way in which she was right. Harry really did recover when Nora killed Greene; she shocked him out of his despair.

The intensity of Harry's devotion to her remains with me. It was a strange affirmation of marriage—that death doesn't weaken love, it only strengthens it. It reminds me of Gabriel telling me about broken heart syndrome. Husbands and wives are linked in ways that a stranger cannot know any more than I understand Wall Street.

That's my excuse, but I should have realized that something was wrong when I saw him on that cot, shivering with cold and despair. I made an exception for him and it was the worst mistake of my life, or so I hope it will remain. There were clues all around every day I'd worked in the Harold L. and Nora Shapiro Pavilion above FDR Drive. The Shapiros had paid for everything: York East, Twelve South, the oil painting screwed to the ER wall.

When I was useful, they bought me, too.

ACKNOWLEDGMENTS

This is a work of fiction but many people helped me with it. On Wall Street: Jane Gladstone, Flavio Bartmann, Daniel Loeb, Boaz Weinstein, and others who prefer not to be named. In East Hampton: Jillian Branam, Ina and Jeff Garten, Frank Newbold, and Janine and Tomilson Hill. In Suffolk County: Jason Bassett, Bill Keahon, Sarita Kedia, Steven Wilutis, and Lieutenant Charles L'Hommedieu and the officers of the Riverhead Correctional Facility. In the world of psychiatry: Don Tavakoli, Eli Greenberg, Jason Hershberger, Michael Walton, Michael Dulchin, Paul Appelbaum, Steven Hoge, and Paul Linde. At NetJets: Richard Santulli and Mark Booth. Elsewhere: Lionel Barber, John Ridding, Nick Denton, Chrystia Freeland, Emily Gould, Ruth Rogers, Frances Gapper, Paul Gapper, Louise Gapper,

Maureen Tkacik, Dusan Knesevic, Philip Raible, Deborah Wolfe, and the Brooklyn Writers' Space. David Kuhn and Gill Coleridge encouraged me to start and to finish, and Mark Tavani at Ballantine made the result much better. It was inconceivable without Rosie Dastgir, my wife and literary foil, and our daughters Yasmin and Rachel.

About the Author

JOHN GAPPER is associate editor and columnist for the *Financial Times* based in New York. He has written about banking for two decades and covered the Wall Street crisis in 2008. He is co-author with Nick Denton of *All That Glitters: The Fall of Barings*. He lives in Brooklyn with his wife and two daughters. This is his first novel.

About the Type

This book was set in Sabon, a typeface designed by the well-known German typographer Jan Tschichold (1902–74). Sabon's design is based upon the original letter forms of Claude Garamond and was created specifically to be used for three sources: foundry type for hand composition, Linotype, and Monotype. Tschichold named his typeface for the famous Frankfurt typefounder Jacques Sabon, who died in 1580.